THE PACK

L M .   P r e s t o n

THE PACK

Published by: Phenomenal One Press

P.O. Box 8231, Elkridge MD 21075

www.phenomenalonepress.com
phenomenalonepress@yahoo.com

First Edition:

Cover Artist: Shoshana Epsilon (http://shoshanaepsilon.blogspot.com/)
Printed in the United States of America

ISBN-10:   0-9841989-7-0

ISBN-13:   978-0-9841989-7-9

Library of Congress Cataloging-in-Publication Data on file.

For my children and my husband, who helped me dream the impossible and gave me the support to achieve it.

More Releases from LM. Preston

www.lmpreston.com

BANDITS, Spring 2011

Daniel's father has gotten himself killed, and left another mess for Daniel to clean up. Saving his world from destruction, he must fight off his father's killers while discovering a way to save his world. Time is running out, and Daniel must choose to either walk in his father's footsteps or to re-invent himself into the one to save his world.

EXPLORER X - Alpha, Feb 2010

For most kids, a trip to space camp is a trip of a lifetime, for Aadi it was life altering. After receiving a camp immunization needed for travel to Mars, Aadi finds that the immunization is the catalyst of an insidious experiment. Lucky for him, he was engineered to survive, thrive, and dominate. Without realizing he is being trained to conquer worlds, and manipulated under the guise of a camp, he unfolds the plot too late for a change of fate.

EXPLORER X - Beta, Summer 2011

Determined to save his friends, Aadi and Eirena prepare to leave the planet Shrenas, but not before they immobilize the evil race of Femoh's from attacking the innocent Nutah. After their final confrontation with the species that tortured them, they race to save Dakota and Carter who is dying. Time is slipping and the possibility of losing a friend is not an option, but the foe that awaits them may be worst than the one they left.

Acknowledgement

Thanks to God for giving me a tenacious spirit of positivity with an active imagination and the energy to do it all. To my devoted Beta Readers, Marie Williams, Samantha White, and Jenny McDiarmid, Willow (Missy), Amanda and Jesse, who helped me create a better story. To my daughter, who challenged me to write another awesome story in which I have come to love the characters just as much as I loved the characters of my previous novel. To all the kids that have gone missing – you are the inspiration for this story and I pray that you all get home safe. To my kids, who continue to give me true and honest feedback for all of my work. I thank you.

THE PACK

T H E P A C K

Chapter 1

She often walked this way home, listening for all the familiar sounds. Adjusting the handle of her small bag across her chest, she strolled slowly on the long suburban block that stretched quietly in front of her. It was night out, but it made no difference to Shamira, for she lived in the dark for most her life. She heard the quietness of the evening while she walked a comfortable pace on her journey homeward. There were no birds, no rustling trees, and no one walking the streets. Only the slight hum of the generators could be heard in the quiet of the late evening while it pumped fresh oxygen into the air.

Suddenly, out of the stillness, she heard someone approach, and she turned slightly to judge who it was. Shamira could tell the footsteps weren't friendly, but then again, neither was Shamira. A mischievous smile crossed her face that some would mistake for innocence, the furthest thing from her mind. The footsteps continued to fall quickly toward her, and Shamira slowed down to lure them closer. She knew that *he* came. *Only one scum for my trap today.* She had dealt with others before, but tonight, she only had time for one.

He grabbed her by the neck. *Typical. Why do they always go for my neck? This is too easy.* She smiled to herself again, and figuring she wouldn't work too hard to bring him down, she swallowed in preparation for the attack. Restlessness rose in her in anticipation of the fight. Time was slipping away, and she had to get home before her mother did. *This has to go quickly*, she thought regrettably, for she hated to rush things. She waited to see what her captor had planned for her, and she stood seemingly docile with his thick arm circled around her neck.

"So, what do I have here? Ooh, I've hit the jackpot tonight, baby!" He shoved his nose in her hair and sniffed, "A pretty, sweet-smelling girl all alone. You have no choice, you know. You're coming with me. I have got plans for you, sweet thing," he growled in her ear. She inhaled the smell of his putrid breath. The coarse hair on his arms scratched her neck. She squirmed away from him a bit, and his bulging belly pushed against her back.

"Hey! Stop, dude! Let her go!" She heard a voice in the distance. *Shoot!* she said to herself, knowing she would have to play helpless now. She had traced this creep for weeks, and now some goofball would-be hero would mess it up for her. *Dang it! No one must know,* she reminded herself, for no one could know what she did when she was alone. *Great, I won't get any information out of this creep tonight,* she grimaced.

She felt her attacker slack up just a little, but couldn't resist the urge to hurt him, like she knew he had hurt others. She lifted her leg high and stomped down on his foot with all her might, cracking his bones on impact. He instantly let up his tight hold. She turned precisely enough to step out of his reach. He yanked her long braid, a move she didn't anticipate, but she smiled at his obvious feeling of superiority over a girl he knew was blind and helpless. A smile slipped to her face at the knowledge that he'd been tracking her for sometime. She thought to herself, *I may be blind, but I'm definitely not helpless, you filthy son of a bastard.* Letting him think he had the upper hand, she allowed him to pull her back into his grasp by her hair. Her back was bent back like a bow, and she sensed his jaw was unprotected just above her nose. *Not surprising. It's always this way. They all get cocky in the end.* She braced herself to head-butt her captor in the chin, hopeful that he would bite off his hanging tongue that dripped a disgusting stream of spittle on her nose.

Then, she heard it. The guy that yelled out in hopes of stopping the attack had run up behind the oaf that was too dumb to realize that the gig was up. Just then, her self-appointed savior stepped in to save the day and snatched her target away by his neck. She heard him drag the scum slightly away. There was a grunt and rustling, and with a *thump*, the fat, smelly attacker was dealt a kick to his head after he crashed to the pavement. *Hum, that sounds familiar, only I kick harder. It appears the kid has some skill. He's sloppy, of course, but skillful enough to do the deed.* She heard the boy land one last kick for good measure, and her self-imposed hero walked over to her rescue. "Great. Now I have to play grateful," she muttered to herself.

"Thanks," she spat out most unconvincingly. She couldn't help it. This was her only set-up for the night, and now she had to find another way to control the rage inside her and solve the mystery of the missing kids on Mars. *It looks like another night in the training room. So freaking unfulfilling.* She rolled her eyes.

"I guess you're welcome," the boy said, "but you don't really sound too grateful." He tried to take her hand just like all the others who thought she was a poor, blind, invalid little girl. Disgusted, Shamira jerked away. She didn't need his help or want him there. He'd disrupted her planned attack, and the last thing she needed was for him to touch or pity her.

"I had it handled," she said and then started to walk toward home. As she headed off, the temperature changed. It was getting late. She could always tell. She tried to ignore him and hoped he would get the message. The last thing she needed was a nosey tagalong.

"You could've fooled me," the boy pressed. "He had his arm around your neck!" He made the fatal mistake of touching her again. She didn't think, only reacted as she grabbed his hand and held it steady, yet firmly before he made more than a whisper of contact. Shamira did not like to be touched. It angered her immensely. Many people touched her freely, like they had a right to simply because her eyes appeared unseeing. They always assumed she needed their help, but they were all mistaken; she didn't need anyone's help. Shamira always fought her own battles—some of which she even created because she hungered to fight. There was an urge inside her, something she barely controlled. She breathed deeply and tried to hold it back, but it was barely at bay.

Nevertheless, he wouldn't stop. He didn't get the message and decided to stick around. He moved a distance away, but she knew exactly where he was. She had to breathe deeply to avoid doing something they'd both regret. She was getting angry again, just like she always did when someone treated her like she was helpless. They didn't know about this rage inside of her, this burning, this constant hunger for a challenge, someone deserving of justice— something she could barely hold in. She stood down, calmed down, and waited, relaxing enough to drop his hand. She knew exactly how this was going to go. First, there would be his concern, then pity, and then his hand again as he tried to help. *I don't have time for this today. I'm already late.*

"Look, don't touch me, okay? I don't like it, and you don't have the right." She moved past him to walk home.

"Hey, I'm sorry, but it's obvious that you need somebody to walk you home," he said then reached out to touch her shoulder just like she knew he would.

That's it! The dam inside her broke. *I was angry before, but now I've had enough playing with this self-righteous imitation hero!* She slid out from under his outstretched hand, smoothly ducked, and then turned around to land a solid punch to the boy's face. She didn't stop, either, but instead punched him again and again in the chest to make him backoff.

He took the battering, but yelled, "I won't fight you back! I don't hit girls."

"Err! Leave me alone! Go away! I can take care of myself! I will hurt you, so just leave! Leave!" Dismissing him, she turned away and ran all the way home. She ran quickly and smelled the sweet aroma of manufactured air and the quiet *hum* that was Mars.

Whoever he was, she would remember him—his voice, his smell, and her dislike for him. *He dares to pity me.* She would teach him to pity alright. They would meet again, and when they did, she would not hold back. She'd make him stay out of her way.

Chapter 2

Shamira's run home was warmer than usual. The Martian summer day that marked the end of school made a smile slip quietly across her face while her light jacket flapped behind her. *I hate school!* It only brought her grief and greatly tested the control of her temper, which could cause terrible things to happen if she were to ever let it go unchecked. The wind blew with the smell of dirt and dryness. She loved the smells here. They weren't overpowering and allowed her time to ponder over them. The smell of that boy had been somewhat musky with a touch of spice, like he had recently washed. *Unfortunately, my captor smelled like he hadn't had a bath in weeks,* she reflected, cringing a bit when the memory filled her nostrils.

On her run home, she took time to calm down and put out the fire of power that threatened to spill over inside her, to go deep, deep inside. She didn't want her parents to know this part of her. They tried so hard to help her control it, but even they didn't know she had her own ways.

She hated being late. When her mom got home from work with her younger brother in tow, she liked to start on dinner right away. She knew her mom's job was demanding and took a lot of the kindness out of her, but Shamira didn't care. Her mom was perfect to her. But Shamira's mom didn't feel the same about her. It was clear that Shamira's brother was the favorite. Her mom adored her brother, and Shamira admitted to herself that she adored him too. He was the only one she truly loved to touch. He loved her just the way she was, even with her imperfections.

Her dad wouldn't be home until late. He was working an extra shift because one of the Elite members of the Security Force had disappeared. This troubled both her parents since they were part of the Elite team. The Security Force kept law and order on Mars, and Shamira's parents worked so hard to accomplish this feat that she couldn't help wanting to help them. It was what drove her out into the night. She had her ways of investigating, and it was easy because most people ignored, pitied or deemed her harmless and helpless. She had heard that there were thugs kidnapping the children of Security Force workers, and she wanted to put a stop to it.

With Shamira's imperfection, it was easy to remain hidden and to collect a lot of information that her parents might never want her to know. She had her ways of investigating, and it was easy because most people ignored or discounted her while thinking her an invalid. She didn't mind, really, because in the end, it made her stronger, or so she liked to think.

She slowed when she approached the house, and the dust and dirt of Mars kicked up when she skidded to a stop at the front door. She took a whiff. *Spaghetti. Mom must have had a good day today.* Her mom only made spaghetti on the good days. The days that Shamira wasn't home to start dinner, her mom always cooked. On the bad days, her mom would order takeout. The pizza delivery driver knew them pretty well, since most days lately were bad ones. Also, lately Shamira was always late. It just seemed to be taking longer to control the burning within.

Her dad used her lack of control for this power within her as an excuse to teach her so much. Everything he taught her, she thirsted for and obsessed to make it perfection. She loved it mostly because it was his gift to her, something that only they did together. Although the raging beast within her was mostly caged, the gift of time and skills her dad gave her were only tools to help her control it. She had gone so far beyond what he had taught her that she had to

15

dummy it down when she was with him. She didn't want them to fully know this side of her, this hunter that she had become. When she was with them, she would always be the daughter they wished for. She refused to lose their love by revealing her innermost raging urges.

The door opened, and she smelled the garlic bread and her brother's unique, sweet smell. She was now at peace, for the beast was caged, and she was home. David met her at the door. She reached out her hand and tousled his warm, silky head. He laughed, then stood up and said, "I'm getting too old for that, Meera!"

"You're never too old for your big sis to do this," she said and tickled him. He doubled up and almost fell to the floor.

Then her mom came to the door. Shamira could feel her contempt as it hung deeply in the air. She could feel her mom size her up before she fussed, "Hmm, I wondered when you'd show up. Do you have a death wish? Do you *want* to get hurt? Mars is not safe, yet you roam around aimlessly like you are in some carefree garden. Shamira, I called you on the earlink. Why didn't you answer me?"

"Mom, can I come in please? You're in the doorway, and I really have to go to the bathroom," said Shamira. She started to move side to side like she really had to go badly.

"Yeah, right. That isn't working this time. Get in here. Now," said her mom. She pulled Shamira into the house, and then quickly closed the door. Shamira figured she'd tried this tactic too many times now. Her mom had already figured out that she didn't have to go to the bathroom. She wondered if she should play her story out or just deal with the argument with her mom.

"Mom, you know I hate wearing the earlink. It interferes with my hearing, the one thing that helps me stay balanced and know when someone approaches. If you interfere with that, then I have to concentrate harder just to get around," Shamira responded. She gave up the bathroom pretense and stood still in front of her mom. She felt David's hand grab hers. He always sided with her in a fight with her parents, and she loved him for that. It was the two of them against the world.

"By the way, where are you coming from? School had no extracurricular activities today. Where do you keep going every night? I'm sick of this. I'm sick of you worrying us to death. It ends tonight. No more side trips from school! No more. Do you hear me?" Shamira knew her mom would be angry. She also knew that she wasn't going to stop what she was doing, at least not until she could find those kids—all of them. So she stood there, bowed her head like she was sorry, and took a deep, soothing breath.

"I'm sorry, Mother. It won't happen again," Shamira said in the small voice she used when her mom got this way. She kept her head bowed since she didn't want her mom to see the rage within her.

"I've heard that before! It's not working anymore. You will get tagged! That way, we won't have any problems finding you on your long walks home!" her mother added with a pointing finger. Shamira held still when her mother's strong finger pushed against her

17

shoulder. It hurt a bit with its heaviness and sharpness.

"Mom, I don't want to be tagged like a dog. I promise! Just give me another chance, please? I promise, Mom. I promise," Shamira said with a broken voice, on the verge of tears. If they tagged her, she would have to stop what she was doing. It was the first time she'd ever felt useful, needed, and free. *Please don't take that away from me, Mom,* she pleaded in her head.

"Fine, but this is the last time. I promise you with every bit of my being that if you get lost or show up late again, no begging or pleading will stop this. You will get tagged if I have to drag you to the doctor myself. Your father won't save you this time. You brought this on yourself." She turned and walked back toward the kitchen.

"Shamira, why don't you want to get tagged? Mom and Dad are. They couldn't be part of the Security Force if they weren't. I thought you wanted to be on the Force when you grow up? You'll have to get tagged sometime if you want to work for them," David reasoned while he absently rubbed her arm.

"I'll never get tagged, even if that means not joining the Security Force. I just can't, you hear me? You don't ever let them do it to you either. I'll always find you, and I don't need a tag to do it," she said and lifted her arm up to rub down the silkiness of his hair.

"I told you, I'm too old for that," David said, then hugged her. He then tickled her sweet spot under her arm, and she instantly came out of her melancholy. Only David could do this for her. Her baby brother was the most perfect boy of all.

"When you're finished sulking, get in here and eat this great spaghetti I made. I was happy when I got home until I didn't see my little girl," her mom yelled from the kitchen. *Of course she rubs it in*, Shamira thought with a smile. Besides, she hadn't been a "little girl" for a while now. She was sixteen and felt even older from all the secrets she kept. She headed to the table, knowing that was her cue to eat. In spite of everything, she was still hungry.

She sat down and waited for her mom to prepare her plate. Conforted by this little thing her mom loved to do for her, the only thing, in fact, that her mom did for her. Shamira was sure her mom did this for David, too, but it still felt nice to be so loved sometimes.

"So, how was work today?" Shamira asked. She grabbed her fork and twirled the spaghetti around slowly, teasing her hunger with the smell of the sauce and cheese.

"Today was better than the rest of the week. We got a lead on Lieutenant McCann. It looks like we're dealing with a new secret organization. How they managed to form it without us knowing is beyond me. Well the good part is we now can figure out who the players are and crush them before they get any momentum." Her mom smiled, and then said, "We're also close to finding McCann. Although there is some interference with the location devices, we're confident he will be home with his family before this coming Monday," her mom said excitedly. Her mom loved being the key Detective and Agent of the Security Force. She was a hunter just like Shamira; only she got paid for it. Her mom's work was also something they both liked to share, and Shamira couldn't help but consider her mother's gift of information.

"Well, do you think they hurt McCann? I like him." Shamira said. She started to think of a way to track him. She decided then and there that she would give the Security Force just two days before she would attempt to find him herself. Her main focus had been on finding the kids, but she didn't like it at all that McCann was now a victim as well. Kids of various Security Force Elite members and the Mars Planet Police were sporadically kidnapped over the years, never to turn up again. Shamira swore she would find them and bring pain to those that took them. As she sat there daydreaming of what she would do to those who hurt the missing kids and Officer McCann, she heard a *crack*. Without realizing she was doing it, she'd pressed her fork so hard onto her plate that the plate snapped in two. She gulped and turned toward her mother, knowing she wouldn't be pleased.

"Shamira! Look at what you did! How did you do that? Oh, never mind. Just clean it up, will you?" her mom said. She knew her mom was disgusted with her now. It was usual for her mom to get angry with her when she appeared clumsy. *Well, it can't be helped now*. She was a bit angry with herself, too, because she was still really hungry. She got up, gathered the mess, and threw it all in the trash. She didn't miss a single piece of glass when she wiped the table clean.

"Shamira, I'll make you another plate," David said. He got up quickly and scooped a big fresh helping of spaghetti on her new plate.

She heard the heavy metal spoon slide against the glass plate and sat down. She liked letting David feel like he could take care of her.

"Thank you, David. You're the best little brother a girl could ask for," she said and picked up her drink to take an embarrassed swallow. She didn't need to turn to her mother to feel the woman's angry glare. Shamira quietly picked up her new fork and ate in silence.

"Well, I have to go back in late tonight. You and David will be here with your dad until morning. We need you to watch him until noon. Don't go anywhere but to the park. Do, you hear me, Shamira?" her mom said with an obvious threat in her voice. Shamira didn't hear her all that well since she was concentrating hard at not breaking another plate, but she answered anyway to avoid further wrath and disappointment.

"Sure, Mom. What time will Dad get home?" she added and then put the fork down.

"He's on his way. We have a surprise for you, but we're going to wait to share it, considering your recent punishment," her mom added. She got up and went to the kitchen cleaner.

"Punishment? What punishment?" Shamira asked. She tried to appear calm.

Her mom hesitated a moment for effect, then said, "Well, you will not be going out without your earlink. If you don't wear it, it's automatic tagging. That's the punishment for at least for one week."

Shamira couldn't win. "Fine, I'll wear it for the term of my punishment," she replied. She didn't want to add fuel to her mom's fire, so it was best to agree quietly.

"Good. Now, come give me a hug," her mom said. Shamira was temporarily in shock. Her mom rarely had time for hugs. *Something more must be going on at work than she's willing to share*, Shamira contemplated. She stood when her mom came over and gave her and her brother a much treasured group hug. Shamira felt an inner peace and joy when she hugged her mom tightly back. Her mom was slim, packed, and firm, a tall woman with a great inner and outer strength, which she needed to do her job well as a Security Force Elite member. Shamira loved the smell of sweet roses that came from her mom's skin, a smell unique to her.

"You know, it's a little unsettling how you appear to have sight. You look at me and move like you're not blind at all. If it weren't for those extreme pale blue eyes of yours, I'd think you could see. Sometimes it makes me forget that you are," her mom said and sighed before she continued,"Shamira, I may be hard on you, but I do love you, you know."

"I know, Mom. I love you too," Shamira said and then hesitated to let her mom go.

"I love you both! Always," David added with a tight squeeze.

"Enough of that, you charmer," Shamira said and then rustled her brother's hair.

Chapter 3

Her mom left to put David to bed and read to him about Earth, part of their evening ritual. Shamira didn't remember anything about Earth. They'd come here when she was newborn. H er parents couldn't turn down the chance to work as Elites on newly colonized Mars. They were right under the head of the Security Force Elite Leader on Mars, a coveted position Shamira had heard them mention to others. They'd been chosen from their birth and trained to serve on the Security Force as Elite members since they were children. On

Mars, her parents' organization was the law, the order, and the leading power. It was an opportunity neither of her parents could turn down. They simply had no choice.

Her earliest memories were faded except for one: the day she died. Her parents said the Security Force were the first ones on the planet. They came a year before the other settlers. However, the oxygen management system had bugs in it that caused it to fail. She was asleep in her room when it happened, and her parents lost consciousness before they could get to her. Shamira was the only child on the planet at the time. She had been born healthy, but when the air system failed, she stopped breathing. Her parents told her that when they awoke after the air was regenerated to find her dead, they were frantic. They carried her to a makeshift hospital.

They tried everything on her to revive her and finally experimented with injecting her with the enhancements only used on the Security Elite in hopes of bringing her back to life. Little did they realize it was a double-edged sword that saved as well as doomed her to a life much different than any other. She finally came back to life after being clinically dead for several hours. It took months for her to recover, and when she did, she was blind.

These pensive thoughts filled her mind, but Shamira pushed them away. Mars was her home. She loved it here, and it was a part of her. She knew and understood its people. She had survived, and that was all that mattered. *I wonder if they know that in order to save me, they turned me into a freak?* Exhausted after her reminiscent thoughts, she went to her room to take a quick nap.

"Wake me up in two hours," she said to the home network system. It would make sure her bed shook at the designated time. She wanted to greet her dad with a big hug when he got home. Unlike her mother, her dad was really touchy-feely with his family and loved to hug and kiss them all the time. He was just that type of guy, and she truly loved that about him. Her dad was the only hero she'd ever need.

The bed shook promptly after two hours passed. Shamira woke up to run to the bathroom and brush her teeth. Throwing cold water on her face, she smiled at the knowledge that her dad would be home in just a few minutes. She brushed her long hair and slipped on the pajamas she was too tired to put on earlier. She walked to the living room and felt the lights come on upon her entrance. Even though she couldn't really see the lights, she could feel their warmth when she walked through the house. She had asked her parents when she was younger why it would warm up slightly when she walked through the house, and they explained that the smart house they lived in tried to make it comfortable for them.

She heard the door open when she entered the room. She instantly smelled her dad, and he smelled like a spicy winter day. She ran into his arms and hugged him. He was built of pure muscle, tall, stocky, and hard with the stubbly beginnings of a beard: the result of being away at work for days. She felt totally safe in his arms. He was her dad, her friend, and her champion. He laughed and squeezed her back, then kissed the top of her head.

"Hey, pumpkin! I knew you'd be up waiting for me. I missed you all today," he said. He pushed her away gently to look down at her.

"Sure you did. How did you have time to miss us when you were working so hard?" she asked with a laugh.

"You're right, honey, I was working hard. Your mom—the poor woman—has to get up in about an hour to go into work again."

He walked past her and put down his suitcase. She heard him walk to the safe and put away his guns, which he rarely ever needed because he was so skilled at martial arts. He could kill a man with his bare hands, and the technosuit all Security Force Elite members wore enhanced his natural strength five times over. He had told her that all of the Elite Force members were fitted with them before they left Earth. The suit was a second skin. She could tell the difference in her parents' skin texture and the feel of other people's skin when she was younger. Yet, they didn't tell her about the suits that only the Elite 200 wore until she was older. She had found out that the Elite leaders of the Force acted as the leaders of each Sector. They were groomed on Earth for the role. The main computer on Earth tracked them until they died and their signal was lost.

As far back as she could remember her father had been training her. He told her it was her job to train her brother. He said she had to learn how to train the next generation of Security Force members since he dreamed of the day her brother and she would take their parents' places. Also, he used it for a technique to help her control the power. The power was something her mom noticed in her when they brought her home from the hospital after her death. When she came home from the hospital, she was much different than the baby they had come to Mars with. They hadn't told her about the power personally. It was something she dug up on her own out of the home network system database bank that held all the conversations and records in the home. They knew she knew how to use the system, but what they didn't know was that she had figured out how to hack into it. She smiled at the thought.

"Dad, what have you guys been working on? Both of you are working longer hours than before. These last six months, we haven't even been able to train together." There was a slight whine in Shamira's voice. She lived for those training sessions. When she worked with her father, he was a worthy adversary, someone that pushed her technique by his sheer strength alone. Her dad didn't even realize that he had long stopped holding back with her and that she'd taken him to the limit of the super strength gained by his technosuit.

"I know you miss it. So do I, pumpkin, but we have a major storm brewing at work. This crime organization is a much larger problem than we expected. Your mom left work on a good note today, but that's going to change when she returns to her office. We lost the one so-called lead we had. I, for one, am not going to be the one to spoil that for her, so I guess she'll find out at work." He sniffed at the air briefly and asked, "Hey, did she make spaghetti?" He went over to the kitchenaid, a wall appliance that served food and beverages, and then touched the front to go through the food catalogue.

Shamira answered, "You know she always does when she comes home happy."

"Yeah, and I'm starving," he said. He got a glass of water from the kitchenaid.

"Sit down, Dad. I'll fix your plate," Shamira said with a smile.

"You spoil me just like your mom. Sure, I'd love that." After he took his seat, Shamira walked over to the kitchenaid and pressed in the request for a plate of spaghetti. It came out warm, ready and on a plate. She reached in and grabbed it out of the dispenser door. Placing the plate down in front of him, she sat down and grinned.

"What are you smiling about?" He lifted an eyebrow, and stuffed a fork full of food in his mouth.

"Well, I'm punished, you know. You weren't here today to back me up or to tell Mom that I just require twenty more hours in the training room," Shamira added with a giggle.

"Your mom's not going to let me get away with that one anymore. I was warned before I got home not to go soft on you," her dad said while he talked between bites. She could hear the smile in his voice.

"Well, that's okay. I guess I can deal with the punishment. Are you and Mom are going back to work together? She said I have to watch David in the morning."

She rested her head on her hand, as if watching him. She did it to goad him, because he often said he was spooked by the fact that she didn't *act* blind.

"Yeah, when I wake her up, we have to go. I was barely able to get away. Look, today you both stay inside. Don't go out. There is a lot going on right now that requires the Security Force's attention elsewhere, and I don't want to risk yours and David's safety, okay?"

"Why? Mom even said we could go to the park. You know David loves to go outside and play with his friends. I don't like being cooped up in the house either, and I know he won't. Dad, you *know* I can protect him. He's starting to take his training seriously. He can fight off most would-be bullies on the playground," Shamira added. She figured it was best to play naïve. She didn't want her dad to know that she had an inkling of knowledge about the missing kids.

"It's just not safe, okay? I think I've shared too much with you as it is, so just take my word for it. You've been staying out later and later. I have a feeling, from reports of injured bad guys, that you have been on a scene or two. I'm not positive yet, but the injuries some of these guys have sustained—near death in some cases— makes me wonder if it's not someone who has been trained to do the job. The only person besides your mother and I to know those techniques lives in this house. I warn you, Shamira, I better not find out it's you. If I do, your training ends. Do you hear me? You will go back to being a normal girl," her dad said with seriousness in his voice. He lay his fork down. She felt his pensive stare, like he was touching her face to find out what she was hiding. She effortlessly displayed calmness and nonchalance.

I'll never be normal. "Dad, you know I need the training. You know it's a good outlet for me. What else can I do? I'm not hurting people. You didn't teach me to seek out a fight, right? So why would you think I could do those things?" she asked, hoping he believed her lie. She fought to keep perfectly natural since he could read her like a book. Those kids depended on her being able to pull this off. She forced herself to relax.

"I know the training keeps your nervous energy under control. But, you could try more meditation or relaxation therapy. And that's exactly all you'll be doing, Shamira, if I find out you're acting like some kind of vigilante. You understand?" he added, sliding his chair back when he stood and wiped the spaghetti sauce from the corner of his mouth.

"Sure, Dad. Hey, Mom said you had a surprise for me. She didn't get a chance to tell me what it was," Shamira added, trying to switch the subject. She was more than a bit curious about the surprise.

"Oh? She didn't tell you because you're on punishment. I can't hold it in much longer, so I'll let the cat out of the bag. I'll tell your mom, and she will forgive me, of course. She can't help it. She thinks I'm hot," Shamira's dad said with a laugh.

"You crack yourself up, Dad." She stood up and started to

jump up and down like a kid while she chanted, "So tell me, tell me, tell me!"

"We got you an appointment to go to Earth and get your sight regeneration surgery. We had planned on getting it done after the accident... I mean, shortly after you lost your sight... but the colonists were coming to Mars, and your date got pushed back. We never planned on you growing up blind. People don't suffer with those aliments anymore, and we're sorry we kept you this way for so long. It couldn't be helped. Flights to Earth are only once a month, and the surgery is a rare procedure. Not to mention we just couldn't get off work. We have gotten approval to do this."

He came over and gave her a hug that she sensed was full of regret for all her suffering. Even though her parents felt bad about it, being blind never bothered her. In some way, Shamira felt like she could see more than anyone else could.

"Wow. Well, I don't know if that is a good thing or a bad thing. Dad, I just don't know if I'm ready to see. I like myself the way I am. I want to be happy, but I just... well, I don't know," she said. She pulled out of his reassuring hold to sit back down in her seat.

"I know, I know. This must be hard for you. I thought you'd be happy, though—happy to see my ugly face, your mom's beautiful face, and your brother," he said, trying to laugh over her discomforting response.

"I already see your faces. I know you. I can really *see* every part of you all that you don't notice yourself. I can find you in a crowded room. I can tell when you're within a mile. I *feel* you. I *sense* you. I see more than you'll ever know," Shamira said heavily.

"I know, sweetheart. You'll never stop being able to see in that way. It's a part of you. It's who you are now. But this is a chance to grow - to improve. Just, think about it, okay? I have to go get your mom, so go back to sleep. I don't want her to know I've been talking to you yet. She'll know by the look on your face that I let the cat out of the bag," he said, then pressed his hand to her shoulder.

"Okay. Goodnight, Dad," she said and stood up. She didn't turn back but headed straight to her room, where she fell on her bed and cried. *I don't want to change.*

Chapter 4

Shamira heard her dad clearly when he said not to go out. She also clearly decided right then and there that she would disobey him. She had logged on to the supercomputer based in the Security Force's Headquarters when she visited her parents at work the week before. She had secretly created a secret account that allowed her undetectable access to the system. The greatest part of it all was that she could tap into it from any remote location. She didn't use her earlink for calling her parents anymore because she had rigged it to be her own personal computer when she was out of the house.

She took a moment to search under her bed for several devices she had pilfered from her parents' weapons case over the years. She never took obvious items and was careful to space their disappearance out over time so her parents did not become suspicious. By augmenting all of these treasures to her own use, she had created an arsenal of weapons that were uniquely useful to her in gathering information and bringing down would-be attackers.

She placed her supply belt on her waist with her stick, metal balls, knives, and such. Walking to her closet, she said, "Open, Level Two."

The door on the wall opened, and she reached behind her clothes to get the black jacket and boots that she often wore when she searched for a lead. She took her long, silky braid, twisted it into a ball at her nape, and put on her sunglasses. They would disguise her extremely pale blue blinded eyes, a distinctive feature that could give her away. Shamira didn't often think about how she looked since she never had a boy approach her anyway. Most of her peers either ignored or taunted her, so her looks didn't concern her except when it came to her missions.

She finished dressing by placing on her gloves. Adjusting her weapons belt to hide it from David, she walked out into the living room area. David waited there for her impatiently, his distinct smell filling the air around her. She heard his shuffling feet.

"You ready, kiddo?" she asked with a smile in her voice. She knew he was ready because this was their usual routine when her parents weren't home. Walking past him, she went to the door. He tried to trick her and jump in front of her, but she quickly sidestepped.

"Darn! I can never get you," he said, then stomped the floor.

"Nope, you never can. So you need to keep trying harder. We really need to get back to the training room," she said and then turned the knob.

"I don't like training. It's boring, and you always win. When are you going to let me win?" He followed her out of the door so quickly he nearly bumped into her. She smiled at his clumsiness.

"Never. I can't make it easy for you. You have to win on your own, because you earn it," said Shamira. She then reached over to him, mussed his hair and pinched his cheek.

"Great. Then I'll always be a loser. Darn it!" He stomped behind her to the garage.

"Open and send Pearl out," Shamira said to the garage. Pearl was her motorcycle. When her dad gave it to her and he told her it reminded him of oysters from back home on Earth. It was a smart cycle, computerized and powerful. Her parents always referred to Earth as "home," but to Shamira, Mars was home. She would never leave, and the thought of going to Earth scared her. Pushing the conversation with her dad away, she waited for Pearl to drive out.

The garage slid open, and her motorcycle revved up its engine automatically and drove alongside her. She swung her leg over, put her helmet on, and waited for David to follow. She felt his firm, well built arms when they encircled her waist, and she took off. She loved the feel of riding her motorcycle. It was a smart cycle that primarily drove for her, but she knew this territory of Mars so well that she didn't use the auto controls as much. As for her sight, she had what some would call "second sight." She just *knew* where things were. When other vehicles passed her by or approached her, she sensed them. She could *feel* them, as if their images were pushed into her mind outlined in white with a black background. She felt the change in the temperature or the energy of her surroundings, which further enhanced her ability to interpret the world around her. It freaked her parents out because the truth was, they didn't know how or why she could do the things she did. They'd given up trying to explain it to her or to themselves.

The two reached the playground in record time. The civilization on Mars was built like most all cities on Earth. However, the Sector she lived in was a bit of a distance from the other Sectors. That distance consisted of some barren land in which Sector Five seemed to rise up like an oasis. Her parents said it reminded them of a place on Earth called Las Vegas, a beautiful place in the middle of a desert. They said the only difference was that Mars Sector Five didn't have glitzy lights or the showy feeling of Las Vegas. Her dad said it was grittier, kind of like New York.

"Shamira, can I go on the virtual game board over there?" David asked and barely gave her a chance to answer. He slid off the motorcycle and threw his helmet on the seat and then took off across the fake spongy grass. The park was the center of three major streets, which fed into it as a place for people to play virtual games, read on the 4D book players, or watch people perform. They also had a track for people who still liked to run outside, though few people took advantage of it anymore. These days, mostly children used the park, but now and then, others appeared, and they often seemed unfriendly. They were most likely the victims of the poison that the crime organization named Monev left behind.

"Sure, but stay there. I'm going to go for a walk!" she yelled behind him. She slid off her motorcycle, took a sniff of the air, and headed toward the center street, Sable Street. She knew where to go. She had followed this lead for a while, and his habits were pretty regular. This Lenny sold scream in an alleyway in the middle of the Sable Street across from the park. Scream was a tag used in virtual reality that gave players an edge, kind of like having a virus on hand to help them win millions in the videogame or gambling hells on Mars, provided they didn't get caught or killed using it. It also contained a highly addictive hallucinogenic drug that ensured its users came back for more. This Lenny was a really bad guy with a really bad habit of getting kids hooked on scream.

"Great, a distraction," Shamira said sarcastically while she smelled the distinct scent of Kim and her groupies from school. Now she would have to play helpless again since she didn't want the kids from school to consider her even more of a freak than they already did. *Wonderful.* "I really don't need this right now," she said under her breath. She felt a change in the wind and knew Kim had stuck out her foot. Pretending to be caught off guard, she tripped quite on purpose, trying to make it look like an accident.

"Hmm... I guess the handicap girl can't find her way. Want some help? Need a seeing eye dog?" Kim asked loudly and with a sarcastic inflection in her voice. She spoke to her like she was born deaf.

"I can hear just fine, Kim. How about you?" Shamira replied loudly like Kim. She couldn't help herself. Playing weak was getting harder and harder the stronger the power grew inside of her.

The energy around her changed again when Kim and her other two friends pushed her between them. Shamira stood in the middle of the circle and tried to appear off balance. Although, when Kim spat on her, the dam of her control broke, and Shamira decided she would play the invalid no more. She punched Kim lightly on the chin and then back-kicked her taller friend Megan in the chest. Megan fell to the ground.

Shamira barely held her anger at bay while she remembered all the times she had allowed them to beat her up just so she could keep her secret abilities hidden. She held Kim firmly by the neck, careful not to choke her. Figuring she would be gentle with Kim, unlike Kim was with her. She felt the air shift when Kim's friend Shannon tried to run away. Shamira threw all pretense of gentleness away and slammed Kim down with the hand that she held firmly to

Kim's neck in order to quickly pull at Shannon's flapping braid.

"Oh, no, we wouldn't want to leave you out, Shannon, now would we?" Shamira asked. Then, she yanked Shannon's braid back, causing the girl's back and head to hit the firm turf.

"Now girls, I don't want to play anymore," Shamira said. She stepped over Shannon's sprawling body. Dismissing them, she walked in the direction of Sable Street.

"I'll get you..you, Shamira, you stupid blind witch!" Kim yelled.

"I'd like to see you try," Shamira muttered. Then, she smiled as she crossed the street.

As she placed her foot on Sable Street, it was like she had entered a different world. The scent changed drastically to a pungent, sour odor, like spoiled food. The street keeper androids that cleaned the nicer areas on Sector Five didn't travel on Sable Street or the poor areas of the city. Many of the people who settled on Mars were thrown off of Earth, supposedly "reformed" criminals who sought redemption. The families who supported them moved with them to Mars. "Unfortunately, no matter where people move, they still seem to bring all of their bad habits," her dad had once told her. And this Lenny was a prime example.

She closed her unseeing eyes and tried to differentiate the smells around her. She adjusted to the foul smell of Sable Street and its inhabitants to follow the familiar scent of her prey. "Lenny" was what he called himself, but Shamira doubted that was his real name. Many of the first-generation settlers changed their names in hopes that Mars would be a new beginning for them. They always seemed to revert back to whatever got them in trouble on Earth. She was part of the second generation of kids on Mars. Unfortunately, many of the second generation were homeless, forced to live in the gaming hells or the Outlands when their parents got addicted to scream, gambling, or got killed. For all too many of the settlers and their children, Mars was not the Mecca they were promised. Hopefully, in time, it would become that. *At least it will after the Security Force takes out the trash that's infecting this planet.*

She sensed that the street was rather empty, which was quite normal for daylight hours. Like most seedy places, Sable Street came alive mostly at night. Shamira knew that her sneaking out at night would be less difficult in the upcoming days with her parents' work schedules so hectic. She wouldn't feel right leaving David home alone, so her adventures into the night would have to take place after she returned from her trip to Earth.

"Hmm," she said. She sensed him up above in his usual spot just up the alley. She walked over to the store window display and appeared to be looking inside when she heard his customer leave. Figuring it was best to attack him right away, she reminded herself that she was pressed for time and didn't want to leave David alone for too long.

She walked into the alleyway and sensed that Lenny stood alone. He was keying in the credits that his last customer paid him for the scream. She could hear him tap on the mini-computer screen that most dealers kept on their wrist.

"Looks like you made out pretty good today," she said and walked toward him. She wasn't in the mood to play victim any longer for the day, so she didn't give him a chance to reply as she breathed deeply to tap into her surge of strength and punched him with enough power to smash his back and head against the wall. His head nodded, and she flexed her gloved hands, which caused the extended claws of the glove to extract.

Cracking his neck to the side, he licked his lips. His voice filled with lust as he said, "Hey! You like it rough, don't ya? I do to, you fine young thing."

She grinned at him, anger building, and with lightening speed she gripped his neck. He gulped out when she tightened her grip on his neck and her knee jabbed into his groin with great force.

"Don't try to sweet talk me. I want information. You know where the kids are being held, don't you? Tell me, and I'll let you go with memories of Earth," she said. Switching hands, she held his neck with her clawed glove. Using her other hand, she reached into her pocket to pull out a truth tick that she pierced into his neck. She waited for the flat mini computerized bug to do its job. It sharp legs sunk into the Lenny's skin and the biological replica of many species, inserted a poison into Lenny that forced him to tell the truth. An added side effect was that it erased a portion of the victim's memory, depending on how long it was attached.

"I'm not talking. I ain't getting killed for no one, sweetness,"

Lenny said with a wince from the tick's deepening claws. His speech slurred while the tick started to do its dirty work.

"We'll see about that. Just give it a moment, *sweetness*," she said and promptly spit in his face. He disgusted her. His kind had no morals. He even sold scream to kids, convincing them to trade their souls for the kick of winning games, only to disappear in the end, suffering who knows what kind of torture before meeting their doom.

The scent in the air changed, and she heard someone approaching. One of Lenny's sidekicks, she could smell Lenny's scent on him. She swiftly took the metal ball out of her pocket, waited for the guy to come closer, and without turning from her captive, tossed the ball at him while she faced Lenny as he weakened. The metal web burst from the ball and slammed its running victim against a wall of the buildings they were sandwiched between. She heard him gurgle while the web drew tightly to strangle its victim within an inch of his life. It allowed only enough air into his lungs for him to stay alive.

"Now, where were we? Oh yeah, you were telling me about where those kids are being held—and as a matter of fact, where Security Force Leader McCann of Sector Three may be," Shamira said. Then she forced him to look directly at her shaded eyes. The drug from the tick finally took effect, and Lenny got the dazed look and grunt of a forced truth teller.

"I don't... I don't know where all the kids are. Some are in the Outlands where the dark isles where built. Some of the kids... uh... I don't know... they didn't survive," he said, forcing out the words.

"What about McCann and the other Security Force Elite that have been kidnapped?" she asked. She forced her knee further into his groin for added balance.

"I... I'll be killed if I tell you. I... I... they're being held in a secret location. I... I don't know where..." he forced out over a thickening tongue, one of the dreaded side effects of the tick. Sometimes the victim would have an allergic reaction that caused the tongue and then the throat to swell, which could lead to death by suffocation. Shamira frankly didn't care that Lenny was allergic to the tick and considered it his fate. The monster was getting what he deserved.

"Lucky for you, that's all I have time for today. I'll be playing with you soon since you're full of information, sweetness, hmm?" She punched him with such force his head hit the wall and he fell to the ground in a deep sleep. She noticed a new aroma in the air, a scent she remembered. *Just great. That's all I need, a self-proclaimed hero lurking around for me to explain things to.*

"Well, I guess you *can* take care of yourself," the boy from before said. "I'm impressed." He came up behind her while she bent down and removed the tick from Lenny's neck. She crushed the tick in her hands and placed it in a pouch on her belt. With a flick of her wrist, the sharp claws on her glove retracted.

"What do you want?" she asked sharply while she walked past him to Lenny's flunky.

"I want what you want—answers. I've been tracking this guy

43

for weeks, trying to find out about my younger sister, who was taken over a month ago," he said. She could tell from his voice that he was confident and sincere. He was also a bit older, and Shamira noticed the newness in the deepness of his voice, as if he was still getting used to his grownup man-voice.

"Where are your parents? Why aren't they doing this for you?" she asked. Then, she pulled off the hook knives that held the metal web in place, and the victim fell loudly to the ground with a cold *thud.* "If your sister has gone missing, why aren't your parents doing something about it instead of just you?"

"I'm pretty sure they're dead. My dad was a member of the Security Force Elite on Sector One. One day when I came home, I found my mom cut down dead in our living room. My father and sister were nowhere to be found. He loved my mom, and I know he would have killed anyone who harmed either of them. He and my sister were just gone," he said and walked cautiously toward her.

"Back up, boy. I don't like people close, so keep your distance," she said. She squeezed the metal ball, and the web retracted back inside. Squeezing it locked, she slid it into the pocket of her belt. "Well, look, I have to go. Just… just stay away from me, okay?" Shamira said. She then turned away from him and ran at top speed to her motorcycle.

"David, come on!" she yelled then climbed on her cycle, and waited for him. She knew the boy hadn't followed, for which she was glad. Hopefully, that would be the last she saw of him.

"Hey, Sis, you ready?" David asked. He already knew the answer from the look on her face, so he quickly put his helmet on and mounted Pearl behind her.

Chapter 5

As they approached the house, Shamira knew immediately that her parents were home. She sensed them while they watched as she drove up with David behind her on the motorcycle. *Can this day get any worse?* she wondered.

"Shamira, get in here at once!" her father said. She could imagine him as he stood on the front porch with his arms crossed, her mom beside him with her condemning stare.

"I'm coming," she said and climbed off her motorcycle. David quickly followed.

"Hurry it up, Shamira!" her dad bellowed. *He's really angry now.* He only yelled at her when she had done something really, really bad.

"Pearl, go park yourself," she said then took off her helmet and placed it on her hip. Her motorcycle followed her command immediately and drove into the garage, which opened then closed behind it. She and David took deep breaths and bravely headed to the door. Her parents stood aside while the two kids walked inside the house.

"David, go to your room. You're grounded for the remainder of the day because you didn't have your earlink in. Shamira, sit down on the couch. Now!" her dad said. She felt him point at the place he wanted her to sit, so she headed to the far end of the couch. Adjusting her jacket so it further concealed her weapons, she tried to look casual since she intended to play stupid.

"I thought I told you last night that I didn't want you to go out today, especially with David," her dad said.

"Nelson, let me handle this," her mom added calmly.

Uh oh, Shamira thought, *this is big trouble.*

Her mom started in. "Shamira, we're tired of warning you and giving you rules you refuse to follow. You, my dear, have given us no choice. When you return from your trip to Earth, you are getting tagged." From the tone of her voice, there was absolutely no chance of coercing her otherwise.

"Katherine, let's wait on that punishment, alright?" her dad

47

begged, trying to cut his daughter some slack.

"For what, Nelson? Why wait? I'll not keep tolerating her total disobedience. She's going to get herself and her brother hurt if she keeps this up!" her mom said.

"Look, don't argue because of me. When I get back from Earth, I'll work harder at behaving. Heck, I'll lay low for the next week and stay in the house, okay? I don't want you to fight," Shamira said quietly.

Her father reached out to touch her shoulder. "Shamira, you are not the reason we're fighting. We're just under a lot of stress right now. Your trip to Earth is tomorrow. We have no choice but to do it now because the opportunity may not arise again. Earth will be cutting off trade with Mars until we can get things here under control. We will not delay your surgery any further. Your mother and brother will be staying here while I take you for your surgery," her dad said gravely.

"Why can't David go? He's never been to Earth. He deserves a chance to see the place he came from, doesn't he?" she argued then stood.

"It can't be helped. It's too dangerous. Several of the last flights to Earth have been attacked. We can only hope we will make it safely there and back. I know you're capable of taking care of yourself if we get in any trouble, but David has been unmotivated with his training. That is something you will have to address, Shamira, when we return," her father added.

"Is there anything else you want to tell me? If not, I'd better go pack," Shamira added and stood to go to her room.

"Yes," her dad said dryly. "You're to stay in your room until we leave. You're grounded." Even though he was still angry, his words didn't have the same bite like they had moments before. Instead, he sounded tired, very tired.

"Yes, sir." Shamira turned to walk directly to her room. She didn't have time to spare thinking about her trip to Earth. She had to upload the information she had gathered into the supercomputer at the Security Force Headquarters. She sat down at her desk and keyed in the code that would send her message in the form of a wrapped virus to the supercomputer. They would never know who sent it or from where.

She got up and took off her jacket and glasses. She knew hiding them would do her little good now that her parents had seen her in them, but she still folded them neatly and placed them in the hidden compartment of her closet with her most treasured weapons. Heading to her shower, she felt the floor warm beneath her feet. She walked directly inside and turned on the hot, pulsing water, unbraiding her hip-length hair while water poured down her back. *This trip to Earth is going to be the longest trip ever.*

Chapter 6

Shamira refused to hurry. She didn't want to go to Earth, and she definitely wasn't ready to have her eyesight back. Not to mention, she was scared to death from all the questions running through her mind. *Will I lose my abilities when I'm able to see? Will I think I'm pretty? How will this change the comfortable world I've build for myself?* She also wondered why this was so important to her parents. She wondered if gaining her sight would make her perfect in their eyes. In any case, she hoped traveling and the surgery would be quick. She had to get back before her lead left town. She slowly folded her clothes and longingly touched the makeshift weapons she would have to leave behind.

After she packed, she was determined to talk to her brother before she left. She closed her suitcase and then tapped in the code on the top to direct it to go straight to the living room. She heard it roll off. It was still earlier than David liked to wake up, but she had to steal a hug from him since it would be at least a week before she saw him again. Quietly, she walked to his room. She could hear her parents while they talked softly in the kitchen, and she planned to practice her eavesdropping skills after she finished with David.

He sat up in bed like he'd been waiting for her. She heard him move slightly when she stepped over the threshold of the doorway.

"Shamira, I wanted to come to your room to tell you goodbye. I wish I could see Earth," David said in a sleepy voice.

"Oh, you will see Earth one day. I wish you could go too. You're the first person I'd like to lay eyes on when I get my sight," she said. Then she sat on his bed and messed with his hair.

"Well, you already know what I look like. I have brown eyes, stupid dark brown hair, and I'm really big and strong. You know... I look like Dad, only a little stronger, actually," he said with a chuckle.

"I bet you do. I can't wait to come home and see you," she said. She then leaned in to hug him.

"You already see me, Shamira," he said hugging her back tightly.

"I have to go, goofball. You better be training with Mom while

I'm gone. I don't want you getting soft on me," she said. She then stood and walked out before he saw the lone teardrop from her eye.

She walked toward the front door and noticed that her parents' voices instantly stopped. *No eavesdropping today, I guess.* "I'm ready, Dad," she said quite unenthusiastically, waiting near the door.

"It's about time. We better get going. I didn't realize how close we are cutting it," he said, then opened the door. She felt the air shift, and her mom moved quietly toward her.

"Shamira, enjoy this. Enjoy being able to see. It's all that I have hoped for you. I always wanted you to have a normal life with all it has to offer you. You'll love being able to see, just wait. Now hurry before your father leaves without you," she added. She tried to make a laugh at the end, but Shamira could hear a tremor of uncertainty in her mom's voice. *Hum, what's that about,* she would ponder that later. She grabbed her bag and walked to the car.

Her dad drove in silence to the spaceport. They flew at a higher altitude than some of the other air drivers. Most people tended to stay on the ground unless they were going long distances. Her dad only went in flight mode when they were traveling from their Sector to another, something they rarely did anymore. The crime level had skyrocketed in all Sectors, keeping the Security Force Elite much too busy for face-to-face meetings.

"We're here, Shamira. Follow me and don't slow down. The androids will grab our bags and park the car. We need to hurry. This may be the last space flight going out for a while," he said gravely. She didn't hesitate when she placed her finger on the panel to release the door. The door slid into the body of the car, and she got out. Her dad touched her so that she would know where to follow him.

"Dad, you don't need to lead me. I can smell you, so just walk." She hated when he treated her like she was weak. He knew some of her unique abilities included being able to differentiate between odors. She could especially pick out the smell of her family. They were the most familiar scents and stood out in the midst of many other odors.

"Hello, Special Nobel. We're honored to have you on our flight. Please follow me this way," said the female android. Androids were not plentiful on Mars because it was very expensive to ship them, but the majority of them could commonly be found in established places like the spaceport.

"Hello. Can you make sure we have a seat near an exit bay?" her father asked the android. Shamira frowned, wondering what made her dad request to be near the escape pods. Again, she thought about the hushed whispers of her parents.

"Dad, why would you request that?" she asked, and he pulled her by her arm to keep her moving.

"Don't concern yourself, Shamira. Let's go," he added, and without consideration to her feelings, he took off in a jog. She reluctantly followed, and before long, they came to a stop. She felt the presence of the massive passenger ship and almost missed her step. Before she could right herself, her father pulled her forward over the threshold.

"Sit down and buckle up. We made it just before takeoff. You should take a nap because it's about an eight-hour ride. I've got some work to do, so I won't be much company until we get you to the hospital, got it?" he asked, and she heard him pull out his suitcase.

Shamira didn't fight sleep. It was easy to doze right off since she'd had a late night and plenty of questions to keep her from sleeping soundly through it. She had tossed and turned, thinking about the kids and the boy she met. For a moment, she had actually felt sorry for him. Even though she had her issues with her mother, she couldn't imagine coming home to find her dead and her father and brother missing. She wondered how he made it all the way from Sector One, because it was a two-hour drive to Sector Five. She wondered how he had known to track down Lenny. She'd been tracking the sleaze ball for weeks, of course, using all her devices to do it, but she wasn't sure how this boy had managed.

As she thought about it, Shamira was certain her mother would be one of the Elite that would intercept her tip sent to the Security Force computer. Then, they would at least have a place to start looking. The Outlands were a pretty tough territory to search. She dreaded the thought but figured that it may be one of the places she would have to venture into with her new sight. She just wasn't sure she was ready to actually see what there was to see there.

In her stupor, she heard various passengers whispering about how dangerous it was to travel and that the Elite Security Force members were being hunted down like animals, many of them killed. Rather than worrying about it, she let their whispers lull her to sleep.

The loudspeaker woke Shamira from her nap. "Ladies and gentleman, we're landing on Earth in just thirty minutes. We thank you for flying with us on Space AirJet. Please remain in your seats until we land in DC," said the voice on the loudspeaker.

"Dad, did I sleep the whole time?" Shamira asked, batting her eyes several times to cure their dryness. She never slept that deeply, but then she hadn't been on a spaceship recently either.

"Yes, you did. Oh, Shamira, you need to be prepared for the slight gravity change when we get to Earth. It'll feel a little heavier when you walk. It usually takes a good two weeks to get used to it, so take it easy and don't try to run. Oh, also, your surgery is scheduled for today. We'll make it in just enough time for you to get checked into the hospital and put under."

"Great." She had very little excitement in her voice, and she figured her dad could tell she was a bit reluctant. She didn't care if he knew she didn't want to be here. He gently patted her hand.

The craft started to descend, and she felt the change in pressure, which was more enhanced than when she flew on Mars. They landed smoothly at the Earth Space Pad.

Chapter 7

She instantly felt what her dad had warned her about, a very heavy pressure weighing down on her, like her clothes were made of lead. Wiggling in her seat to adjust to the change, she stretched out while she tried to fight against the pull of gravity.

"Ladies and gentleman, please take the injection from the vial administered by the robotic arm in the seat in front of you. It will speed up the adjustment to Earth's gravity pull," the voice on the speaker said cheerfully.

"Shamira, it's okay. The doctor told us this won't affect your surgery, so go ahead," her dad reassured her.

"Fine. Will it hurt?" she asked then straightened her arm. Before her father could answer her, the metal robotic hand held her heavy arm in place, and then she felt a suction of her skin just under her shoulder. She felt tingling when the medicine sank in. Almost instantly, she wiggled her arms and noticed the effect.

"Better?" her dad asked.

"Yep. Just like home," Shamira added.

Her dad pulled her up beside him and again dragged her forward. She was really starting to get ticked off with his manhandling. He had never treated her like this before, like some kind of helpless ragdoll. *Why is he acting like I'm so helpless all the sudden?* She pulled back from him and jerked her arm away. "Dad, stop it! Stop treating me like I can't find my way, okay? You're ticking me off," Shamira said. She stood straight and wouldn't budge, and her dad didn't try to pull her anymore.

"I'm sorry, pumpkin. I'm just worried because I know this is all new to you. Just keep up with me, okay? The Earth Security Force has a car waiting for us at the gate. Just follow closely. It's not much safer for us here than on Mars right now, so let's go," he said and walked toward the exit. She followed him and felt the press of others around them while they ran through the Space Pad. She focused on the scent of her father and the path before her. Earth smells were rather overwhelming to her. The odors were so different it started to smell acidic instead of pleasant, and she started to feel dizzy from the onslaught of foreign scents. When they arrived at the vehicle, her dad grabbed her hand and pulled her inside its warmth.

"This place has so many smells. It's giving me a headache," Shamira said. She placed her hand over her nose and shook her head side to side to try to orientate herself to this new environment.

"I'll close the windows. Hey, Jake, I didn't know you were picking us up!" her dad exclaimed. He leaned forward to pat the driver on the shoulder.

"You know whenever you come to Earth, I have to be the first friendly face you see. I nearly tackled the new guy down to get to the car so I could pick you up. Hey, your little girl grew up to be a beauty! Man, her eyes are stunning. I've never seen eyes such a pale blue. She's got that burnt brownish gold hair just like her mother. How is Katherine, by the way? Still a bad ass?" The guy named Jake laughed.

"You know it. That's why I married her. I wanted a woman that could keep up with me. Oh, and Shamira's eyes are a result of the accident. Hopefully, they can fix the color when we get the surgery today. Shamira, this here is my old friend, Jake, one of the guys that started training with me in the Elite Security Force for Mars," her dad said. *He sounds so happy to see his friend,* Shamira thought. She wondered if he regretted his decision to leave his family and friends to move to Mars.

"Hi, Mr. Jake," Shamira said in a flat tone. Her thoughts were not on being polite, for she knew that by this time tomorrow, her life would be changed forever. She took a whiff of the air and realized that Jake had a nice, strong smell to him. It was a bit musty, so she figured he was a larger man. Most large people had a heavier scent. *He must be bigger than Dad.* She sniffed again and also realized he must be rather hairy, too, because his odor held a deeper smell of heavy cologne. It had to have somewhere to linger at this late time in the day, and usually people with hair carried false scents longer.

"Oh, she's a quiet one, I take it. Why did you wait so long to come back to visit? We've been hearing a lot about Mars at Headquarters, and it isn't good. After we drop her off, you only have a short while before the emergency meeting. You'll not want to miss that," Jake said, his voice growing heavy. They'd been moving at a steady pace and now were coming to a sudden stop. "Here we are— Johns Hopkins Hospital. Let yourselves out and go to the first floor. They're waiting for you. Here on Earth, Security Force members are treated exceptionally well. I'll be back for you in forty-five minutes, Nelson. Don't be late," he said.

Shamira felt the air pour into the vehicle when the door opened. The overpowering odors hit her at once. She focused on getting out of the vehicle without making a fool of herself and walked around it to the other side where her dad stood.

Jake couldn't believe how well she got around with her disability. "Hey, Nelson, you sure that girl can't already see? I didn't expect a blind person to have that much sense of their surroundings!" Jake laughed.

"She's my girl, Jake. What else would you expect? See you in a few," her dad yelled back. He grabbed her hand and walked inside the hospital.

"Dad, this place smells nice. Or better yet, doesn't smell so intense like it did outside. You sure this is a hospital?" Shamira asked and then removed her hand from his.

"Oh, it's a hospital alright. We haven't gotten to the prep room yet," he said. Someone walked up to Shamira, and she instantly knew it was an android because it didn't have any scent at all. It touched her shoulder before she could jerk away.

"Welcome, Shamira Nobel. Come with me, and I'll get you settled while your father finalizes the paperwork. My name is Kylin 5, and I'll be your android for your visit here at the hospital. Please follow," it ordered. It gently placed a soft hand on Shamira's shoulder and led her toward the operating prep area. Shamira sniffed while walking, concentrating on any smells she could recognize. As she walked further, she smelled a very faint tinge of blood. This was not something most people would notice, but it was an old sort of smell, like it had been cleaned over and over again but never quite completely removed.

"Here we are. Your room is right here. This room is where you will change. After you change, lay down on the bed, and it will move to the room next door where the operation will take place. The operation will only take about thirty minutes per eye. Your father mentioned you are to regain your original eye color of hazel brown.

Is that correct?" Kylin 5 asked.

"I'd like to keep my original eyes and my original color," Shamira said with a frown. She crossed her arms over her chest defiantly, for this was one thing she refused to compromise on. She wanted to remember being blind. It was so much a part of who she had been for all these years. She wouldn't let her parents just try to erase that away like it was something wrong.

"As you wish. In that case, the surgery will last a bit longer per eye since we will have to do a repair instead of a replacement, but that's no problem. We're here to accommodate. Now, please hurry. The doctors are waiting next door," Kylin 5 said and then moved to the door. Shamira knew the android was still in the room because she could hear the slight *hum* of its internal battery. She didn't care, though. She was ready to get the whole thing over with. The sooner this was done, the sooner she could go home.

She yanked off every stitch of clothing and then jerked up the gown on the bed. Doing as she was told, she didn't have to like it. She pulled the gown over her head and got into the bed like she was told. The lights in the room grew brighter, and heat warmed her from under her gown. She felt a shift on the floor and heard a slight grinding like gears were turning, and her bed moved through a set of sliding doors to a much brighter room than the one she had left. She forced her mind to go numb. Being in this new place was making her feel just a bit out of place.

"Hello. My name is Doctor Hawkins, and I'll be completing

your surgery today. I heard you requested that we repair your actual eyes, and I'll do my best. It won't be that difficult, but it will take a little longer. I'm sure your android already explained. Your father will be here when you wake up in a few hours. Now, we're going to put some tubes in your nose, and they will make you a bit sleepy. Enjoy your nap," he said. That was the last thing Shamira heard before she felt the tubes going into her nostrils, smelled a strange aroma, and was thrown in total darkness.

She awakened with a start and jerked straight up. She tried to open her eyes, but they were taped shut.

"Oh, great!" she said. *Now I have to wait to open my eyes. What kind of cruel joke is this?*

"Shamira, have patience. You can see. They just didn't want you to open your eyes before I got here. I wanted to be the first person you saw when you opened your eyes. I was running a little late, pumpkin, that's all," her dad said. He put his hand on her shoulder. "Well, are you ready?"

"Dad, just remove it, okay? Take off the tape. I want to get this over with," Shamira forced out. She bent her knees up and wrapped her arms around them. She was shaking slightly as her fear and doubt built.

"Uh, Shamira, before I take these off, I should warn you that your eyes are a bit more advanced than, say, a normal person's. Since I hoped you'd one day be a Security Force Elite, I asked the doctors to enhance your sight. You will be able to see an extreme distance away.

You will also be able to see through walls, but that's our secret, okay? It's going to take you a few days to get your mind used to controlling all of these features your eyes have, but it will be well worth it. Ready?" her dad asked. For once, Shamira was speechless. With all that her dad added to her eyesight, how could she not appreciate his thoughts? This would help her immensely when she got home, and she smiled at the thought and nodded for him to proceed.

Her dad's right hand was on the top of her head. He held her steady while he gently removed the tape from her eyes. She held her eyes closed and waited for him to remove his hands, and then she slowly opened both eyes. She marveled at the light peeking through her eyelids, and opened her eyes just a little. She breathed in deeply, then threw caution to the wind and opened them up to see her dad just an inch away from her. He had dark brown skin, a strong chin with a dimple in it, brown eyes, dark brown wavy hair, and a goofy smile on his face.

"Daddy, you are funny looking!" she said. She reached out and hugged him and laughed out loud. She looked past him and jumped back. The wall of white appeared to be within an inch of her nose. She cautiously put her hand up to her face and then reached it out to the wall that seemed to move. She shook her head. *What kind of eyes did they give me?* "Dad, the room is moving! Ugh! Stop it!" she yelled. She placed her hands over her eyes to take her back to her place of peace, the darkness she had known for so long.

"Shamira, you have to open your eyes. It's the only way you

will adjust and learn to use them," said Dr. Hawkins.

"How long is this going to take? I want to get out of here and go home! This sucks!" she spat out vehemently and then banged her heel on the bed. The confused vision made her feel helpless all over again. For the first time in over thirteen years, she had no control. She had to start over.

"If you open your eyes, it will only take twenty-four hours for your brain to adjust. But, if you hide in the darkness, it will take longer. Do you want to stay with us for a week instead of just a few days?" the doctor asked in a condescending tone.

"Fine," Shamira spat out. She opened her eyes to focus on her father's angry face.

"Shamira, your attitude stinks. This is a good thing, and you should be more appreciative. Now, take it slow and concentrate on getting used to managing the images in this room. I hate to leave you, but I've got an important call I have to take in private. I'll just be outside the door." As he stood to walk away, Shamira tried to focus on him, but he appeared to be moving in a blur toward the door. The doctor was staring at her now with a stern look on his face, and she promptly stuck her tongue out at him.

"Your dad is a good friend of mine, and I know he raised you to be better than this—stronger and willing to fight to improve. Let's show him that you can make him proud. Open one eye at a time. Look at the wall with the open eye and concentrate on looking *through* it to the other side. Push your sight through the wall with your mind, Shamira," he said in a deep, forceful voice.

Shamira concentrated with her left eye closed, and her right eye pulled the image of the wall closer. She commanded, *Go, push, go away,* and the image moved back to where it was supposed to be. Taking a deep calming breath, she told her eye to look past the wall, and she saw her dad looking like he was arguing with himself. She figured he was using his earlink, and he clearly wasn't very happy with the way his conversation was going. Switching eyes, she repeated the exercise. Smiling to herself, she opened both eyes and could see through the wall and past her father. She thought, *Further, push inside him,* and she saw blood pumping. The nanonytes that roamed through his body, through his technosuit caught her eye, and she laughed and said, "This is sweet!" In a much mellower, grateful tone, she looked up at the doctor, and said, "Thanks. Thanks for... you know... setting me straight."

Chapter 8

Her father walked in at that moment. She noticed his mood had changed. The look on his face was gloomy for a moment, but he shook himself out of his thoughts and smiled at her.

"You want to see something beautiful, Shamira? I bought this mirror. I want you to see the beautiful little girl I see. Here, take it," he said, handing her the mirror he held behind his back.

She lifted her hand and hesitantly took the mirror from him. Never having thought much about what she looked like, she didn't realize that at this moment, it meant something to her. She was scared that she wouldn't like what she saw. In the dark, she could be anything—a warrior, a fighter, and beautiful. But now that she was in the light, would she like what she would see? She held the mirror reflection away for a moment. Closing her eyes, she slowly lifted it up to her face. Opening her eyes cautiously and slowly, she lifted the mirror up higher and looked at her face for the first time. Pale blue eyes looked back at her. She blinked and saw her dark brown lashes flutter, and she poked out her full pink lips in a pouty fashion. She slowly smiled at herself, noticing a chin dimple that she obviously inherited from her dad. Her smile grew, and her full cheeks plumped under her olive skin. She took her hand and smoothed away the wayward golden and chestnut brown curl falling over her face. Then she touched her light brown eyebrow and caressed the side of her face.

"Not half bad, Dad. I don't look half bad. I was worried I would be a hag. Not bad at all," she laughed. Her dad lifted her up into a bear hug and laughed with her. Then she heard it. In the middle of his laugh was a slightly wounded whimper. Something was wrong. She felt it; she knew it.

Her dad pushed her slightly away from him, and he looked down at her like he did before she could see, "Look, Shamira, we can't stay long. We have to go home as soon as you are able. I have to go to the Security Force Headquarters for a few days. I hate doing this to you, but it can't be helped. We have to fly back in a private Security

Force cruiser. Earth has locked off outgoing airspace travel unless it's for official business. Shamira, please hurry and get well. I have to go. I'm proud of you. I love you, pumpkin." Then he got up and abruptly left.

She wanted to throw the mirror at him. He was holding something back, she knew it. Since her father had left, Shamira looked over at the doctor and took her anger out on him. "What are you looking at? Get over here and help me get better. I'm ready to go home," Shamira spat out. Tossing the mirror at the foot of the bed, she growled in frustration, and squeezed her bent knees.

"Look, I know you are a lot more than you seem. I've read your medical records. You will heal in half the time of any other patient in this hospital." He flipped opened her file and said, "Because I'm a longtime friend of your dad's, I'm going to give you some advice. Keep your secret to yourself. Don't let any other doctor here or on Mars examine you if you don't trust them. I have sealed your medical files. There will be another doctor attending you tomorrow, your last day required here. Make sure you keep your rage under control. We wouldn't want him to see what you're really capable of, Shamira, now would we? Now practice, and good luck to you," Dr. Hawkins said then he left.

Throwing off the cloak of self-pity, which she'd never been too good at wearing; Shamira climbed out of bed and practiced controlling this new gift. She had been given the gift of sight beyond what she could have ever imagined.

A few days later, her dad barged through the door during one of her personal training sessions. She didn't look at him but kept gazing out the window through the wall of the building across from them. She was intently watching some kids play a virtual videogame that she knew her brother would love. Shamira was good at many things, and holding grudges was one of them. She was still ticked off at her father and wasn't about to speak first, so the videogames provided her a welcome diversion. He had left her there for days without one call. *No word at all,* she seethed. *Oh yeah, I'm definitely ticked.*

"Hey, pumpkin," he began humbly, "I'm so sorry I had to leave you, but we need to talk now," he said. Her huge dad tried to sit in the small gray metal chair near her bed, but he barely fit. She walked over to where he sat, and he motioned for her to sit on the bed.

I will not say a word. She knew he was about to spill the beans, but she didn't know if she was ready to hear what he had to say. She felt the heat of his body rise. She looked deeper and saw his heart was pounding faster. *Oh, yeah, this is going to be bad,* she contemplated. She sat down with a feeling of dread when a tortured look passed across her father's face.

"There has been a tragedy at home, Shamira. Your mother and brother were out riding their motor pads when they were ambushed. During the fight with your mother, as some sort of distraction I believe, they stole your... your... oh, God, pumpkin, they stole your brother," her father said in a broken voice, barely able to keep it together. He was trembling, and tears were pooling in the corners of his eyes. She felt it then—a building sadness, anger, and fury that felt as if it might overtake her right in that moment. *Down, down, down! Don't lose control here!* She would save it, save it for them all. Tears fell heavily and unchecked from her angry eyes. Her lips thinned, and her fists balled up so tightly that her hands started to bleed. The sanitary whiteness of her room was tainted with small specks of blood dripping from her fingers biting into her hand. Droplets fell onto the white blanket.

"Shamira! Shamira! You're bleeding. Stop it. Stop it!" her father yelled, and jumped out of his chair to shake her. She came out of it, but not without the sting of frustration. They had to leave— NOW! Being here wouldn't help her find David. *Oh, and I'll find him and kill anyone who hurt him*, she thought menacingly. She turned quietly and took a deep breath. She grabbed her clothes from the bag near her bed and went to the bathroom. She had to get dressed, and fast. She got out of the shower and quickly put on her clothes.

She walked out of the bathroom and looked at her dad. "Let's go save him." Walking past him to the door, she was determined to leave immediately.

"You're reading my mind, little girl... reading my mind." He walked past her to lead the way.

Chapter 9

She didn't worry about looking at the boring white walls that surrounded them while they walked down the hallway. All she could think about was getting back home to Mars to save her brother and kill the monsters who would dare to steal him away.

"Shamira, this way. We don't have to drive to the Space Pad. There is a direct path to it down this hallway." He pointed ahead. The hallway they went down was white like all the others but had a sliding door just midway down.

Her dad had his eye scanned, and a voice welcomed him with, "Nelson Nobel, please enter."

Shamira watched the door open, and they went into an elevator.

"Level Minus Two," her dad said.

Shamira looked into the mirrored walls of the elevator. She peeked behind her and noticed that her bottom protruded much more than her dad's. "Hey, Dad, why is my butt so big?" she asked with a frown.

"Don't blame me! You're shaped like your mom," he laughed.

"That's not funny," she said. Then she folded her hands behind her back. *This is useless.* She hadn't seen her rounded behind before and didn't mind then. *I just have to accept me for what I am.* She dropped her hands to her side and looked straight ahead at the back of her dad's head.

"Our stuff is already loaded on the ship. You'll be helping me fly. I want you to use your experience from all the simulation exercises we did on Mars. I know you did it without sight and thought it was a joke," her dad said, regret in his voice.

"Stop beating yourself up about it. I'm fine, and seeing has its benefits, but there are some things I could have gone without seeing," she said, peeking back at her protruding behind and smiling.

"Here we are. Let's go straight to the cruiser. Not many of the staff is around. They're all preparing for the lockdown on Earth," her dad said when the elevator door opened. They walked through a large garage that held the private space jets for Security Force members. The space jets were sleek with retractable wings and a silver sheen of paint accented with black and gold trim.

"These are beautiful," Shamira said in awe. She walked over to the one that lit up for her dad when he approached and touched it. She closed her eyes, using the second sight she'd depended on for years, and walked from the middle of the space jet to the end. Joy spilled from her belly, and she smiled with her eyes still closed.

"I'm glad you like it. Now get in so I can go over the controls with you. " He was smiling at her when she opened her eyes.

"Sweet," she said and ran to the door. The door slid open smoothly, and she climbed in and to the back of the jet. The leather seats were comfortable and plush. Shamira got comfy in hers, and her dad climbed in and closed the door. She stretched out her legs and placed her feet on the pedals.

"Sit back in your seat. Your console is coming from the ceiling," he said and worked the controls. She watched the flat gray ceiling adjust, and the secondary console came from above. A detailed screen was attached that showed the back of her dad's head, the view in front of her, and the mappings of their route to Mars.

"Dad, this is amazing. I'm so ready! Can I drive first?" she asked. For the first time she could ever remember, she got butterflies in her stomach. She felt guilty for it, because she knew she should feel no joy knowing that David was probably somewhere hurting. *Oh, I'll definitely kill whoever took him and the others.* The smile on her face turned to a frown then she pushed her moment of happiness away. She was ready, raging, and angry to get home and do what her hunger wanted her to do—hurt, kill, and avenge.

"I'll lead, and you mimic my moves. Everything will come back from the simulations we did at home. And Shamira, whatever you do, don't close your eyes. You need to really see what we're doing. There are space bandits roaming free now that the Earth Security Force has locked down space travel to Mars. We have to be quick, fast, and focused. Above all, we must reach Mars safely. I have some snakes to track down and kill." He spoke with the most hate and venom she had ever heard from his usually jovial lips.

They took off, and Shamira tried hard to stay focused and not get swept away with her awe at seeing the ceiling of the building open up to a clear sky. The space jet seemed to go straight up and take off slanting skyward.

"I'm not going to waste time here. We're going into low hyperspeed to get into space as quickly as possible. If all goes well, we will be on Mars in about six hours. Brace yourself."

Shamira couldn't help but peek at the blue sky. The sun glared brightly, and she gave in to her awe at her new sight. Nevertheless, the muted windows softened the glow as their craft got closer and closer to the clouds. In a blink, they pushed through Earth's atmosphere leaving a tickling in the pit of her stomach. She skimmed the screen bio of their space jet and the control descriptions. She was impressed to realize that their space jet had major firepower. It also had the latest laser shooting technology that not only fired, but also found the power source of another ship and defused it, causing instant destruction to any opposition. The lasers were smart beams that hunted and fired on the selected enemy with the precision of a magnet.

"Shamira, study time is over. You need to mimic the controls with me. Split your screens so that you have them on each side, and then you can see me clearly and through the window ahead." She easily followed her father's lead. He smiled at her progress then said, "Now, we're in space and leaving the protected area. I'll need you to take over controls if anything happens to me or when I have to concentrate on firing."

She looked out to the black void of space lit up by sparkling stars. Refocusing on the controls, she grabbed the small forked wheel in front of her. Every move her dad made with the controls and the wheel, she followed, and they started to move completely in synch.

"Perfect, perfect. Now that you got it, I'm going in hyperspeed Level Two, heading straight for home," her dad said and focused on the sky in front of them.

They flew without incident for several hours, and Shamira loved her newfound joy in flying. She remembered hating the simulation sessions she had with her dad, using the computer that projected a visualized drawing of light in the shape of the vehicle in her mind. The simulation also pushed heated points on her body to simulate her touching or maneuvering certain controls. She used to think it was a waste of her time, but now she realized that she had simulated flying so much that it was a second nature to her. It was like she had done it for years before and was just getting reacquainted with it, as if she had actually flown before.

They heard a boom of laser fire pass by, "Shamira, heads up! We're being attacked. Damn! These are some nasty bastards, so shoot to kill," he yelled furiously.

"Who are they? What do they want?" she asked, quickly putting in the sequence to aim the laser missiles.

"Damn bandits. They're probably part of the scum crime organization that took your brother. Just prep everything for me to fire and hold on! I'm about to do some fancy maneuvering." He swerved out of the way of a laser shot from one of the other ships. The two attacking ships were smaller but had firepower and were gaining on them. Her breath caught in her throat when her father swerved and dipped, evading all the constant fire to their ship.

"Shamira, I want you to fire at them. Get it right, now. I don't want to waste any shots. I don't want them to have time to run and tell their friends we're on the way," he said and growled in anger.

She knew how to do it. She'd practice this from the time she could touch a computer. Her hands roamed over the controls and put in the locking sequence. She confirmed on the screen that her approaching targets were coming up quickly. She also put in a sequence to counteract against their fire and smiled to herself with triumph when each and every one of their missiles were met and destroyed.

"Show off. That's my girl! Ha ha!" her father laughed. She smiled widely. She realized she loved this just as much as hand-to-hand combat. *Ok*, she thought, *maybe not as much as that.*

"Dad, I'm going to shoot now," she said. She was hit by sadness again and anger. Eyebrows frowning, she fired then blew up the two attackers. Her dad pushed them into hyperspeed Level Four. She looked out the window to see streaks of white where stars once hung in the sky. The jet slowed down, and she looked ahead to see the bright reddish ball that was her home—Mars. A feeling of happiness filled her.

"Shamira. Fire! We're being attacked again. Quick. They're coming up from behind," her dad yelled. He cleverly maneuvered back and forth out of the way of the lasers.

"Dang!" she said. She saw countless fire come their way. She could have kicked herself for dazing out. She quickly locked on the targets, fired, and counter-fired. Breathing hard, she noticed one got away and returned fire. Just as her dad tried to outmaneuver their fire, she managed to hit them.

"Get him, Shamira! We will survive the hit!" her dad commanded. *How dare he get away!* She fired two missiles at them: one to counteract the missiles they fired, and one to hit them head on. The ship tried to outrun the missile, but Shamira used a smart missile for this creep. She had always thought the possibility of killing others would be a line she wouldn't cross, but it was in this moment she discovered that when it came to life or death, she would always choose to live, even if it meant her attacker had to die. She shrugged off the temporary moment of guilt. Their ship flew through the orange and blue fire and debris from the blast. Pieces of the ship flew in their path. Her father dodged them, and she let out the breath she'd been holding as they flew home.

Chapter 10

Her dad wasted no time landing their space jet at the Security Force Space Pad. He didn't speak, and she knew why, because she didn't feel much like talking either. She wanted to get home now and find out what exactly happened so she knew where she needed to go next. She needed to get on the streets to find out what else her target knew to get more answers.

They climbed in his company car and drove in silence. She couldn't help the temptation to look around and take in the beauty of her home. Red, blue, and gold hues came from the packed sand, windblown and a bit wild in its comparison to her brief observation of planet Earth. Her father flew home.

Her thoughts turned dark. The fury was building in her again, just as it always did when she spent too much time pondering things that made her angry. She remembered to push it down, down deep. She didn't want to tip her parents off to where her thoughts were leading her. If they knew what she was capable of doing, they would definitely lock her inside. Now with real physical sight at her disposal, nothing could stop her from pursuing those creeps that tried to control her world. They wanted to infect the world that she loved and use kids as pawns to control the Security Force that was in power. Her father's voice jerked her out of her thoughts.

"Shamira, we're home," he said with relief in his voice. There was heaviness there, and she felt it too. Sadness flowed within her, and a tear fell from her eye. Her eyes closed, and she pictured the David that she knew from her unseeing past.

The car landed in the driveway. Her dad quickly hopped out of the car, not looking back at her. She took a moment to stare at the gold from the setting sun on the house. The front yard was scattered with rock decorations of various colors and hues. They'd a cottage-style house with angular sharp edges that made it appear like it was part of the land around it. There weren't any other houses nearby, and she had to push her sight in either direction to see the neighboring homes.

The heat generators were kicking up. She closed her eyes and listened to their humming. Most people couldn't hear them, and she guessed they just sort of automatically tuned them out, but she had always heard them and felt the slight tremor where she stood when they kicked up the heat. Being blind had made her sensitive to those things that other people took for granted. It seemed that her senses hadn't lost their sensitivity. *It's good to be home.* She inhaled the Mars air that she knew so well.

Closing her eyes briefly, she pondered on how they had drilled miles under the planet's surface to add heating beams to make Mars as close to Earth temperatures as possible. Breathing in, she wondered about the towers throughout the planet that pushed clean oxygen and powered the heat generators buried deep within the ground. She raised her chin and felt the winds and sun, which generated the power on Mars every day and night. *The people on Earth take so many more things for granted.* Although the heat generators made Mars warmer than it would be without them, she realized that Mars was still much cooler than Earth.

Opening her eyes, she shook off a slight shiver when the coolness of the evening air hit her exposed face. Pulling her jacket closer, she took a deep breath, caged her anger, and walked toward the door. She opened the door and was hit by warmth. She looked up to see her dad as he embraced her mom. Shamira's mom had hair slightly darker than her own. Her face was pale with a sprinkling of freckles over her nose, giving her a youthful look. Tears fell unchecked from her mother's eyes, and her mom pushed away from her dad. She ran to Shamira and snatched her up in her arms. Her mom and she stood about the same height, but her mom was thicker. She had a firm grip when she pulled Shamira tightly against her. Caught off guard, Shamira didn't have a chance to return the embrace.

Shamira pulled slightly away from her mom to get another look at her and realized that she looked similar to what she had imagined. She closed her eyes and sniffed, smiling slightly at the familiar scent.

"Hi," she said, smiling. Her mom smiled at her through her tears, and Shamira noticed a deep dimple on her mom's left cheek. She reached out and touched it.

Her mom took her hand, and turned to her father. "It has been horrible. Nelson, everything is falling apart at Headquarters. They're tracking us down one by one and snatching our kids. I will kill the bastards. I will. If it's the last thing I do, I'll hunt every one of them down and make them pay!" her mom said, releasing her hold on Shamira.

Her father paced angrily and said, "Katherine, I know, baby. I know, but you will have to beat me to it," her dad said. His anguish showed brightly on his face. Growling out his grief, he punched his hand through the wall, and tears ran silently down his face. Her mom rushed over and hugged him from behind, whimpering while she cried.

"I'm so sorry, so sorry," her mom cried. Shamira stood and

watched them and thought this wasn't the way she wanted to see them for the first time. Again, her anger started to build. She had to go, to get out of there. She wanted to start looking for David. Her fist balled up and she tried to regain her slipping control. She would not cry. Refusing to give the slime that did this to her family the satisfaction, she would find the mastermind behind this. She was sure of it.

"Nelson, we have to go. They're waiting for us at Headquarters. We're having an emergency tactical meeting. This is a lot worse than we anticipated. A member from each of the Sectors arrived early today—or what remains of them anyway. They're waiting on us to get there. We must go." Her voice broke while she tried to regain her composure. She pulled away from her husband, whose head rested on the wall above the hole he'd made.

"What about Shamira? Should we take her?" he asked and pushed away from the wall.

"I think I'll be safer here, Dad. I want to get reacquainted with my home and spend some time in David's room. Please?" Shamira pleaded, bending her head down and trying to look pitiful. She didn't want them to notice the anger burning within her. It would give away her intentions to her dad. He knew the other side of her nature, the fighter, the hunter, and her inner beast.

"She's right. There'll be so much going on there. I don't even know if Headquarters is safe anymore," her mother said.

"Fine. Shamira, lock up," her dad said. He grabbed her mom

by the hand. They gave her a quick hug goodbye, and were out the door.

Taking a deep breath, Shamira looked around the room, which was bright, even with only few windows. She looked around and realized that the room was pretty open. There were no walls separating the main rooms. She looked toward the only wall in the room and knew it led to the bedrooms. Testing her ability to see through walls, she pushed her sight deeper into the room that was David's. She saw his bed and a picture of the two of them at the videogame dome. In the picture, she was leaning toward him with her hands tangled in his brown hair. She wasn't smiling, but he had a big grin on his face.

She shook off the memory of the day they'd taken that picture. Turning, she went straight to her room and took a selfish moment to look around, realizing that she liked the dark pink and purple colors. Taking a moment for research, she sat down at her desk and tapped into the Security Force main computer, still undetected. She wanted to know exactly what she was up against and what the Security Force knew about this crime organization, Monev.

"Jackpot!" she said when the screen came up with the results of her search. *Hum, the scum is trading drugs on Mars and Earth.* Now she realized why the Security Force on Earth locked down their airspace: They were cutting off the source of the drug that was not only highly addictive, but also gave its host extremely aggressive behavior when the addiction grew worse.

Shamira knew about the drug trading, but she still didn't know how the missing kids fit in the picture. She wondered how they tracked and captured the Security Force members. The Security Force members were extremely well trained and stronger than the average person. It would take ten average men to bring down just one Security Force Elite member.

Her research reached a dead end, and she decided it was time for her to do some digging of her own. She got up and threw off the jacket she had worn home. She quickly grabbed her hunting clothes and her weapons. Smiling, she placed her shades on her eyes. She still like the way they felt. *I'm ready.*

As she walked out onto the driveway, she felt something strange, as if someone were watching her. *Man, this sight is making me lazy.* She closed her eyes and inhaled. It was that boy. Tingling started in the pit of her stomach, so she took a calming breath. She was curious what he looked like, but she wasn't about to let him know that. She stood up straighter and turned around slowly. Her breath caught when her eyes landed on him. He was beautiful. A bit taller than she was, he was dressed in a black form-fitting jacket and jeans. He had billowy blonde curls, dark green eyes, and dimples on each cheek. He smiled at her with the cocky, self-assured grin. She slowly lowered her glasses and frowned at him.

"What do you want? I thought I told you to stay away from me - boy," she spat out and put her hand on her hip.

"My name is Valens, and you are not getting rid of me. Also, from the way you look, I'm older than you - girl," he said with a lift of his eyebrow. "I want the same thing you want—to find the bastards who are stealing kids and killing the Security Force members."

He sauntered toward her. She didn't want him to come too close, or he would see how uncomfortable he made her. Taking a deep breath, she thought, *I better work really hard to fake it.* She didn't want him to go with her because she worked best alone, and she was sure he'd make her lose her concentration.

"Well, it's up to you to try and keep up. I don't like partners - they're sloppy," she said, and then turned from him.

"Come out, Pearl," she said to her motorcycle.

"Who said I was giving you a choice?" he replied and reached to touch her arm. Remembering that she didn't like to be touched, he pulled his hand back. She looked at his arm retreat, and lifted an eyebrow.

"You're different somehow. Can you see me now?" he asked, studying her with his eyes.

"Does it matter?" she snapped.

"I never thought it did," he said with a shrug.

"Yeah, I can see. Doesn't matter though, I could have tracked them when I was blind – and *alone*," she snorted and smirked.

She turned away from him and hopped on her motorcycle. She was getting ready to pull off when she felt the weight of Valens press against her back, and his hands gently held onto her waist. She didn't trust her voice to speak clearly, so she took a deep breath.

Kicking the motorcycle into full gear, she headed toward Sable Street.

Chapter 11

"Hey, let's go to Snake Ice, that gaming room on Black Snake Avenue. I have a lead there," Valens said way too close to her ear. She was not in the mood for his demands.

"Look, I have a lead on Sable Street, and that's where I'm going," she said, irritated.

"That lead you had is dead. Trust me. He's dried up, and his cold, dead body has been tossed into outer space. We'll get more information at the Snake Ice gaming hell. Trust me, okay? We're on the same team," he said, as his hands squeezed slightly on her waist.

"Fine. We'll go to Snake Ice then," she spat out. She wished he wasn't so close. He really made her feel uncomfortable. It seemed like everywhere he touched felt heated. She took a breath to steady herself.

"So, since you are seeing me for the first time, how do you think I look?" His sweet smelling breath caressed her ear when he asked the question.

I will not give him the satisfaction of the compliment he's fishing for. No way. "I saw you before I got my eyesight. Smelly, cocky, and a sloppy fighter. Now my eyesight just confirms it," she said with a smirk. She figured her comment must have worked, because he pulled away from her and only held onto her jacket, not even touching her waist. She felt a little chill, but she brushed it off. *This is better. He needs to save his flirting for someone else. I don't need the distraction.* Her brother came first, period.

"Here! Turn here. We still have a few miles to go to get to Sector Seven. When we get near, park where we won't be seen. I know a kid that will let us in from the back entrance," he said, pointing to the turn.

Shamira thought about Sector Seven, which she'd heard was falling on hard times. Sector Five may have had its bad areas, but Sector Seven had many more. It was like a virus was spreading on Mars, and crime, poverty, and homelessness were taking over. With the Security Force members coming up missing, the infrastructure that held Mars together was breaking apart. It was like a war was brewing, and the kids and innocent people of Mars were about to be swept up. Shamira couldn't help but wonder, *How are they able to hold the Security Elite down? What are they doing to them? How are they tracking them?* "Valens, do you know what they do with the kids? Why are they even taking them?" she asked, figuring he may know something she didn't. Adjusting in her seat, she tried to focus on the dark road ahead. She passed cars, squeezed between trucks, and drove at top speed. No one knew the leader by face or name. Whoever led them stayed extremely hidden.

"I don't know about the leader, but I have an idea of why they're preying on the Security Force Elite. The lead I'm following has his hands dirty in the dream pushing business. That business is booming. Especially in the Sectors that have missing Security Force members. The kids are probably an insurance policy for Monev, to make sure that the Force stays too busy taking care of their own," Valens spilled.

"Did you have a chance to check out the Outlands? My lead said he believed some of the kids may be held there," Shamira said.

"No. I have to get some gear first. That place is dangerous. Not to mention it's cold as hell there. The generators are few and far between out there, and we'll freeze before we get to their hideout if we go unprepared," he said. He was feeling a little at ease now, because his hands rested back on her waist.

Just great. More delays. She was getting angry at all this waiting, but she had limited time tonight to search. "Well, your lead better be a good one," she said.

She hit the clearing and turned into a hidden parking space behind the building. Lights of the city shined brightly in the dingy night air, and sand blew by in the two-moon Mars sky. The magnetic fields buried in the north held most of the sands to the south at bay, but they didn't always work as well at night when the sandstorms were the strongest. Shamira climbed off her motorcycle and ignored Valens behind her. Pulling her jacket closed, she yanked up the zipper at the top and then pulled at the bottom zipper to open up the bottom part of her jacket, which would give her access to her weapons. She heard him slide off the motorcycle. He came up behind her, and she felt his hand reach out again. The air changed when he pulled it back.

"Let me lead the way this time. I know it's hard for you, but I have connections here that will help us get in without paying or jacking in to the games. Give me a minute though. I have to call Tim to let us in," he said. Dismissing her before she could argue, he walked ahead to the alley entrance to the club. She frowned at him. *How dare he.* She worked alone and didn't need his help, or at least she wouldn't after this.

She followed behind him, looking around at the brown and black buildings huddled together on the city block and sand swept ground separating the bundles of buildings. There were people hanging out around the buildings, most of them trying desperately to get in, and many of them clearly strung out on dream. She pondered over the different products Monev sold. Dream, they sold in order to hook people on the euphoric feeling of happiness. It was basically a cheap street drug. Scream was sold to get their upperclass clients addicted to the gaming hells they ran. It seemed to Shamira that Monev had no bounds to the poison they tried to push. They found every angle and exploited anyone and everyone at their evil whim.

Shamira continued to watch people huddle around the club entrance. The people hooked on dream had a glazed look in their eyes and were not talking or aware of their surroundings. They were like human zombies while the drug had them in the pleasure phase. That would change once their fix was over. They would become angry, anxious, and violent, depending on how deep their addiction went.

Looking at Valens, she could tell he was waiting for the boy named Tim, their ticket into hell. Snake Ice was one of the most dangerous places on Mars, so she braced herself to prepare for what was within. Her eyes closed and she inhaled the gritty smell of her surroundings. She felt a brief change in the wind and realized that Tim must have opened the door. Opening her eyes, she followed Valens into the building. The hallway was dark, and Tim walked ahead of them. Tim was tall and lanky with a shot of green hair that stood straight up to a point. He smelled of dream, the drug that was infecting Mars like a disease. She grabbed Valens by the jacket. He turned slightly toward her.

"Look, I don't want any dreamhead identifying us. They can't be trusted," she pushed out in a whisper, nodding toward Tim.

"He's okay. He just sells it. If he became a user, they'd kill him. They don't want users giving away their information to the Security Force," he told her in his deep voice. She continued to follow but refused to trust this kid who smelled like sour perfume - like dream.

The club played loud music, and there were huge screens on all the walls with games and various tournaments. Games of death, destruction, and addiction were played here. Winners took home millions of dollars in debits. Losers sometimes lost their lives. This was what her parents fought to keep off of Mars and what Earth fought to keep here.

Shamira looked at the games with her eyes for the first time. They were vivid in color, images of the players held within. Some players, the serious ones, jacked in using bio conductors that were lodged into their brains. They would go to an underground surgeon to get those shot in and then would wirelessly connect to the games they played in the different gaming hells. People that were just experimenting started off with nanoshots. She could tell who they were by the blue hue around their lips, a known side effect. Nanoshots were vials of microcomputers that users would drink. The vials were laced with a drug that enhanced the virtual reality of the games. It came out in their bowels within twenty-four hours, taking the euphoria of the game with it right down the drain. The experience would cause the players to seek it out again if they weren't strong enough to resist.

"Hurry up, dude, before they see us," Tim said, gesturing for them to follow. Shamira pushed her sight past the wall above them and saw two men arguing over what she presumed was money. One guy with jet-black hair and a scar slanted on his lips gave the other guy some dream. It was enough to sell to a small army.

"Tim, who runs this place?" Shamira asked while he walked them through the crush of people watching the games, drinking, dancing, or high on dream.

"I don't know the guy, but he comes and goes here a lot. You'll know him if you see him though. He has an ugly-ass scar right down his lip," Tim said, pointing them toward a corner behind the bar.

"Thanks, man. Remember, if you need a place to hide, I got one for you," Valens said as he slapped hands with Tim.

"I know, man, but I think I can help you more from in here," Tim said, and then walked away.

"How do you know all these guys?" Shamira lifted an eyebrow and leaned back against the wall. She took a moment and closed her eyes, seeing with her other senses. She inhaled the overpowering scent of all the different odors in the room and tried to find something different.

"Hey, stop closing your eyes. That freaks me out," Valens said. He was looking out at the crowd as if he were looking for someone he knew.

"So, who are we hunting for tonight, Valens?" Shamira asked, gazing over the crowd of gamers and partiers.

"This guy that works for the thug that runs the human pushing ring here on Mars," he answered.

"What do they do with the people they capture?" she asked and moved off the wall to look more intently at the crowd.

"They go after the genetically gifted, so to speak—types like the Elites. People pay for muscle grafting, good health, and the best body transplant specimens available," he said, disgusted. She looked at the blond curl falling over his eye as his eyebrows frowned. His lips frowned and a look of recognition showed brightly on his face.

"Who are we looking for?" Shamira asked again, this time with an edge of anger and frustration at having to wait to find out who her target was.

"There he is. Fisher. The kids around these parts warned me to stay away from him. They say he will try to add as many kids to his collection as he can get. He's the one who collects young meat. There's another that collects the grownups," Valens said. His eyes followed the guy named Fisher.

She looked at Fisher, a big guy with a broken nose and brown hair. He was feeling up and talking to some woman. The woman was a blond with her hair pinned up and her breasts falling out of her slinky purple dress. Valens' gaze paused over the woman and looked her over from head to toe. Shamira smirked. *Figures he'd be after the double-Ds just like every other guy.*

"Look, I don't want to wait here all night for him to leave. Let's roam and talk to some of the kids here that would know his habits,"

Shamira suggested. She started to walk along the side of the crush of people, and Valens followed closely behind. As they walked around, she saw a boy cleaning the floor around the bar on his hands and knees.

"Hey, why don't they have the android doing that?" Valens asked, bending down to slip the boy some credits for information. The boy hesitantly took them and shoved them in his back pocket.

"They make me do it for punishment. I messed up the pass of the dream, and my boss threatened to give me to Fisher. I would lick the toilets clean before I would willingly go with that sadistic bastard," the boy spat out.

"Dude, what's your name? I got a place you can hide if things get sticky for you," Valens said.

"Naw, that's alright. I don't want to bring my boss down on you. He can be a son of a bastard, but he's better than the alternative," the boy said.

"Hey, what's your name? I need some information," Valens said lowering his voice.

"Kevin," the kid said, scrubbing the spot under his hand with serious vigor. Shamira glanced down at the kid and wondered why he didn't take Valens up on his offer for help. She turned away from them and looked out for Fisher among the mass of people crammed on the floor.

"Do you know who Fisher works for? Where they may be holding some kids that were kidnapped?" Valens asked and then looked around briefly to make sure no one noticed him.

"Oh, man, you don't want to know where Fisher's boss is. Where he is, death is. Believes in the old ways of torture and punishment, they say. I think Fisher is a fake compared to Slasher," Kevin said, and then moved up the floor of the bar. Shamira noticed one of the guards observing them a bit too closely.

"Hey, c'mon, Valens. Someone's onto us," Shamira said and tapped Valens with her boot heel. He looked in the direction of the door and saw the muscle-head guard walking their way with a distrusting scowl on his face. Shamira hurried toward the back entrance, and Valens followed.

"Go to the left. That hallway leads to the exit near your motorcycle," he said while he pointed.

"That guy is on us. This way," she said and took off down the middle hall. They ran at top speed to the door and heard the muffled sound of an argument. Shamira looked back to make sure the guard wasn't still following them. She slowed down and put her hand up to Valens to signal for him to stop. He ran into her and caused her to slide a few feet. The sound of their clumsy collision was silenced by the distant sound of the music. Shamira walked softly toward the hallway off to the side of the entrance. She put her finger up to her lips and motioned to Valens to be quiet. Just ahead she saw two thugs tugging some kid back and forth. She heard the boy scream and the voices of two men arguing got louder.

"You can't save him now, Danny. I'm going to kill his sorry ass right here. The little bastard spent my money, and he will pay for it with his life," a deep voice yelled.

"Don't be a fool! This kid sells more dream than any of those slack ass runners you have. He's worth more alive. We just need to rough him up enough to teach him a lesson. Like this," a guy with a softer, more menacing voice said. Then she heard a *thump,* and the boy cried out while she watched his body crumble from the punch.

Her anger rose, and her adrenaline started to pulse. She wanted to save the boy, but she wanted even more to hurt these men. She stepped into the hallway in front of the three, took her metal ball out of her belt, and threw it at the tallest guy on the left. The ball flew at him, its metal net opened, and the hooks extended. It slammed the man's head against the wall. She ran full speed at the shorter, bushy eyed man. Quickly, she twisted her glove, which extended her claws and slashed him on the face. She felt power now. Her heart was beating, and she couldn't stop. She couldn't help herself. Beating this man's head to the wall made her feel better, like she was getting a little revenge on someone that was part of the gang that stole her brother.

"Shamira!" she heard. She didn't stop, but the guy she was beating did. He fell against her in dead weight. She smelled blood and moved back as the man fell dead to the floor. Turning her head toward the boy she'd saved, she saw a look of guilt written on his face.

"Sorry, but he was going to kill you. He went for his gun while you were beating him. He likes pain and isn't really fazed by it. I didn't want him to hurt you like he did my sister," the boy said. Shamira looked him up and down, studying his jet-black hair and his piercing gray eyes.

"What's your name?" Valens asked. Shamira crossed her arms and continued looking the boy over from head to toe.

"Mitch. C'mon. We got to get out of here, quick!" Mitch said, dropping the gun to run toward the door. Valens took off and grabbed Shamira by the jacket. She jerked away from him.

"I can't leave a mess," she said. She ran to the man held by the metal net. Taking a pill from her belt, she forced it into his mouth. Then she kneed him in the groin to make him swallow the pill. "That will take my face out of your mind, you scum."

She yanked the hooks from the wall. The ball retracted the net, and she put it in her pocket. She turned around to follow Valens when she saw a look of irritation on his face.

"Duck!" he yelled. She ducked, and he threw a boomerang-like device at the guard that had been tailing them. The silver boomerang hit the guy and knocked him out cold. He fell in a heap on the floor. The device returned to Valens, and he compressed it and jammed it into his pocket. Valens grabbed her by the jacket, and they ran out the exit door to her motorcycle. Mitch grabbed a nearby hummer board and followed them as they sped away from the scene on her motorcycle.

"Go near your home, two blocks up. My motorcycle is there.

I'll take this kid to my hideout and get some answers out of him when we get to my cycle," Valens said from behind her. Shamira sped, and the boy was right behind them, his slim body fitted with a light jacket for the cold Mars night. She focused on the road ahead of them. Taking several deep breaths to calm down, she felt a sensitive tingling on her skin from the remnants of the fight. She wanted to hurt someone. The training room will have to do for tonight.

She pulled up to Valens' motorcycle and paused to look up at the two moons in the sky. *Crap, nothing is going as planned.* He slowly slid off, letting a hand linger on her waist. She turned to him and frowned, and he smiled a dimpled smile back at her, and then walked toward Mitch. She got off her cycle and followed him. *Valens, you won't be the only one to get answers from this kid.* Frowning, she looked Mitch over. This kid looked her age, but he was now a killer.

"So, Mitch, what's your story?" Valens asked, his hands on his hips. Shamira walked over, crossed her arms over her slightly bloody black jacket, and frowned at Mitch.

He rubbed his hand through his hair. "Well, about a year ago, I came home to a massacre. My aunt, who moved here to help my dad with my sister and me after my mom died, was stabbed, lying on the living room floor. My dad was missing, but he gave whoever took him a fight. Everything in the front room was broken, and there were holes in the walls. They didn't find my sister. She was hidden in a spot I showed her when we played hide and seek," Mitch said. His eyes watered. He got a dazed look, as if reliving that horrible moment.

"What's your dad's name?" Shamira asked. She distanced herself from his pain, not wanting to think of that as a reality for her family.

"Carl Poole. He was one of the Sector Seven Security Elite. A lot of good it did him, since he got taken and got my aunt killed," Mitch said.

"So, where's your sister?" Valens asked. He crossed his legs when he sat down and faced them on his bike.

Mitch started to pace slowly and said, "I don't know exactly. I found my sister and figured we'd better hide. We contacted the Security Force in our Sector, and they helped us out for a short while, and then they just forgot about us. We got hungry, and street junkies tried to take us and sell us to Fisher." Mitch stretched, and then crossed his arms in front of his chest.

"Did they sell you?" Shamira asked flatly, sizing Mitch up to see if he was telling the truth.

Mitch frowned back at her and said, "What do you think? Anyway, that guy I killed back there, his name is Snake. He... well, I thought I had bargained with Fisher's cronies. I decided to sell some dream for them so Kate and I could eat. I started working for Snake and Kimble."

He shifted and turned to Valens, "They work under Fisher, the leader of the human trafficking part of the gang named Monev, or The

New World , they sometimes call it. Well, they took Kate and promised me that Slasher, their leader, would not hurt her if I did what I was told. Then, they put me on the street to sell dream. I haven't seen my sister since, and I haven't gotten paid." A lone tear dripped from his eye, and the anger he felt showed through his pain.

"You can't go back," Valens said.

"I know. They have my sister and my father – that is, if he isn't dead already. You don't know what they're capable of. I also know where they may be keeping some of the kids and maybe the adults too. If we go, we have to go with guns, or we're dead," Mitch said, his eyes now dry.

"Oh, we are going. You can bet on it. But for now, boys, I have to run. I'll see you tomorrow," Shamira said sternly.

She heard Valens say to Mitch, "I got a place for you, dude. Follow me."

"Meet me here tomorrow!" she yelled back. She hopped on Pearl and rode home. She had to go to the training room to exercise away the excess energy from the night's events. *Crap.* She hated waiting. As she came up to the house, she let out a breath of relief. Her parents were not home. She climbed off her bike and walked toward the house. "Pearl, go park and clean yourself," she said.

She walked in the house and straight to her room. Opening up the clothes compacter, she told it to clean her soiled clothes. Then, she walked naked to the shower to wash off the blood and dust from her night out. She couldn't wait to go to the training room. Sleep was the furthest thing from her mind. She was filled with adrenaline that she had to shave off before she could face her parents when they returned.

Chapter 12

In the training room, Shamira worked herself to exhaustion and slept just a few hours before returning to the training room again. The training room was underground like many of the Elite had in their homes. This fact was unknown to anyone not on the Elite Security Force, including the support staff.

Her parents both worked out in the training room, though her mom did most of her training at the Security Force Headquarters for their Sector. Her parents led Sector Five and were virtually the rulers of their Sector. When the Security Force members started turning up missing, the second in command would lead, but those Security Force members were not enhanced, only the Elite few were. The Elite had certain abilities they gained from training at a young age, and their special suits only left them vulnerable on their heads and groin areas. Shamira wondered again how Monev was able to bring the Elites down. The tags or tracking devices they wore were only traceable from the supercomputers at Headquarters, and even she couldn't break in that deep. It would take her years to get past the barriers to access that information.

She punched the bag in front of her again. Her preference was working with the punching bag and sparring with the android when her dad wasn't available. Today though, it wasn't doing the trick. Turning away from the bag, she touched the control on her wrist to activate the fight simulation. The punching bag disappeared into the ceiling.

Besides the punching bag and the sparring android, the training room also had an obstacle course, weights, and a simulation room for learning flight maneuvers and finding information about a particular enemy that would allow her to build a replica and find their weakness. She went to a nearby table to get some dot tags that stuck to the vulnerable parts of her face to simulate a punch on either one of those areas. Its purpose was to make the trainee used to accepting pain, which was something Shamira did rather well. The simulation created a virtual reality with the enemies she programmed in with her wrist controller. She knew it would effectively replicate the pain and even the smells associated with being hit, and she was ready. She zipped up her form-fitting simulation suit that covered her from head to toe.

"Multiple fighting sequences with obstacle course," she said to the computer in the training room. The lights dimmed, and she closed her eyes to get her former rhythm. She readied herself and made sure she was able to sense all things around her. The simulation created a twenty-man attack on her home. She was thrown into a replica of her living room, and bad guy Fisher that she created for the simulation burst through the front door. She ran toward him and front-kicked him in the face, feeling the adrenaline rush she was searching for. His cronies came from behind, and she followed through on a back-kick just as another nameless foe punched her on the side of her face. She smiled. This is what she needed—a good fight. She was just getting started when the simulation suddenly ended.

"What? Restart simulation now!" she yelled.

"Not Today, I need a sparring partner, so I cut off your simulation," she heard her mom say. *Now this is rare*, Shamira frowned. *I've never sparred with her before, so why does she want to do this now?* She didn't want to hurt her mother by turning her down, but she was afraid to let her mother find out what she was capable of. Especially know that she was all keyed up from what she'd seen and heard that evening. She just had so much anger and frustration built up in her that she didn't think she had the control to hold back from hurting her mother or concealing her hidden strength.

"Mom, I kinda want to do this alone today," Shamira said as she took off her simulation gear.

Ignoring her, Shamira's mother said, "Computer, we're going to the sparring room."

Great. Her mother was wearing a green form-fitting sparring suit. It had a zipper up the front, and her feet were sticking out at the bottom. Her mom was in better shape than Shamira realized. She had strong legs, a muscled stomach, and firm, yet softly muscled arms.

"Don't worry, Shamira. I can take anything you can dish out. The question is, can you take what I dish back? " her mother said and squatted into a fighting stance.

Taking off her simulation tags, she tossed them to the floor. Shamira followed her mom's lead, and the lights in training room lit up brightly. The wood floor beneath Shamira's bare feet felt cold, and she looked into her mother's eyes and saw a fighter there. With no hesitation, she lunged and punched at her. Her mother dodged the attack with speed. Her mom followed through with a punch to Shamira's stomach, but Shamira didn't flinch. She was used to hits and responded with an uppercut. Her mom quickly moved to the side to escape her punch and landed a punch to Shamira's face. Shamira was getting tired of holding back, and her threadbare hold on her control started to slip. She dipped and punched her mom hard in her stomach, which pushed her mom back about two feet.

"Shamira, I do believe you are stronger than you let on. Don't hold back. Push it, girl! Let it go," her mom said, not a bit out of breath from Shamira's punch. Shamira released her hold on her strength, and she and her mom did a fighting dance of punching and kicking across the room. Even with Shamira pushing to maximum strength, her mom kept up. Her mother landed more punches, jabs, and kicks than Shamira did just by attacking Shamira's weak points. At the end of their sparring session, they were both out of breath and Shamira felt much better, having let off the steam of her frustrations.

"Shamira, I'm impressed. You're a worthy opponent," she panted, "You even found some of my weak points I had forgotten about. Thank you! It was fun." She rubbed a sore spot on her shoulder.

Shamira was stunned. She had rarely gotten compliments from her mom, and she felt joy spill over inside her. Now she knew she was ready to do what she had to do. She also realized that the power that was within her grew the more she challenged it. Her mother had taught her to push harder than she would have with her dad.

"Thanks, Mom," she blushed, "Are you going back to Headquarters? Have you all found some answers?" Shamira asked.

"Well, now you are going to get me all angry again. As we suspected Monev is behind the attacks. Of course, you realize that Monev spells V-E-N-O-M backwards, right? I guess they use that

108

name to describe the drugs they're pushing. Anyway, we didn't plan for this type of attack, and a lot of families of the Elite have been lost in the process of the Mars Planet Police efforts to control the crime. Earth wants nothing to do with this, of course, and won't allow any travel between Mars and Earth until we get control of the problem here," her mom said while she folded her legs to a crossed-leg sit.

"How are they finding the Security Force Elite members," Shamira asked, folding her legs in similar fashion to her mother's.

"Well, we don't know exactly how they're doing it, but we figure they are using the Security Force Elite's tracking devices against them. They've obviously found a way to find us," she answered while stretching.

"Okay, well finding you is one thing, but how do you catch an Elite?" Sharmira asked frowning in thought.

Her mom sighted, "We're pretty sure they have also probably spent years spying on us and building a device that scrambles the nanos that give our suits their strength. Besides, we're strong even without our nano boost. So, the truth is, I don't really know how they're bringing us down," her mom said then started to stand.

"How close are you to finding David?" Shamira asked.

"Not as close as I'd like to be—not nearly as close." Her mother winced a bit at the question. "Hon, I've got to go. Your dad is coming home in the morning to check on you. Please take your earlink if you leave the house," her mom said before she headed out the training room door.

After her mother was gone, Shamira's thoughts moved to her next meeting with Valens that night. She pictured his face, and her breath caught at how beautiful he was. She knew it was stupid to think of him this way, he was simply too beautiful for her. *I just don't deserve him for myself—not like that, anyway,* Shamira's thoughts teased. But part of her wouldn't let the desire to have him for her own slip away.

She took a deep breath and thought to herself how things were a lot easier when she couldn't see. Being blind, she wasn't captured by a person's outer beauty. She could stay in the safe shell she created for herself. Now, she had to work harder at not being charmed out of it. She forced her mind to put thoughts of Valens away.

Reminiscing on her brother, she couldn't help but picture the horrible things that could be done to him if she didn't find him soon. She didn't want to involve so many others in her quest, but unfortunately, she realized that for now, she needed Valens' and Mitch's help. She needed them as backup and for the information they were easily able to gain from their friendships with other street kids. She put her face in her hands, took a deep breath to relax, and went to change to meet Valens in a few hours.

When she drove Pearl to the designated meeting spot, they were waiting for her. She was not surprised. Valens was always punctual. He was wearing black leather pants and a matching jacket. His wavy blond hair escaped from his black hat. Mitch cleaned up well, too, with jeans and a matching jacket.

"Shamira, we figure we can hit the hideout in the Outlands if you're up to it. Mitch knows the way there. We'll have to walk about a mile to get to the place, but I brought something to help us with that too. These shoe tags will help us glide at a faster speed to get there and escape if we have to. They also have guns there, so Mitch and I are wearing bullet- and laser-proof jackets. I brought one for you, too, if you want it," he said with a sly smile, holding the jacket out to her.

"Sure, I'll take it. You lead. I'll follow right behind," she said and hoped he wouldn't ask to ride with her.

"Um, Mitch is driving my cycle." Valens cleared his throat and said, "How about I ride with you and direct you where to go." He looked back at Mitch who appeared temporarily shocked at the statement before putting back on his angry guy face.

"Oh, yeah, that's definitely best. Let's go," Mitch said flatly as his expression recovered. He got on the motorcycle quickly, as if he didn't want to catch Shamira's eye.

Just my luck. This is not going to be easy. Valens climbed on her motorcycle behind her. She took off her jacket and replaced it with the much safer one he had brought for her. He helped her put it on, and Shamira wasn't sure whether to be annoyed or flattered. He leaned in toward her neck to adjust the collar. The skin of her neck tingled as his breath touched it.

His hand left her collar to rest on her shoulder, and she stayed perfectly still, not wanting him to know that he was affecting her. He leaned close to her ear and spoke softly, "That should do it. Mitch is leaving us." She felt his breath on her ear, and then shivered.

Snapping out of her embarrassment, she grabbed her helmet from the handlebar and put it on her head. Then, she leaned forward and took off at top speed behind Mitch. She drove thinking of how they would get into the facility unnoticed. She had brought some devices that would help. Her heart started to pound when she thought about the fight ahead of her. She was thirsty for it—the hunting, the fighting, and the joy of finally seeing David again. *David, David, David.* Seeing his face in her mind was the best way to keep thoughts of Valens away.

The Outlands were rarely traveled. They were extremely cold and windy. Sand kicked up at high levels, causing gritty mountains of red dirt to form out of the ground. The visor on Shamira's helmet protected her eyes, but she replaced them with her shades for their journey to the criminal compound. Getting off their bikes, they took a look around and tightened their jackets.

"Here. Take these and put them on the heels of your shoes. They will allow us to hover a couple of feet above ground to get to their hideout faster," Valens said while he handed them flat metal plates that hooked into the soles of their shoes.

"Mitch, what do you know about this place? About the security? Where are the innocent people held?" Shamira questioned as she attached the hoverplates to her boots.

Mitch turned toward her with an angry look on his face and said, "Well, from hanging around Fisher, Slasher, and Kimble, I know more than I'd like. The compound is very hard to find. I know the general location, but it's completely out of sight. We may have to observe the location before we attempt to enter. The security there is very tight. I've no idea how we're going to get in, much less how to get out. You got any ideas, Valens?"

Shamira lifted an eyebrow and said, "I'll find the hideout. Trust me. I have my ways to get in. I have scrambling devices for all of us that will make us invisible to any surveillance." She scanned the area briefly. "As far as sneaking up on them, I don't have anything that will keep us out of the view of any armed guards, but I don't think they have any in plain sight. If they did, they wouldn't try so hard to conceal their hideout. I'm willing to bet they don't have guards posted outside. I bet they're relying solely on electronic surveillance that keeps them hidden and picks up on any movement outside. Now, let's go," Shamira said, then walked past Mitch without sparing a glance at Valens.

Valens looked at Mitch and winked. Mitch didn't budge, and Valens said, "You heard Warrior Girl. Let's go, Mitch."

She stopped when they didn't immediately follow. Shamira eyed Mitch, who looked her, then to Valens and shook his head. Ignoring his reluctance, she turned away from them to continue.

Shamira knew that Mitch didn't want to follow her. He seemed to trust Valens more than he trusted her. Valens was good, but he wasn't her. She knew *she* was going to save David. Valens was just along for the ride as far as she was concerned. She hoped he had improved his hand-to-hand combat, because they were probably going to have a fair share of it trying to get out of this place.

She stomped down on the sand-packed ground, which activated the hovering mechanisms Valens gave them for their shoes. Her legs bent as she balanced about three feet from the ground. Mitch glided in front of her, and they followed him across the windy terrain. The wind tore at her, causing some hair to escape her braid. The sand hit her face painfully, and she smiled.

She was so angry. *I should have taught David to fight better,* she scolded herself. *If I did, maybe he would've been able to escape. I should've trained him instead of letting him whine his way out of it. I screwed up. If I had just taken more time with him, he would have been able to fight back, to run and get to safety.* She was angry with herself for having failed him. *This is my fault,* her anger boiled all the more, *but I'll fix it, and I'll bring them all down to their knees in the process.*

Mitch came to a stop, and Shamira and Valens stopped behind him. "How much farther?" Valens asked. He was looking around for a sign or something to give away the hideout location.

Shamira looked slowly and pushed her sight beyond the wind dunes and what appeared to be the road ahead of them. Then she saw it—a huge building standing right in front of them about half a mile ahead. "The hideout is a half a mile ahead of us. There seems to be a level on the entrance that has guards patrolling it," she said. She turned to look at Valens and Mitch to see their mouths open in surprise.

"How in the heck can you see that building? We can't even see it," Valens said with a surprised look on his face, and he reached out to touch her shoulder.

She sidestepped him and replied, "I just can. Let's go. Put on the scramblers. We don't want to alert them. I see a weak point in their facility that we can sneak in through. It will be tricky, and we'll have two guards to take out, but we can get in. I'll take care of the guards. You both head inside, and I think we'll find what we're looking for on the lower level," she said and then started to walk toward the complex. They followed and looked around for a sign of what she told them she saw.

"Mitch, what made you stop here?" Valens asked.

"They talked about a small beacon and two sand hills in front of the complex. I saw the sand hills but missed the beacon. Fisher mentioned you're at death's door if you pass through the sand hills unaware, so when I saw them, I stopped," Mitch said while they followed closely behind Shamira. Mitch's voice was almost drowned out by the sound of the wind kicking up.

"The scramblers seem to be working. They don't see us. The opening is over there. When we go through the door, there will be a guard on the left and one on the right. I'll take the guy on the right. You both take the one on the left and follow me down the hall between them," Shamira said above the wind.

"Shamira, why don't you go down the hallway, ahead of us? We'll handle the guards?" Valens suggested.

She turned to him and smirked. "Valens, I can take both the guards, but I want you boys to have some fun too. Let's go," she said and stalked forward. Valens and Mitch walked on either side of Shamira as she led the way.

"Hey, follow me. They're not paying attention, and the opening is right in front of me," she said softly, and they crouched down to follow her as they flew at top speed toward the camouflaged door. They came up to the door and hovered before landing. Valens and Mitch followed her, ready to attack. She kicked in the door and attacked the guard nearest her. Her eyesight adjusted easily from the dark to the dimly lit hallway. She punched up with such force she heard his teeth crack, and blood spattered out of the side of his mouth. *Yes!* she thought. *One step closer.* She knew that Valens and Mitch were engaged when she heard their scuffle while they worked on the other guard.

She jammed her fingers in the eyes of the guard that fought to grab her. Then, she punched him in his neck and stuck him with a truth tick, using her forearm to hold him to the wall. "Where are the prisoners? Where are they!" she screamed at him.

"I ain't telling," he spat out. The tick started to work and his tongue got heavy.

"Don't fight it, scum. Tell me, or I'll slice you now," she said,

116

putting even more pressure on his neck. He coughed, and his eyes started to tear up. The tick was working, but they were running out of time. She could hear heavy footsteps in the distance, not far away.

"They're on the lower level, in hell," he forced out. She pulled the tick out and sprayed his face with a drug that knocked him out. She turned to see Valens with his knee in the back of the other guard as Mitch punched him in the face. She pushed Mitch out of the way and sprayed the guard's face. The guard's body instantly fell limp as his head hit the floor. Then, she motioned for them to follow her down the hall and the stairs to the lower level the guard had called "hell."

The halls were dim and dingy, like they were hardly ever cleaned. Sand from the outside went unchecked along the corners of the walls and kicked up as they ran down the hallway. They ran to the stairway on the side of the elevator straight ahead. Shamira concentrated on the sounds around her. She heard steps coming from above and figured they had enough time to run down the stairs undetected.

She ran at top speed down the empty hallway with Valens and Mitch at her heels. She glanced behind her to see Mitch sticking small bombs that stuck on the wall. She kept running, and Valens ran past her to the door. She slid as she got to the steps. Valens kept his balance and grabbed the door to the stairway. He yanked at her jacket to pull her into the stairwell. Valens took the lead when they ran down two levels of stairs with the pounding of feet coming down several flights above them. Mitch was close behind her. Shamira pulled out the mapping device she had on her hip and stuck it to the corner of the wall. It would send images of the building and the inhabitants to her home computer long after she and the others were gone.

Pushing her sight past the walls, she sped up and ran down the narrow hallway that led to the holding cells. Shamira didn't see anyone walking around in the cells. She saw guards patrolling ahead and heard them making up ground behind them. She saw a hidden vent on the floor just before the doorway leading to the cells and pointed to it as she ran to it in top speed. Valens passed her in a running slide and stopped in front of the vent. He bent down and snatched a knife from his pocket, then pried the vent open. Valens grabbed her leg, and Mitch pushed her down into the vent before he followed. Valens followed while he held the vent in place with his gloved hand.

Shamira closed her eyes to block out the distraction of sight and listened. She heard the many guards moving rapidly in their direction. There were maybe twenty of them pounding down the stairs and through the hallway. Listening deeper, she heard the boys' labored breathing, and she forced her lungs to breath at a normal pace. She heard heaviness in the footsteps beyond the vent and knew they were carrying guns. They were ready to kill, and she smelled their heightened state of anticipation. *I won't die today,* she thought, *but I can't say the same for you.*

She heard the deep commanding voice of their leader. "Where'd they go? Find them now, or you'll all die. If I don't kill you, Slasher will. Go!"

She wanted to get them all, but her father taught her to fight when the odds were with her. She knew she could handle ten of them, but she didn't know about Valens' or Mitch's skills. Trusting someone else to do the job was not her style, and leaving them behind was not an option.

Valens turned to Mitch and gave him a pair of form-fitting leather gloves. He then looked at Shamira and cautiously took her hand. She jerked her gloved hand out of his, and he leaned toward her and whispered, "Trust me. I have something that will help us get out of here in one piece." Shamira hesitantly let him take off her gloves. He took some webbed gloves out of the inside of his coat, and she squinted at him with a look of distrust. He whispered to her, "I made these especially for you," and placed the webbed gloves on each of her hands.

Most of her hands were exposed, but the webbing had some weight to it. The stretchy fiber crossed around her fingers and hands, as tightly as a second skin. At the tip of each finger was a form-fitting elastic plastic that was heavy like it had some sort of moveable metal inside. He took her finger and touched it to her nose very lightly, and she felt an electrical shock. "It has a slight shock that intensifies when your adrenaline rises in a fight," he whispered. She pondered on the tickling his breath made at her ear and then flexed her hand to get

119

used to the gloves.

"Well, they seem to have moved on. We can get out now and investigate the holding chambers. I suspect there are hidden chambers, but my device will reveal that to me when I return home. The scrambling devices are still working. Their cameras can't see us, but if we come across a guard, the scrambling devices won't work." She crawled closer to the vent, "Mitch, do you know of a way out of here besides the way we came?" Shamira asked.

She didn't hear the heavy footsteps of the guards near, but she knew from looking through the wall that four patrolled the area they planned to enter. Lifting a lip in thought, she knew she would have to knock them out because she didn't come here to leave without the information she sought.

"The best way is the way we came. I have it rigged. Valens has the detonator, and we can fire it up when we escape," Mitch said and flexed his hands in the gloves Valens gave him.

"Okay. Look, there are four guards in that other room. It's a hallway with cells on each side. The hallway stretches pretty far down and then flows into another hall. Follow me, and hopefully we can get past this first hallway tonight," she whispered before she turned and removed the vent cover.

She hopped up from her knees to a squat and stood. The boys followed, and Valens walked toward the door with Mitch beside him, guns drawn. Shamira walked backwards in the opposite direction and ran at top speed while Valens opened the door. Valens threw the door open, and the large, heavily armed guards drew their weapons.

Shamira sped through the hall and threw a flat disk that extended with knives and sliced off the fingers of the two guards nearest the door. They fell to their knees, writhing in pain as their weapons dropped. Crying out, they fell and the burning smell of flesh filled the air when the weapon cauterized the wounds it left behind. The guards in front of her fired at them, but their jackets deflected each shot. The boys raised their hands to their faces to protect their weak spots from shots that scattered. Shamira went for the tallest guard of the two remaining ones.

Hearing the thunder of numerous guards in the distance several levels up, she yelled, "Work fast! We're going to have company!"

The moaning noises from the prisoners held in the cells along the hallway got louder. She felt her power build, which caused the gloves on her hands to let off a magnetic shock. Running at top speed toward the heavyset guard, she punched him with all the pent-up anger she had held within. The blow shook his body as one punch knocked him out cold to the floor. She glanced back at Valens, who was doing a good job of beating down the remaining guard with a well formed kick to his head. Mitch used a cutting device to cut through the metal bars of one of the holding cells.

She looked around and saw the prisoners for the first time, now realizing why she didn't see them walking around their cells when she was hidden in the vent and looking into the hallway. All of the prisoners appeared to have their bodies imprisoned in the floors. Their heads were exposed, but they had a pain emitter on their foreheads, an evil device that poured excruciating pain through the veins of the victims like liquid fire.

"The guards are coming from both sides! We have to go now and fight our way out. Crap! We won't be able to save them," Shamira yelled at Valens and Mitch, who were working on the bars.

"Now," Shamira yelled. Pulling Valens and Mitch away from the cells, she started to run in the direction they'd come. The image of the dazed, pained eyes of the men and woman she had to leave behind forced tears down her cheeks as she ran. The boys were close behind her. Her anger built, her rage burned, and she felt it. The beast of power deep within her was now unleashed and climbing up her back. She ran head on toward the guards that stood between her and her escape.

"Brace yourselves! We're about to fight our way out of here. Guards ahead!" she yelled back at them.

"No prob! I came prepared," Valens said with a slight laugh in his voice like he looked forward to the confrontation. They ran at top speed past the fallen guards, up the stairway, and to the door in which they came. Just as they opened the door to the hallway, the elevator opened, and guards poured from the elevator and the stairs. Valens threw small bombs in the direction of the mass of guards that charged them. They ran down the hallway toward the door. Mitch detonated the bombs behind them, but a number of guards stood with guns to block their exit at the door.

Shamira attacked the guard in front of her with a side-kick to his neck. Another guard attacked, and without thought or fear - only anger, she allowed him close enough to nearly land a punch. Dodging his blow, she followed through with a punch to his face, consciously commanding the surge of power to flow to her gloved hands. The blow knocked her attacker through the jagged door that separated them from the outside. Several guards came upon her, wanting a piece of bringing her down.

Shamira's anger only grew stronger with each assailant's arrival. The ball of fire within her raged, fought, and clawed for release. She let it go and lost control. It was if she were watching herself from above. It overtook her—this sensation to punish. She fought with quickened speed and punched with the precision of a trained killer. Finding the weak points of her opponents without thought, she used her reflexes born from years of training. She punched their necks, groins, stomachs—anything in her way to finish them off—and left them in quivering heaps on the ground. *Back, back, back in.* She had to regain control of this power that had plagued her all of her life. *Focus!* The wind of power pulled back within her. She looked behind her to see Valens throwing a smoke bomb, which brought the remaining guards to their knees.

"Hurry, let's go. Kick on the hover tags!" Valens yelled at her. Then he and Mitch flew past her as she kicked on her tags and was lifted up in the air. She flew to the door and followed behind them.

They had a small lead. She looked back to make sure they weren't being followed and felt a slash of fire from a laser as it cut her neck. The shot didn't hurt since her adrenaline was still at full blast from the chase. There were guards on them and coming fast.

"Get on the bikes, fast! I'm about to cause a huge sandstorm!" Valens yelled. He threw several discs on the ground behind him as he flew through the air. The discs illuminated as they landed, and sand immediately swirled up as high as twenty feet, causing a moving sand barrier that rose up from the ground to form between them and the guards.

Shamira's breathing was heavy while she balanced herself on air. Valens slowed alongside her, then pointed to his foot and tapped his foot on air, causing him to pick up speed and pass her by. She had to adjust her balance and shades while she picked up speed and stayed on Valens' heels.

They got to the motorcycles, and this time, Shamira didn't spare Valens a glance when he hopped on behind her and she kicked the cycle in gear. They took off, and Valens yelled, "We're clear! They're gone! The devices will work for an hour, and then they detonate."

Shamira shook her head and thought, *He has the coolest toys.* Smiling at her thought, she and Mitch raced to their original meeting place near her home. Bringing her cycle to a stop, her breath continued to race, and she talked herself into pulling back and breathing normally. Finally at peace, she slid off her bike. She glanced at Mitch and winced a bit from the dull ache of her wound. Valens got off the bike and walked over to Mitch. She noticed that both Mitch and Valens were breathing hard and smiling from the adrenaline rush of their adventure.

Valens turned to her. His eyes lowered, noticing the gash on her neck. He reached out to touch her bleeding wound then rubbed the blood between his fingertips, and said, "You're bleeding. Let me help you."

"It doesn't hurt." Shamira jerked away from him to put her hand on her neck.

"How the hell did you do what you did back there?" Mitch asked with a look of shocked recognition on his face. His laughing face closed up instantly when his eyes fell on her.

"It's what happens when I lose control. It was them or me, and I knew it wouldn't be me today," Shamira said, crossing her arms over her chest.

"So, I guess we won't be able to return there without considerable backup, huh?" Valens said.

"There won't be a backup, but I'm returning. I did leave something behind that will give a better advantage the next time," Shamira said.

"Shamira, Mitch told me about another possible location. There is a place where the kids are more likely to be held. The story of what they do to them there ain't pretty. Anyway, we need to go to Shadow Hell to meet up with Mitch's contacts," Valens said. He stepped forward and reached out to put pressure on her slightly bleeding wound. Not bothering brushing him away this time, she gave in to the guilty pleasure his soft but firm touch gave her through the sting of the wound.

"Look, I don't want to involve all of these people. They work for the organization we are trying to bring down. Why should they be loyal to us? Why should he be?" she forced out, nodding in Mitch's direction with a suspicious glare. Anger filled her at the thought of involving other kids in the mission to save her brother. She couldn't trust them; she wouldn't trust them.

"Trust me, they are safe. Mitch is safe! None of these kids choose to work for Monev—they are forced to. They're blackmailed, beaten, threatened, or much worse than your nightmares. You can't imagine the abuse they suffer. I will not leave them to suffer. I know they all share the same desire that you and I do—to bring down Monev," Valens said, placing his hands on her shoulders.

That's it. He's gone too far, she screamed in her mind before she yelled at him and said, "Get off of me!" then jerked away.

"Chill, damn it! Shamira, he's right! I hated being held hostage by them. You have no idea how evil those men are. No idea! These kids I know work on the inside and have valuable information about the way these dudes work. They will have the answers we need, and they will want a way to help and escape like I did. We promised each other if one of us got out, we would save the others. It seems to me you only care about your damn self, but right now, you need us, and we need you. You need Valens and me to get you one step closer to saving your beloved brother," Mitch growled out. "And, by the way, you're not the only one who has lost someone to these monsters, just so you know."

Slightly humbled but not convinced, she cast Mitch a distrustful glance. "I gotta go. We'll meet here tomorrow night to go to Shadow Hell. Valens, bring your own cycle, or you will be walking," Shamira said with contempt at Mitch's statement.

She walked away from them and climbed on Pearl. Anger and frustration built within her from this escalating situation. She had no choice. Like Mitch said, she needed them, even if she hated needing anyone. If she wanted to save her brother and the others, she needed them. All the years she had been blind, she never tried to create friendships. She buried her happiness, fears, and desires so deeply that she didn't know if she would ever be able to reach them again. Valens seemed to have befriended kids everywhere. Everywhere she looked, he was there, and for now, she had no choice but to accept it.

Crud. Why does he have to be so beautiful? She wouldn't allow him to trick her again. He would ride his own cycle tomorrow. She would get the answers she needed to save David and bring down Monev.

She drove without focus. Her mind knew the way home like a reflex, and Pearl would get her there safely anyhow. As she pulled up to the house, her stomach sank. Her father had beaten her home. *Can tonight get any worse?*

Chapter 13

Shamira pulled up her collar and tried to conceal her weeping wound. Climbing off of Pearl, she adjusted her jacket and stood to prepare herself for whatever her father may say. "Pearl, go park yourself," she told her cycle and walked to the front door.

Opening the door, she saw her father sitting on the couch. He leaned forward with his elbows causally balanced on his knees. She didn't bother to speak, knowing it would be a waste of breath and energy. Her beast now slept within her and she was exhausted. Neither of them said a word as she walked to stand in front of him.

Looking at him, she took a deep breath and waited for him to yell at her.

His expression angry, he said sternly, "Shamira, you will be going with me to the Security Force Headquarters tomorrow. I don't know what you have been up to, but it stops tonight. Go to your room."

It was worse than she thought. He was beyond angry, but she figured he was lax on the punishment because of his grief. Swallowing back her words of explanation, her eyelids closed and she controlled the impulse to argue back. She quietly walked past him and went to her room like she was told.

Awaking early, with her mind heavy after reviewing the data she had captured from the enemy hideout in the Outlands. She was happy they got out of there unharmed. After realizing the compound they had broken into held atrocities that went unseen to them in their brief journey within, she wished they could have done more damage to bring it down permanently. The data proved the organization had a highly complex lab in the lower levels of their Outlands post. It was where they did many of the extractions of human body parts they sold on the black market. She figured the prisoners they held in the upper levels were waiting to be processed below. From the snapshots she captured, she knew that although they had some state-of-the-art equipment, their methods were barbaric—probably purposefully so.

"Shamira, it's time to go. Meet me in the car," her dad's voice called through the intercom in her room.

She shut down her computer. Grabbing her bag, she walked to the car, where her dad was waiting for her. He looked straight ahead, like he couldn't stand to gaze at her. For a moment, she felt self-conscious, wondering if the wound she had treated the previous night had healed enough to be concealed under her necklace. *Has he seen it? Does he know what I've been up to?* She wouldn't give in and admit to anything. If she did, they would lock her in the house, and that was a risk she could not take. David needed her too much, and now, so did Valens and maybe even Mitch, if he were telling the truth. Taking a deep breath, she got in the car.

Her father didn't say a word when he took off, and neither did Shamira. She looked straight ahead at the sky while they flew in the air speeding toward Headquarters, which stood about twenty feet high. Headquarters had many hidden secrets—rooms no one from the outside was aware of—but Shamira knew them all because she had tested her 3D simulation device there. She wanted to see if she could extract images of every level and person to put in her training simulations. It didn't take long for one of the security guards to destroy her device, but not before she had gotten the data she had sought to extract. The simulation device the doctors of Earth had sent her father for simulating her surroundings worked by emulating the sensation of touch. She would put the visual of an environment in the simulator, and in turn, it would simulate her walking through that environment, touching the walls, smelling it, and emit flashes of light into her mind's eye to give her a mental visual memory of the structure.

She looked forward to seeing the place she had visited with her parents many times while she was blind. It was much larger than she had assumed. The deep silver metals that covered the structure made it look imposing and aesthetic. It rose out of the ground like an iron giant with a sleek, curved base that was scattered with reflective windows that looked like mirrors. Various vehicles of all sizes drove into the landing pads that opened with sliding doors throughout the structure. *Amazing,* she thought, her eyes glued on the imposing building before her. She spared an excited glance to her father, who still sat stoned face and silent as he drove forward. This was a side of her father she had rarely seen. *It's to be expected,* she guessed. *His son is lost, and I'm is pushing my luck, worrying him to death.*

They pulled into the car pad on the second level of the Headquarters building. She looked at him and waited. Her father stopped the car, and squeezed his hands on the steering wheel. He turned and looked at her.

"Shamira, I don't know exactly what you have been up to, but I know something is not right with you. It's got to stop. Your mother and I have so much to deal with right now, and we don't have the energy to deal with you acting out. When we leave you at home, home is where you will stay, or else I'll have no choice but to drag you with me to work every day," he said steadily. Seeing the hurt and disappointment in his eyes, she looked away. She was unfamiliar with seeing emotions so vividly, and seeing it with her own eyes caused her sadness to rise much faster than it ever had before. A tear dropped from her eye at disappointing the one person who had been her champion all of her life. Angrily, she wiped the tear away. Mostly, she was angry at the way her family was being torn apart because of Monev. She would hunt and find her brother, then find the mastermind behind it all and bring him to justice. In this, she had no choice.

"I'm sorry. I'll do better, Dad. I don't mean to upset you," she said blankly. Her emotions were so jumbled that she felt numb, and the tears stopped as quickly as they had started. Feeling her father's strong hand on her shoulder, she relaxed, and he pulled her into a hug.

"Oh, Shamira, it's not you. I'm not upset at you. I'm just angry at the lack of manpower we have to bring this crime organization down without them killing our kids with it," he said. They pulled apart, and he glanced at her with sorrow in his eyes and gently pushed her away to open the car.

Walking inside Headquarters, she closed her eyes to sniff in the familiar metallic scent she was used to from her numerous visits with her parents. She'd come to know many of the Elite in the upper levels of the organization. Often, she looked forward to visiting Headquarters, since many of the Elite had become like family to her.

They walked by her dad's friend on the way in. "Nobel. Shamira, it's good to see you, squirt," Broc said with a nod. She recalled that he wasn't an Elite Security Force officer, but was a second in command that supported the Elite on one of the other Sectors. He didn't hold the enhanced strength of the Elite, but all support staff were trained to be just as dangerous.

"Hey, Broc, it's good to see you too," her dad replied. He stopped to shake his hand and gave Broc a slap on the opposite arm.

"Shamira, congratulations on your eye surgery. I heard it was a success. I see you still have those stunning, unique eyes. Nobel, I'm sorry to hear about your son being taken. Those bastards! Man, they're getting worse, and worse. Anyway, I get to skip out of the emergency meeting with Cal today. Lucky me. I've got to go check out a lead we have. Hang in there, man. Just one step closer and we're going to bring these bastards down and get your son back," Broc said. Then, he slapped her dad on the shoulder and went to his car.

She followed her dad to the elevator and up to his office. Her mom's office was directly above her father's, and she would often go to visit her when she got bored waiting on her father to return from meetings. Looking around, she noticed the hallways were bright and the floor was still squishy soft like she remembered. Only now, she noticed it was gray. Entering her father's office, she saw the videoconference wall to the left. The sound was low while it displayed an ongoing meeting, and her father ignored it as he went to his desk to get some paperwork.

"I'm going to a meeting. You stay here, and Valerie will take care of you. After my meeting, you can join your mom and me for lunch. Do not leave this office, do you hear me? I repeat - do not even think about stepping out that door unless you're going to the restroom. I don't have time to hunt you down today," he said, then grabbed his briefcase and walked out the door.

Yeah, He's still mad at me. Well, it can't be helped. She wouldn't stop until she had saved David. She tapped on his video pen, which displayed a 3D computer that projected a keyboard. *Wow! Impressive! My keyboard at home just has old-fashioned keys.* The screen was a solid model that afforded the user privacy that a 3D monitor did not. Stretching her neck to the side, she started to type in her password to check the supercomputer database. She wondered if they were yet able to find out how the Elite were being tracked like animals and captured. So engrossed in her search, she didn't hear someone enter the office.

"Is Nobel here?" a brown haired man asked. His tall muscular frame filled the doorway. She jumped at his surprise entry. Her eyes studied him and noticed he was rather attractive with dark brown hair and hazel gray eyes and extremely fit. He stood about two inches taller than her father, who was over six feet. He had an edgy look to him, which indicated to her he was a rather strong and deadly opponent to any who would try to cross him.

After her observation, she decided to respond to his question. "No. He went to a meeting. Can I leave him a message for you?" she offered. She tried to play off the fact that she had been snooping.

134

Hopefully, he wouldn't notice her guilt.

"Tell him Cal came to see him," he said, then studied her closely for a moment.

She squirmed, a bit uncomfortable with his inspection and the look of contempt on his face that passed in an instant, immediately covered up with a fake smile.

Lifting an eyebrow she said, "Cal? You act like you don't know me. You know I don't like jokes." She hesitantly returned his faux smile with one of her own. She took a deep sniff to seek out the scent she usually noticed when Cal, Commander in Chief of the Security Elite, came around to tease her in the past. She didn't recognize his scent. Grimacing, *this eyesight is making me lazy again.*

"Well, you know me. I'm full of jokes. I'll go meet your father," he said, then teased her once more with a guarded stare before he turned to leave.

Relaxing, she watched him leave. Reading the screen, she searched for information about the missing Elite, and her breath caught. She realized how they had been tracked. The Elite were the Security Force members that headed up the Sectors, and they had a specialized tag or tracking device located in their heads. The device was only accessible by Headquarters computers on Earth, and Earth sent direct encrypted responses for inquiry of the Elite only by members of the Elite that had special code keys to access the information. Unfortunately, when they were captured, their tagging devices were deactivated, which made the remaining Security Force

135

believe the captured comrades to be deceased. Chewing on her fingernail while in thought, she guessed this turn of events would mean all the Elite were now under suspension.

Something is definitely fishy here. She pondered on these thoughts further. *This still doesn't justify how they're able to subdue and manhandle them. The Elite are the only people on Mars with superhuman strength enhanced by the skin suits they wear that can never be taken off. This is a secret only the Elite know—or so we think. They don't even tell their wives or kids this. The only reason I know is because I was blind and depended so heavily on my other senses that I immediately noticed a difference.* She frowned in thought, *Hum, how did Monev know of the Security Force's secret weapon, and how did they know that weapon's weakness?* She logged off the computer and looked at the video wall at an empty conference room.

She looked up, hearing someone enter the office. "C'mon, Shamira, let's go. Time for lunch," her dad said while he walked into the office.

They walked to the lunchroom, the one place she really enjoyed when coming to Headquarters. It had distinct smells of coffee and nice, comfortable overstuffed chairs. For the first time, she actually got to see if the room was as pleasant as she remembered. The room had soft colors of green and brown and video streaming walls of oceans and beaches on Earth. A fountain built into the wall went from floor to ceiling, which made the soothing sound of a waterfall.

She saw her mom waiting for them, and she wasn't smiling. Her mom sat in one of the large brown overstuffed chairs with their lunch on the cushioned ottoman that also served as a table. Shamira was determined to act unaffected. Her mom could be more difficult to face than her dad sometimes. Sitting down next to her mom, she said a quiet, "Hey, Mom," and stuffed a sandwich in her mouth before she said something that would give away her eagerness to go home.

"Shamira, take this. You will need it the next couple of days," her mom said. She gave Shamira an earlink and a temporary tracking tag.

"Your mother and I unfortunately have to go on separate missions to start to track down some leads on the crime organization that's doing this. Problem is - no one at all is talking. People here are scared. These goons believe in manipulating people by stealing their families and using that to control them. This is turning out to be much harder than we thought," her dad said, stuffing a bite of his sub in his mouth.

She glanced at him, noticing he rarely ate in this hurried way and that he had lost some weight.

"Finish up, Shamira. We have less than two hours to be at our locations. Unfortunately, we have to leave you home alone for a few days," her dad said.

"Um, Dad, Cal came by your office today," she mentioned and watched him closely to see if his expression would reveal that he felt the same disconnect as she did about Cal.

"He did? Well, he didn't mention he saw you when he came to the meeting," her dad replied and paused a minute in thought.

"He acted like he didn't know me. I told him I don't like jokes," she said and watched again to see how he would respond.

"He's different these days. I think the effects of losing control of the Security Force's hold on Mars is starting to get to him, and he's angry about it—like we all are. He just isn't his easygoing self anymore. Now, it's strictly business, and his smile's a put-on," her dad said and shook his head in understanding.

"Shamira, we better go. I'll take you home," her mom said. Shamira hoped for once her mom would not speak to her on the ride home, and her wish was answered. The silent ride home gave her time to think.

She had to ask some questions about the leader of the crime organization and a possible connection to the leader of the Security Force. *Maybe the crime organization leader has a vendetta against the Security Force.* Tonight, she would get some answers. Tonight, she was upping the pressure. The time for waiting was over. Her mom didn't bother to go in the house, and for that, Shamira was glad. Shamira walked through the door and straight to her room to get ready for her meeting with the guys.

Chapter 14

Valens brought his own cycle, and Shamira let out a sigh of relief. *Thank God.* She didn't have to fight the uncomfortable tingling she got with Valens riding behind her. She looked at him and couldn't help curling her lips into a small smile.

"If all I had to do was ride my own bike to make you smile, I would have done it yesterday. You look different when you smile," Valens said, his voice dropping deeper. He returned her smile, and then winked at her. She looked away and turned to Mitch, who was impatiently looking ready to go.

Mitch nodded at the road ahead, "Follow me. I know were we can park and be concealed."

Valens and Shamira followed on the busy street leading to the outskirts of the city in Sector Four. Shamira had never been in Shadow Hell, and she wondered if it was as bad a place as the rumors she'd heard. Kids at school talked about sneaking into the underground club often, but it was one of those places a member had to invite you to before you could get in. She hoped Mitch's friends could get them in safely, because she had a feeling some of the prominent people of Monev would be there. She only needed to get one alone to get the information she sought. Her gut was telling her there was some connection between Cal and Monev. She just didn't know what it was, but she would find out.

They drove until they got to the business district of Sector Four. She noticed the Sector was more upscale than where she lived, and she was shocked to realize that a skuzzy place like Shadow Hell was located there. Sector Four was the professional Mecca of Mars. The street cleaning androids were doing their jobs. Night had come, and the chill of its fingers stretched before them. The Sector lit up with lights and signs promoting shops, stores, and merchandise. She wondered why Monev chose such an upscale area for one of their members-only clubs when they sold junk that turned the other areas in Mars to ghettos and slums.

Following Mitch and looking around, she realized this part of the city wasn't too busy. It had a few cars coming and going on the

140

ground with none in the airspace above the buildings. She wondered if the Mars Planet Police shut down the airspace in this Sector in order to keep it safe. The Mars Planet Police worked under the directive of the Security Force and acted as beat cops who secured each Sector on a personal level.

Shamira found out during her visit to her father's office that the Mars Planet Police members were no longer able to keep their restraints on the crime rate. It was also becoming known that Police were being murdered at an increasing pace with weapons much more advanced than their own. Since the Mars Planet Police didn't have the enhancements the Elite had, they were much easier targets—not to mention a direct way to gain control of the Sectors.

They parked in an underground parking lot, and Valens took out covers to drape over their bikes. The parking lot was spotless and had video advertisements on the polished metal walls.

Valens turned to Shamira and said, "Okay. We're going to meet Hedi and Anthony. Hedi is a computer genius and has hacked into Monev's database to create fake entry card keys for us. Anthony is what they call a runner. He's pretty strong and has run goods to all facets of the organization. He knows all their dirty little secrets. Hedi's parents were members of the Mars Planet Police Force." Valens looked at Mitch who nodded in agreement, and continued, "She found her father dead in his sleep with her mother missing and was taken before she could run. Anthony has a brother being held by Monev, and his dad was the lead for the Mars Police on Sector Two.

He's also one of their best and oldest runners at age sixteen. Most runners don't last that long, so give them the respect they deserve. They're risking their lives and the lives of their families to help us."

Mitch threw an angry gaze at Shamira. "Yeah, well, just tell *her* to keep her attitude in check. They aren't going to tolerate her lack of gratitude, dude."

With a tightening of her lips, she choked back her response. *I'm so not in the mood for this*, she thought before regulating her voice to respond. "Are any of the members of Monev going to be there tonight?" She returned Mitch's angry gaze.

"There are several of them that come here a lot. I think Thor and his cronies hang out here the most. They like the torture chamber. It's one of their favorite spots, and Shadow Hell is the only one of their clubs that has one," Mitch said.

"What's the torture chamber?" Shamira asked.

"You don't want to know. Just know you don't ever want to go there," Valens said, and then started walking toward the stairs with Shamira and Mitch in tow.

Arriving two levels up, they walked out the door. Mitch stood in front of what appeared to be an office door. The only door in the hallway, it was wooden with a metal plate on it that said "New World Technologies." She couldn't believe how bold they were. *Why hasn't anyone put two and two together?* She closed her eyes, focusing on the sounds and smells around her. The faint scent of dream tickled her nose. She heard nothing but their breathing. It was definitely too quiet.

Valens slid in his key, and they followed him into what appeared to be an ordinary office. She looked at Valens and started to say something, but before she could speak, he raised his hand up to his mouth to tell her to be silent. Listening now more intently for hidden sounds around her, she heard the very faint beat of music. Her hearing was more sensitive than that of the average person, and she was sure the boys did not hear the music. She looked beyond the walls in front of her and pushed her eyesight behind the reception area. Seeing the elevator beyond the door on the left of the receptionist desk, she wondered if that's where they were heading. Looking up at Valens to see him pointing in the direction of the elevator, she nodded at him.

Thinking for a moment, she wondered how they planned on getting out of there. She'd brought some of her gear, but these walls were thick, like they'd built this place with the intention of it staying hidden from any device that may try to see beyond the obvious, like some kind of bunker.

The elevator took them up five floors. Shamira turned to Mitch and whispered in his ear, "Do you have a way to get out of here if we get in trouble?"

Mitch turned to her and smiled for the first time, then winked at Valens. Valens smiled and tapped his fist against his heart. She placed her hands in her pocket and looked through the elevator doors to see completely empty levels of floors, realizing the entire building was nothing more than a front. She zipped up the form-fitting leather jacket and adjusted its bottom over her tight, shiny black pants. Bending down, she pulled up her boots to prepare for whatever waited for them at the end of the elevator ride. *What have we just walked into?* Shadow Hell was definitely starting to fit its name.

The elevator opened to reveal an entirely different world spawning out before them. Music, loud and throbbing, filled the elevator. They were drenched in the dark purple hue that was Shadow hell. The smell of smoke and fire drowned out the faint smell of sweat from the crunch of bodies before them. She noticed the built-in fire pits on several walls that had videogames playing. The players were on platforms just above the built-in flames in the walls, obviously using scream to give them an edge over the games they played. She sniffed for dream, and it was so faint she realized that for this high status club, dream was not the poison of choice. The smell of stale burning flesh filled Shamira's nostrils, strangely mingled with the scents of flowers. *I'm going to be sick.* Unconsciously, her hand went to cover her nose, and Valens grabbed her wrist before she could complete the movement.

"Act natural, like you can't tell what you smell," he whispered in her ear.

"Can you?" she whispered back.

"We can't smell like you. I smell flowers. C'mon," he said and followed Mitch.

As they walked through the crowded floor, Shamira noticed a muscular pale blond man dancing with three gyrating females on the floor. The man stood several inches above all the people on the floor, brawny and ripped. She figured he was about the same height as her dad, if not taller. If she were a betting girl, she would say he was in the gang in some way, and from his looks, he could be this Thor that Valens had mentioned.

Looking ahead, she spied Mitch slipping in a side door on the right of the bar. The bar extended the length of the club. It had open spots for tables and large, comfortable chairs for mingling. She glanced up at the ceilings to see women in cages suspended by chains from the ceiling, held just high enough that they could not be bitten by pit-tigers nipping at their toes. One woman had streaks of tears falling from her eyes while she struggled to keep her legs bent and out of the jaws of the vicious pit bull/tiger male. Shamira's eyes watered in frustration. *One day I'll end this*, she swore.

Valens tugged her by the jacket, and she walked forward. She followed him through the doorway. Mitch was standing in the hallway, which was painted black and had video walls with pictures of people burning in the fires of hell on them. Some had music videos and flashed the dancing and gyrating bodies on the dance floor. Shamira blinked, and a tall, brown-skinned boy with a light mustache came up and hugged Mitch, then punched him playfully on the arm.

"You came! I can't believe it," the boy said, and he easily lifted Mitch from the ground then shook him like a ragdoll.

"Put me down, you giant. Hey, this is Anthony. He and Hedi are going to join us in the private viewing room. We can see the action from there and get a feel for where everyone we need to know about is," Mitch said with a smile.

Humph, Shamira thought, *Mitch really does have friends I guess, though I can't see why.*

"Hey, Valens, I've seen you around. Glad you saved Mitch. He's a good kid," Anthony said and slapped a huge hand on Valens. Valens was caught off guard by Anthony's strength and jutted forward a few inches with the force of the friendly slap.

"Well, Shamira was the one that initiated the rescue," Valens said and looked at her. She looked at Anthony, unsmiling, and then shrugged nonchalantly.

Anthony sized her up, and then a look of disbelief crossed his face before he said, "Thanks, Shamira. Follow me. It's not safe to hang out in the hallways here."

They followed him to a private lounge. It had large, comfortable couches and viewing screens on the three walls that sat across from the couches. Each screen had a real-time video of all the rooms that were obviously hidden and not on the main floor.

"Shamira, I guess you haven't been to this place before. This room is called the sanctuary. It's a place for high paying customers to voyeur through the secret rooms of the club while they select a victim for their night of private fun—a place where we sell memberships to the atrocities that can be enjoyed only by high paying customers.

146

You'll be shocked to realize that even some of the Security Elite have paid to enjoy some of Monev's merchandise," Anthony said with a look of distaste visual on his darkly handsome face.

Shamira directed an angry gaze at Anthony and asked, "What are you talking about, some of the Security Force Elite? That's impossible."

"I didn't stutter. I said some of the Elite have been here. Not obvious, but I would know them. If you are looking for some of Monev's most influential, check out Thor down on the dance floor." Anthony eyes turned to the screen in the middle of the wall, "He's the head of the drug trade division. He doesn't personally touch the stuff, but he markets it to the people of influence here on Mars and on Earth. People of influence seem to go for scream. They like the edge it gives to their gambling. Little do they know that Monev laces it with highly addictive byproducts of dream. His cronies, Kip and Stan, run the sales to the average guy here on Mars."

Anthony pointed them out, "There they are—those guys in the body exchange room, picking out a new face for Kip's girlfriend. Kip is known for his fetish of having a different woman every couple of weeks or so, and his current girlfriend, Flame, indulges him by changing her look anytime she sees him searching out a new woman." A look of digust clouded his face.

"Let's go after this Thor. He will have the information we need. I need to find out where they may be holding the kids and who their leader is," Shamira said and followed Anthony's gaze to the screen that showed Thor dancing and kissing the women glued to his large frame.

Anthony looked her up and down. "He'll be easy for you to catch. He likes them young, beautiful, and shapely, and you fit the bill perfectly."

Shamira didn't like the way Anthony inspected her. She stifled a squirm, and moved her gaze from his head to toe.

He smiled in appreciation of her grit, "If you want to play bait, we can trap him alone," Anthony said.

"We'd rather not use her as bait. Is there another way? Hedi is more experienced at luring men and a bit older. We can ask her," Valens said. Shamira turned an irritated gaze on him.

"He's had Hedi, and she barely recovered. Trust me, she doesn't want to go anywhere near him. She's been through hell here over the last year. We just want out," Anthony said. He crossed his arms, indicating to Valens that Hedi was off limits.

"I can do it. I can handle him," Shamira said evenly, glaring at Valens as if to dare him to say anything.

"You can do what?" asked a tall red haired girl with flawless skin and full lips when she entered the room. She closed the door behind her.

"She's going to lure Thor away so we can find out where they're hiding the kids. Hopefully, he can give us the name of the leader of Monev," Mitch said.

Hedi caressed a hand down Mitch's face and turned to Valens.

Her face turned to look at Valens, hungry while she gazed at him. Shamira took a deep breath and reminded herself he wasn't hers anyway. *I don't want him,* she tried to convince herself, but jealously filled her blood, and she turned away.

"He'll like her, but he'll hurt her. She looks too weak." She flipped her long hair back, and touched Valens arm. "Valens, it's good to see you again. Thanks for saving Mitch for us," she said sincerely to Valens.

Valens replied with a smile and crossed his arms. He looked at Shamira and subtletly moved out of Hedi's reach.

"Hmm. Well, I'm impressed. Maybe she *can* handle Thor. I couldn't," Hedi said, her voice lowering as she looked Shamira up and down.

"Don't worry, Hedi. We aren't leaving without you two. I have a place for you to be safe—a place they won't find you," Valens said.

Hedi leaned closer to him and hugged him, her face buried in the crook of his neck. Shamira's fist balled up. She took a deep breath and reminded herself again that he wasn't hers. Valens stood still and hesitantly returned Hedi's embrace.

"I'm sorry. I had started to give up hope of ever escaping. I'm too afraid to wish it. They have recaptured others so many times. What they did to those others... I can't even begin to get the nightmares out of my dreams. It's what has kept many of us from fighting. Kids don't last long in this place, but I refuse to die here," she said with tears in her eyes then she turned out of Valens' weak

149

embrace. Mitch came over and took her in his arms, and Anthony patted her shoulder.

"Is there a place I can lure Thor that's near an exit? You know... a place where we can get out undetected and fast?" Shamira asked in order to refocus on their purpose.

"I know the perfect place—the employee exit. The only problem is, there may be guards there. If there are, we have to go down the side of the building, and since none of us can fly, that's not possible," Mitch said, scratching his jaw in thought.

"I have something we can use if we have to go through that window. If it comes to that, one of you has to take Hedi down. I can take Shamira. Here, put these on your hips. I brought them in case it got sticky getting out of here. Just push this button and it will do the rest," Valens said. He handed them a metal clip that they hooked into the belt loops of their pants.

"Let me put some makeup on you so Thor will think you are more mature," Hedi said to Shamira, then dug in her blouse.

"I won't need it. I have my own way of luring him, and it's not for what you're thinking," she said, refusing to put on the makeup. "Valens, I need you to be my dance partner. The rest of you wait by the exit. Redirect anyone from entering and speak out loud to each other if there is danger," Shamira said. Walking to the door, she opened it.

Anthony took the lead. Shamira unbraided her hair on their way down the hall and ran her hands through its silky, wavy brown and gold spun curls that fell to her curved hips. Sucking at her lips to darken their hue, she unzipped her black form-fitting leather jacket and straightened her spine, pushing out her chest. Valens glanced back at her with a shocked but appreciative look on his face. She winked at him and smiled as he opened the door to the club entrance for her to walk through. Valens followed. The music pumped, and they stood for a moment near the doorway.

"Look, you go straight to the meeting place. Open the windows in case we need a quick exit and call the cycles to come out of the parking garage and park on the street. Shamira, can you tell your cycle to follow ours?" Valens asked.

She put her hand in her pocket and pushed a button on her remote. It vibrated in acknowledgement of her request. "Done," she said and spied Thor with the three gyrating women she had seen earlier. She started to dance toward him, and Valens followed. Finding a spot where Thor could easily see her, she started dancing seductively with Valens in front of Thor. Rubbing her hands down her chest and then to her hips, she looked at Thor and commanded him to return her gaze. Noticing Thor was becoming interested, she pouted out her lips, and coyly lowered her eyelids framed in dark, curved eyelashes. Then, she slowly raised her gaze to his and smiled.

Dancing her way gradually in front of Thor, she glanced at his hand, noticing a deep red ruby ring. Deciding how she would lure him away, she shimmied closer to stand in front of him. His hands were on his hips, and she gently placed hers on top of his and tapped softly to the beat of the music. He smiled, and she tested his ring to see how loose it was. She smiled back, stepped closer to his moving hips, and danced in rhythm with him. She lightly tightened her grip on Thor's lax hand, and then slid it easily off his ring finger without his knowledge.

Her hand dropped from the top of his, and she turned away from Thor seductively. Throwing a smile back at him, she danced quickly past Valens, who was watchful of her while he danced with a curvy brunette. She danced to the meeting place and knew Thor would follow. When she reached the hallway, she stopped dancing. Her heart raced, knowing she would be able to get the information she came for. Adrenaline started to pour into her blood, and she turned to look for Thor, who was slowly, helplessly making his way toward her. She held up his ring for him to see and kissed it. He thought she was playing a seductive game with him, wanting him, but the look of hunger in his eyes sickened her. Valens followed slowly behind him, and the others were hidden in dark corners of the hallway. She didn't need them there. He was manageable; she knew she could handle him on her own. *I have been waiting for this moment since I laid eyes on you, scum*, she smiled.

She walked deeper into the hallway and stood midway in its dark depths. Thor approached. He was a large, muscled beast and a great opponent. *Definitely worthy of my full power.*

He came closer, not saying a word. She heard his heart beating slowly. He was convinced she was the prey, and he wasn't even slightly agitated, but he was mistaken. His pale blond hair and gray eyes sickened her further, but she wanted to laugh out loud because she could tell he thought he was in control. He stopped the pretense of smiling as he stood in front of her. She waited. He placed his hands on her shoulders and jerked her toward him for a kiss. She sped up the pull and yanked back her head to land a head-butt to his nose.

Blood splattered as his nose cracked. Power built in her, and she landed an elbow to the side of his head that brought him to his knees. She yanked the truth tick out of her belt, and Thor roared. He jumped up with such force that he threw her against the wall. She shook her head, dazed for a moment. He charged her and went for her neck, then dragged her up the wall. Lifting his hand to punch her, he frowned as he saw her smile. She licked the drop of blood off her lip.

Her hate poured out, and her desire to hurt him rose. *Awake*, she reminded herself. He had to be awake in order for her to get the information she came for. She lifted her legs, grabbed his pale, spiky hair, and pulled his head down to connect with her knee. He staggered back and quickly recovered to stand. Dropping, she landed on both feet to the floor. She heard scuffling in the distance and knew the others were fighting off guards. She had no more time to play. Running to him, she pushed him against the wall. He fell back against the wall with a bounce. In perfect time, she threw her metal ball at him. His head slammed against the wall as the net held him in place.

She put the truth tick in his neck, forced his mouth open, and pushed in a pill that would help him to forget this when it was over.

"Where are they holding the Security Force's kids. Tell me!" she said and punched him to force the pill down his throat.

"I ain't telling you nothin!" Thor grunted in a choke as the net tightened.

"Yes, you will. I don't have time for this!" Shamira took out a syringe of the poison that was in the truth tick. It would speed up the effects since Thor was so large. It was taking longer than she had to work. She jabbed it in his neck. He roared and quickly recovered. Then a sick smile formed on his face and he licked his lips suggestively at her.

"I had some plans for you, pretty girl. Big plans," he coughed. The drug finally took effect, and his tongue thickened.

"Where are they holding the kids?" she demanded again.

"Olympus Mons, deep within," he coughed out while he fought the poison.

"Who is the head of this? Monev? What is his name?" she said, then jerked his face toward her.

"Re-nu," he said, as if he were in pain from fighting to hold back the words.

"Where is he?" she yelled at him.

"No one knows. I... I don't - know," he slurred. The poison was thickening his tongue to the point it was difficult for him to speak, even to breath.

"Hurry. They're coming fast. Valens, we gotta get out of here now! Now, damn it!" Anthony yelled. She heard glass breaking and saw Anthony push against the door by the window.

"What does he look like?" she said loudly over the noise of music and fighting.

"Brown hair. Shit," Thor coughed and choked on his tongue as the net pulled tighter. She pulled the net off of his face and punched him before he fell to the ground with a *thump*, knocked out cold on the floor. She heard running and looked up to see Valens coming straight at her. He grabbed her around her waist as he ran straight to the window. He held her tightly against his waist while his device clamped onto the wall. It pulled slightly on the loop of his waist and they went flying out of the window on a metal rope. Anthony held Hedi, and they followed. Mitch brought up the rear; firing shots back at the guards that looked down at them from the window several feet up.

They landed on the ground with a *thud,* rolled, got up swiftly, and ran fast to their motorcycles. Shamira hopped on Pearl, and Valens eased in behind her. Snuggling closer, Valens pressed his firm chest to her back. He embraced her tightly and put his head on her shoulder as if he had no intention of getting on his own bike.

"What are you doing?" Shamira asked, turning toward Valens.

"Anthony had to take my ride with Hedi," he said as Shamira sped off to their hiding place.

"Wrong way," he called out in her ear, "we need to go to my

hideout first." She hesitated only a moment before she headed in the direction he told her to go. He gave her the directions and the others followed them.

Chapter 15

The street weaved in front of them, and Shamira took flight on her motorcycle, not wanting to waste one second in their getaway from would-be pursuers. Looking in her rearview mirror, she confirmed the others were close behind. Pearl landed in outside of Sector Five in the barren land heading to the Outlands. Shamira looked behind her and saw the others land. Looking out before her, she saw nothing except barren land of sand. Valens slid off her cycle, and she watched as he walked a few yards in front of them. He stood there while the ground parted wide enough for a truck to enter into it. A ramp extended from the hole, and he returned to the back of her cycle. *Impressive.*

"Drive down the ramp," Valens said. She drove forward without hesitation. She heard the last cycle behind her on the ramp, and the sliding door closed shut behind them. Their path lit up and she saw the smooth cement ramp that led to a large metal garage. There were several other vehicles parked and covered, so she looked around and found a place for Pearl near the corner. Shamira slid off her cycle and stretched.

"Wow, Valens, this is the best hideout I've ever seen. How did you find it?" Hedi asked and slid off the bike behind Mitch. She walked up to Valens and placed her hand on his arm to balance while she looked around.

Shamira slanted her eyes at Hedi and held a growl at bay. She reminded herself yet again that she did not want Valens. Saving her brother was her only priority. She walked over to stand next to Anthony, who stood near the metal door she assumed led to the rest of the refuge. Folding her arms, she put a bored look on her face and looked toward Valens.

"Thanks. My father built this place. It was here when I first got here. We didn't join him until he had been here the first year to settle the planet before everyone else arrived. He had this place and another where we lived in the other Sector. This place was his favorite, though, and we spent most of our time here. Anyway, let's go in," Valens said, then detangled himself from Hedi. As he got to the metal door, he glanced back and motioned for everyone to come closer. He pressed his thumb to the wall, and the large metal door opened. "Hurry up! It's timed," he said. They followed him through the door, and it started to close on Anthony, who barely squeezed into the open room.

Glancing around, Shamira noticed the red, gold, and blue stripes. It looked like a kid's game room. It was large and had two huge couches with large, multi-colored pillows thrown around the room. A large video wall was to the left, and a virtual game room enclosed in glass was in the corner.

She watched Valens walk to the far wall, and when he placed his finger in the middle, it opened to a hallway. The others quickly followed, remembering what happened to Anthony when he was the last person through the entrance. She came up behind Anthony, who she bumped into. He stumbled forward a bit, looked around, and winked at her, revealing dimples. He smirked at her with a look of respect. She winked back, starting to feel a small kinship with them all. *This is dangerous. Kids have never accepted me before. Why should now be any different?* She pushed away that false feeling of hope, of true friendship, something she had always looked for when she was younger.

The friendship she had tried to give many times as a younger child was only thrown back in her face and used to make her the butt of their jokes. Her younger years of hope had been torn to shreds when her friendship was used for trickery. It caused her power to be revealed and become harder for her to control. She had almost crippled a kid with her strength, a kid that almost killed her as a joke. That was behind her now, and it was a lesson she would always remember. It was this lesson that would keep Valens and this group of misfit kids away from her. She would never give her trust to another; they always used it against her.

A tug at her jacket came, and Mitch's frown came through her thoughts. *Yep, just like I thought,* she contemplated to herself. Mitch didn't trust her anymore than she trusted him. *Maybe,* she thought, *he's a kindred spirit.* It seemed to her that Valens trusted too easily, and she knew it would burn him in the end.

Glancing at the open doors along the way, she saw a bedroom with two sets of bunk beds. Then, she turned and looked ahead to see Valens at the end of the hall. He scanned his eye and placed his finger in a DNA scan. The wall opened up into a doorway at the end of the hall. Following the others, she took a look at the lab and training rooms beyond and swallowed. *Wow! This is way better than our secret room.*

"C'mon. We can sit at this table over here and come up with a plan. We can't go into the next hideout without being ready," Valens said and pulled out a chair to sit down. He looked at Shamira and motioned for her to sit next to him. Averting her eyes, she pulled out a chair opposite him at the foot of the table. Slowly she sat down, looking directly at him with a smirk and a nod. Hedi gladly took the chair next to him and placed her hand on his shoulder. The twinge

Shamira felt in her belly was squashed down by the image she placed in her mind of her brother. *No distractions,* she reminded herself.

Shamira moved her eyes from Mitch to Anthony, "We need to capture some of the heads of Monev. I want to bring down their leader. I got a feeling their organization has a mole in the Security Force. As a matter of fact, maybe more than one, I'd bet. If we save the kids and don't bring them down, they will retaliate, and it'll get ugly. They know how to bring the Security Force down, and that's dangerous for everyone here on Mars—everyone." Her eyes finally ended on Valens.

"Shamira, we need to get others to help. We need to go out and recruit more kids. I've ways to give us the edge and the ability to bring down these guys physically, but there are just not enough of us to do it," Valens said and stared back at Shamira. The desire in his eyes faded and was replaced with a steel look of unmoving resolve.

She returned his stare, and lifted an eyebrow. *Good. I'm tired of his flirting. It was an unnecessary diversion.* She liked him to be angry at her. It was safer that way. "I think we have recruited too many already. You never really know who we can trust. How'd you know the kids we might recruit are not devotees of Monev, in line to be trained for leadership? Besides that, I don't want to endanger others," Shamira replied.

Mitch stood up and pointed at her, "Look, you don't know a damn thing about Monev, but we do. No kid wants to stay a part of that team. In order to make it up their ranks, you have to go through

161

an orientation. All kids but three came out of that hell dead. The three survivors being trained for Monev's head have been with Monev since they were born. Those kids were groomed to take over, and the other kids that went through the orientation only did it to live longer. Your life span with Monev is eighteen, and we're all too close to that to risk it. Their promotion process starts when you turn seventeen. It's Monev's way of killing off kids that come to know too much about the organization. You've no idea of the evil you are playing with. If you think you can bring them down by yourself, you're a fool—a fool with a death wish," Mitch yelled.

Shamira turned her gaze to Mitch as she conceded reluctantly. "Fine. Then Valens, you choose our recruits. I'll train Mitch and Anthony with some skills they can teach these kids so we'll survive. I don't want their deaths on my head, you got that? It's not my choice, but yours. You can get them ready," Shamira threw at Valens.

Valens smiled. "Good. Hedi and I will come up with a list of kids we know we can trust," Valens said with a nod.

"I know all the kids in Monev. There are also some kids that haven't been caught or recruited by Monev that have no place to go and would love to help us," Hedi replied, then threw a saucy glance at Shamira while her hand rubbed possessively on Valens' arm.

Shamira cleared her throat. "Good. Mitch and Anthony, come with me to the training room. I have some leftover energy to get rid off," she said and stood up.

Anthony leaned on the table and turned to her. "Wait. You

162

need to tell us how you did what you did back there. What the hell happened?" Anthony asked, not budging. His large frame tensed as he waited for her answer, and he studied her with his dark brown eyes.

"What happened was my anger, and that's all I'm saying about that. All you need to know is that I'm not angry with you... yet," Shamira said before she pushed back her chair and walked to the training room without so much as a backwards glance.

"I like her. She's tough. We're going to need tough," Anthony said. He slid out his chair and followed her. Mitch also followed but remained silent. Shamira smirked. *Glad they had the guts to follow. This is going to be fun.*

Taking off her jacket, she stretched out her back like a cat and then grinned. Her back was to the door. She waited for her prey to arrive. *I really need this*, she thought, picturing Hedi's arms wrapped around Valens. The power within her slept, but she knew that one day, she would release it. *It's too hard for me to control. Sometimes I fear it will consume me. I don't want to think on that now*, she chided. She only wanted to think of her playthings that would help her push Valens out of her mind. The full skill she used during her hunt would not be tested today. Teaching was what she had to do now, and they needed it. Fast, easy moves that would help them become allies would be useful in bringing down Monev. *Trusting them is not possible, but using them is necessary*, she reasoned.

They came quietly into the room. She smelled them and heard

their calm breathing. *They're fighters within,* she confirmed, as she cracked her knuckles in preparation for their attack. Most people who were not used to trauma went into a fight with heightened breathing. *These boys have seen a lot more than I could've imagined,* she considered. They were calm, yet apprehensive. Seeing her earlier, she sensed, gave them a sense of respect of her ability to hurt them. She wouldn't, of course, because they were too useful. *If they become traitors, I'll destroy them,* but she would ponder that later.

Anthony tried to sneak up behind her, and her leg quickly shot out in a back-kick that landed just under his testicles. She didn't look back because she didn't have to. As a blind child, she could sense a person's location and the anxious and quick moves which caused their breathing to heighten. They were all dead giveaways to an unseeing person with her tuned abilities. Anthony groaned and bent over in pain just when the heel of her foot moved up and caught him abruptly in the chin and held it there. As if she were a ballerina, she turned, perfectly balanced, to face him and then lowered her foot to his chest. She briefly glanced at Mitch, who stood unmoving with his arms crossed. She figured he'd be a ruthless opponent. She remembered the calmness of his kill the night they met. Her foot pushed Anthony, power slipping through her, and he stumbled back, caught off guard at how a slight kick could pack such power—and from a girl, no less.

Crouching into fighting stance, she motioned for Mitch to join in on the fun. She sensed no hesitation and his desire to hurt her. He

164

didn't like her, and she knew it, felt it. *I don't like him either. He's just too unstable, and Valens should not trust this one,* she contemplated. *Time will tell which side he'll take,* she thought, and then ducked his punch. She dropped to one knee and kicked him in the shin, causing him to slide. Anthony charged her, and she smelled his anger.

She met Anthony with a slice of her hand to his neck and then grabbed him and held him there. Squeezing her hand closed while puncturing his pressure points, she waited for him to gurgle in response. He held it longer than she thought he would before his protest slipped out in a grunt. She was barely winded.

"Fight, don't give up! Push through it and never hesitate. It'll kill you!" she yelled. She wanted them to learn not to be intimidated. They needed to learn to fight through fear. It was a lesson she'd learned herself -a hard one. Anthony growled and punched at her. She easily swayed out of harm's way and ducked to land a light punch at his neck. Mitch took the opportunity to punch down with doubled fists to the back of her head, but she shook it off and head-butted his chin. Mitch recovered quickly and snaked an arm around her neck. Anthony came forward and landed a punch to her stomach. Air rushed for her lungs.

Yes! she thought. *This is it. They're doing it. No more playing. Now that they have confidence, I can challenge them to push further.* The pain she felt could not stop her. She'd fought through pain all her life. She pulled her knees up, giving the appearance of protecting herself, waiting for Anthony to get cocky. It didn't take long before his features relaxed a little. He thought he had the upper hand and grew arrogant, but she was quick to take it back with a swift kick to his chest. Mitch's arms grew slack, but he didn't hesitate. He pushed her to the ground and climbed onto her chest.

She was starting to like him. He was a fighter, as she suspected. She let him punch her only three times because she wasn't going to make it that easy for him. The angry look on his face showed he was digging into the pit of his soul for inner strength, summoning up his deep anger and hate. She felt it as each punch grew stronger. She smiled at him, as she elbowed him near his privates to draw his attention. He didn't feel it and kept punching.

She moved her head quickly away from his pounding fist. He had no control, so she punched upward, hitting her palm up his nose and forcing his head back. Jerking her hips up to throw him off balance, she flipped to stand. Then, she quickly turned around and climbed on top of him as Anthony tried to pull her off Mitch from behind.

Her legs were wrapped tightly under Mitch with her knees pressing down his arms tightly. She asked, "Can I punch now?" then laughed at the scowl on Mitch's face.

She punched lightly at his neck and head. She didn't want to hurt him but rather to teach him. Anthony didn't give up. She sensed his fist lifting to land a heavy blow. He was stronger than most his age, she figured, and she quickly moved out of the way of his punch as it landed on Mitch's chin.

"Enough!" Shamira yelled. Anthony stopped and was breathing hard. Mitch's heart beat fast underneath her, and she laughed. Hesitantly, Anthony and Mitch followed.

"Girl, you can kick ass and take names. I'm glad you're on our team," Anthony said and helped Shamira up.

"Well, I hope you guys learned your lesson well enough to teach the rest of the recruits. Remember... go for the opponent's weakness. Push through your pain and don't give up," she said. She walked over to her jacket and picked it up off the floor.

"I learned mine. Don't trust you," Mitch spat out. Slowly getting up off the ground, his angry gaze stared at Shamira.

"I hope you don't plan on being a problem, Mitch. If you go traitor on us, I'll make sure you pay. No one is going to risk me losing my brother. No one! You got that?" Shamira warned, her eyes frothing with anger as she glared at Mitch.

Valens stood in the doorway. "Hey, cut it out, you two. Remember trust? We're a team. We're all fighting for the same cause," Valens said and walked in the room.

"You just make sure the kids you recruit are really on our side. I'm out of here," Shamira said, then rushed past Valens and Hedi. Walking as fast as she could to the door, she kicked it when she couldn't get into the garage. Her hands outstretched on the door as if she planned to push it down to get out.

Valens came up behind her. Touching her shoulders with both hands, he came up closer to her and whispered in her ear. "You can trust me, Shamira. I would never hurt you or put you and your brother in danger, but I'm patient. I'll earn your trust—the hard way if I have to," he said. Slowly, he stepped back and leisurely slid his hands from her shoulders to the middle of her arms. He moved aside and put his hand to the wall to scan his finger. The door opened, and she walked to her motorcycle, not looking back.

She sat on Pearl and pretended to let it warm up in case he was still watching. The ceiling opened, and the ramp extended. Her body still tingled where he had touched her, and part of her wanted to trust him so badly. But trust had only bought her pain, and she was done with that kind of pain. Physical pain was easier to deal with because it only got her angry. The pain of trusting Valens would tear her apart. With a shake of the head, she drove home, and a tear fell from her eye. Now there was regret, yet another emotion she didn't have time for. It was just something to remind her that Valens would bring her nothing but pain, but she couldn't help remembering how good his hands felt—almost so good she was tempted to think he was worth the risk.

Chapter 16

Home, her place of refuge, was the only place she could be free to laugh, trust, and play. She sat outside and stared at her home, drenched in moonlight. Home wasn't the same now, though, at least not until David was back. *Funny, David was always my best friend.* He loved her just the way she was and had no expectations. These other kids had plans for her. They wanted her to be part of their team for the purpose of getting their revenge, their freedom, and regaining their families. She didn't think their relationship would go any farther than that, and she wouldn't risk believing that.

"Pearl, park yourself," she said and slid off her motorcycle. Walking up to the door, she realized no one was home waiting for her. For once, that made her sad. She missed her parents, her brother, and her life before Monev started their campaign to take over Mars. This had changed her. It had made her unleash the power within her that she fought to keep hidden. Now all she craved was revenge.

The lights came on when she walked through the door. She didn't stop but went straight to David's room. Grabbing his picture of the two of them as she lay down on his bed, she kissed his face on the miniature video screen. She held it to her heart and then fell asleep.

"Shamira. Shamira, get up," her father's voice vibrated through her mind.

"Um," she groaned and snuggled deeper in the covers that smelled like David. She smiled and played through the dream of the tickle game of hide-and-seek they would play when her parents were working. She dreamed of picking him up from school. They would race home to chase and play through the house before their parents got home.

Warm hands lifted her upper body, cradling her in warmth. She inhaled and thought, *Daddy.* She snuggled deeper. Home hadn't seemed this good in a long time. Their family was ripped apart with grief.

"Shamira, I'm so sorry. We'll find him. David is coming home,

I promise you. I promise," she heard her father's broken voice soothe. He laid her down gently and left the room.

It seemed as though a lifetime had passed. She jumped up, in shock that she had fallen asleep. She looked around the room for her father and saw no sign of him.

"Computer, is Dad in the house?" she asked.

"Negative. He left a message for you. He said you can reach them at Headquarters. They'll be there for two days straight working around the clock. Stay put," the computer stated in its usual happy female voice.

"Go in secure mode," she commanded. Then, she quickly got out of David's room. She had to meet the gang that night, but she wanted to do some research first on Cal and some of the members of Monev. There was this nagging feeling that something wasn't right with him, and she just couldn't shake it. Walking to her room, she got on the computer and searched the Security Force databanks for anything about Cal, Thor, or Monev. She found nothing.

"C'mon! What are you hiding? Why are all these files hidden so deeply? Every other Security Force member's file I can access, but not Cal's. Hmm... let me try something else." She left the Security Force files and started searching the Earth birth records.

Nothing. There is nothing on him. Nowhere is there anything on him. This is unbelievable. Well, I guess they would have to seal the files on the head of the Security Force. Any information on him could be used against the Force. Dang it, she thought, and then she kicked the desk lightly in frustration.

"Let's see. Let me search this Renu," she said. Tapping her foot lightly, she typed in the name she got from Thor. Nothing came up, absolutely nothing. She typed the name "Thor" and pulled up his criminal record from Earth.

"Oh, I should have hurt you worse, much worse, you scab," she growled while looking at his criminal record. Murder, prostitution, and drug trafficking were the reasons he had served time in jail. He got a new lease on life, it seemed, when he was chosen to move to Mars. Many convicted criminals that showed no improvement on Earth five years prior to the Mars colonization got exterminated. Earth's new directive to become a world of peace and prosperity meant those considered unfit were sent to the Waters.

The Waters was a place on Earth where they drowned and disposed of criminals who were too deadly to make the cut to be moved to Mars. Those criminals couldn't go through the chemical and programmable rehabilitation to be moved to Mars. The government and Security Force Elite members were the only people that knew of the plan until the year when the Security Force left Earth to build Mars.

"Hmm... Thor, with your record, you normally wouldn't be chosen. Oh, but I forgot, you did these crimes five years prior to the directive for the Mars movement. Who told you to behave, Thor?" she asked the screen, looking at a much younger Thor. Rubbing her eyes, she ran her hands through her hair. She stood up and decided it was time to get dressed. Stripping, she walked to the bathroom. Her clothes fell on the floor and she walked to the shower. She was in a hurry but really wanted to disappear in the warm shower. Thinking of David, she wanted to make a pit stop before she headed to meet the boys—somewhere that would remind her of him.

After showering, she dressed in full gear. Glancing down at her hand, she frowned, realizing she still had Thor's ring on her finger. A smirk formed on her full lips. *Serves him right.* Then she tucked her collapsed saber in her belt. She took her damp, wavy hair and wrapped it at her nape in a firm ball, put on her glasses, and decided she was ready to go.

She slid on Pearl and looked up at the darkening sky. *Funny how now that I can see, all I see is darkness.* Realizing she was staying up all night and sleeping during most of the day, she chuckled to herself. Valens' face came to her mind, and she wondered if he did the same. She erased his face and focused on the road ahead of her. Ending up at the playground where she had last taken David, she climbed off her bike and walked around in thought.

Remembering David, she wondered if she could catch a faint scent of him here. *I know I can't, but I'll take what I can get.* Just the thought of this being the last place she brought him made her feel close to him.

She looked up at the sky and closed her eyes. Placing her hands in her pocket, she was relieved that no one was out there that night. She didn't want to share this peaceful memory of David running off to play. Inhaling, she thought of David and caught scents of others approaching. *I guess time for dreaming is ended. I'm back in hell.* Slowly, she placed her left hand in her coat and touched the hilt of her saber.

The saber was one of her favorite weapons, and her dad had it made especially for her. She smiled at the thought. It fit her hand like a glove and was collapsed to appear like a small club. When she held it and swung it with a specific amount of pressure, it extended. It was controlled by various sequences that would allow it to change from a club to a saber to extend sharp miniature knives from the length of the saber's blade. *Yep, this is definitely my favorite toy for an unfair fight,* she confirmed and tapped into her power.

With her eyes held shut, she sensed them. One was running fast toward her. Unfortunately for him, he would get cut today. She opened her eyes as he was several feet away, smiled, and swung her saber down his coat. It met skin and sliced through his scream. Her mind was calm, but her beast was excited, and she smiled then swung at the next man to run in for the attack. Then, she saw him. It was Thor in the distance, sending his feeble minions to do his dirty work.

He looked at her calmly, and she knew he wanted his ring back. *He tracked me to get it.* She quickly grabbed a flat disk from her belt, and with a flick of her wrist, it cut the hand from the attacker who attempted to shoot her with a gun. She looked around and realized there were twenty or so ready to attack. She knew running would be her best option, and letting her power free could be dangerous. She was more afraid of it than these men.

Squinting, she saw two motorcycles approaching in the distance. Rapid and steady feet followed. She sniffed and knew Mitch and Anthony were bringing up the rear of the group. Maybe she could win today, or maybe she would be dragging them away with her. She fought, kicked, punched, and ducked numerous blows as they came like a river to attack. Her eyes never left Thor, who stood in the distance and watched with detachment as his men attacked her and she fought. He studied her with hatred, and she made sure he saw the ring on her finger. Taunting him, she got careless and took a blow to the face. She growled as another blow hit her in the stomach and someone grabbed her from behind.

Two men held each leg and her arms. She growled, the beast fighting to get out, and her skin started to tingle. "No!!!" she screamed to back the power down. She looked up to see Mitch and Anthony beating down opponents one after the other to make their way to her.

"Get him! Get Thor!" she yelled at them. A burst of fire from her gut forced out a flame of strength and adrenaline, and released her rage. She jerked her feet from her captors to land a kick in the face of the men closest to her. Her saber, once slack in her hand, was now firmly in place as she tighted her grip. She jerked her weight down to land on one knee as the men scrambled to regain control. A flick of the wrist, and her saber blade was riddled with small protruding knives, and she swung it at the largest of the gang that

175

had grabbed her neck. "No thoughts, no hesitations," her father always taught her. She suppressed any emotion, pity, or compassion while she fought through the men that had tried to capture her. They fell around her, and an opening appeared.

She ran to her motorcycle and climbed on. Looking past the men who had tried to attack her, she saw Mitch and Anthony take a sedated Thor with them to their bikes. They lifted him as if he weighed nothing. *How can this be?* Mitch wore a form-fitting leather riding suit with a tight hood and motioned to her to follow them. The attackers started to shoot at them, and they took off at top speed. Shamira caught up and flew behind them. Laser fire jerked her forward as it hit her shoulder after she took off.

Forcing away the pain and the smell of burning cloth and flesh, she was glad the beast now rested. She was so close to losing control. The last time that happened she was younger, much younger. That time, she almost killed someone. She didn't remember exactly what happened, all she wanted to do was forget it.

They led her to the Outlands, several miles from Valens' hideout. The land was barren, and the only light was from the moons above. Halting their bikes in an unknown location, Shamira noticed they were talking to Valens from their earlinks. Mitch motioned for her to come closer, and she slid off her bike to follow him. The wind was heavy in this part of the Outlands, and sand kicked up in her face. Her eyes had night vision and allowed her to see Mitch while he dug into the sand for something while being directed by Valens.

Anthony held Thor in a neck hold that would break Thor's neck if he tried to awaken. *Impressive. Anthony definitely knows how to take care of himself, and he has the size to do it well. Maybe he was holding back in our training session*, she wondered. Mitch stepped back while a transparent cylinder rose out of the ground. The cylinder was about seven feet in height and about ten feet wide. Shamira observed it had a metal bar in the middle and strapping off the bar that could be easily adjusted.

She watched as Anthony threw a sleeping Thor over his shoulder like a sack of potatoes. Mitch put in a sequence on the side of the cylinder door, and it opened. Anthony secured Thor to the pole. As Anthony stepped out, Mitch quickly punched in a code on the door. They stepped back and watched the cylinder lower into the ground with Thor contained.

Mitch motioned for Shamira to come closer. "Hey, are you okay? You took a hit back there," Mitch said, looking Shamira over like she was a speck of dirt.

"I'm fine. It's just a scratch," she said, and then stood straighter.

She didn't want to appear weak or hurt in front of these guys, but the truth was, the wound hurt badly. Luckily, when it came to lasers, wounds burned closed, so they seldom proved fatal, provided no poison was purposely ejected with the laser or no vital organs were hit. She figured if it had been poison, she would be lying flat on the ground by now, so she could deal with the pain and the scar. It

177

was the second scar she had gotten since she gained eyesight. *Yep, sight is definitely making me lazy.*

Mitch lifted an eyebrow. "Suit yourself. Help us put dirt back over this. Valens said his dad used the cylinders for his experiments. We need to keep this thing hidden," Mitch said while he bent down to push the dirt into the hole.

"Hey, how's he going to breathe in there?" Anthony asked Mitch. "But then on second thought, after what the creep did to Hedi, he can suffocate for all I care."

"Valens said that thing is monitored from his place. He said since it was used for experiments, he controls the air and temperature. We can see and communicate with this scum while we're at Valens'," Mitch said, and then grunted with a powerful push.

"I'd hate to be him. There ain't a toilet in that thing. Damn," Anthony said while pushing more dirt over the top of the canister.

Mitch pushed another mound of dirt over it. "That's his problem. Lucky for him, there are vents in the bottom that release liquids. Trust me, when he wakes up, he's not going to be so damn arrogant," Mitch spat out.

"He deserves much more. He's an evil bastard. What were Earth officials thinking to let this guy pass the board to get here? Mars was supposed to be for petty criminals trying to start a new life. Looks like someone cut a slimy deal, and Mars got stuck with the junk," Anthony said while he stomped down the ground with Shamira and Mitch.

Shamira snorted at the comment. "Oh, someone tipped him off all right. He was a real good boy for five years before the program launched. He came highly recommended for rehabilitation on Mars. I smell a stink of corruption somewhere."

"Corruption? You don't know the half of it. We'll talk more at Valens'. Since I've been most all places Monev is involved in, I'll clue everyone in on the sadistic bastards we're dealing with," Anthony said and stood with a stretch.

Shamira studied them for a moment. "Hey, what happened back there? You both were super strong."

Anthony slowly took off his hood, and wires connected to flat metal tags on his scalp. It appeared to be attached to something under the skin.

"Does that hurt?" she asked.

"Hell, yeah. These are his prototypes. The new ones won't have to stick into the skin. Valens was tracking you and wanted us to be able to help you, so we volunteered to try them out and make sure you were safe. He thinks Thor's ring is a tracking or homing device of some kind. All of Monev's head henchmen have one. Valens knew you still had Thor's and thought Thor would come looking for it. Mitch and I just wanted to come to kick some butt and get some revenge," Anthony said, shadow boxing with a big grin. He looked silly. He was a huge kid, almost as tall as Thor, and sturdy in frame. She turned to Mitch, and his unfailing frown found her.

"I just came to save a comrade—a life for a life," Mitch said, then turned and walked to his cycle.

She smiled. *Hmm. He called me "a comrade,"* she thought. *Coming from Mitch, that means a lot.* She followed them to Valens', holding her warm feelings of true acceptance deep within her and pushing down the sharp ache from her burned skin.

Chapter 17

They waited at the designated spot, and she took a look around to make sure the area was still deserted. With the lair Valens' dad made, she knew he had surveillance around the perimeter also. Most of the high-tech equipment on Mars had to be shipped from Earth. The Mars Security Force didn't allow any technology to be manufactured on Mars, knowing it could get out of control. The ramp opened, and they drove forward to park their motorcycles. Standing in front of the hidden doorway in the wall, she closed her eyes and felt the slight warmth of a beam. *Leave it to Valens to take security to a whole new level,* she smirked and opened her eyes.

She followed Mitch and Anthony as they quickly walked forward. The door wasted not a second in closing behind her when she entered.

"Come back to the lab. The door is open," she heard Valens say from the speakers in the ceiling.

Walking down the hall, she remembered her last encounter with Valens, and a tingling in the pit of her stomach reminded her she wasn't doing a good job at pushing him away. Actually, after that night, she wanted him so badly that she disgusted herself. Well, she wouldn't give in—not now, not ever, and especially when there were so many people at risk. She couldn't afford a soft spot for anyone, except for David. Her family was the only sure thing she knew of, the only people she could count on and trust. Remembering that would save her heart, her trust, and the walls she had created to protect herself.

The door to the lab opened, and she hung back, slowing her walk. She walked through and smelled the fresh woodsy smell she knew was Valens, and she inhaled deeply, hating herself for it.

"Shamira, you're hurt," Valens said. Hard as she tried not to look at him, his nearness made it impossible not to turn toward him. He came to her and touched her arm and neck above her wound.

"It's fine," she said and jerked away. *Crap, that hurt!* She winced.

His lip turned up with a smirk. "No, you're not. Here, let me give you a shot of a healing agent to speed up healing and take away the pain. Besides, I saw you wince," he said with a chuckle.

"Hey, Valens, can we take the gear off?" Anthony asked.

"Yeah. Can you and Mitch take the table in the outer room? Hedi, would you grab that box over there and set up the contents on the table? We can play my favorite game while we figure out what our next move is," Valens said with a glance to Hedi.

Hedi walked passed him to the table. "Sure. No problem, Valens," Hedi said with a dip of frustration in her voice.

"Thought I'd never get you alone," he said in a low, seductive whisper. Then he stuck her wound with a shot of the healing agent. He rubbed in the pain with his thumb.

Swallowing a grunt, she tensed. His soft but firm grip held her steady while he wiped the area clean, and then he leaned in and kissed it. Her arm shivered, and her eyelids closed.

"Stop it," she forced out, and she knew it was a lie. She didn't want him to stop. The longing for the kiss on her lips was so strong she had to swallow her desire.

"Open your eyes, Shamira. It's what my mother used to do to me to take my mind off the pain whenever I got hurt. I didn't mean to offend you," he said sincerely.

She felt his gaze on her but didn't want to open her eyes to see him, but just to get this over with, she slowly opened her lids and saw his beautiful, kind face.

"It's fine. Thanks for the thought," she said, ending in a hard swallow. She stepped back out of the reach of his hand. *Breathe, inhale,* she told herself, trying to regain control of her emotions. Part of her wanted him to grab her and kiss her, to give her the first kiss she had so yearned for since she was twelve. She never thought any boy would want her beyond her difference, so she pushed those hopes from her mind. Valens had been around and kept coming around even knowing she was blind. *He didn't seem to care about my anomaly; at least, that is what appeared to be the case.*

He relaxed and smiled at her. She could tell he was as nervous as she was. She smelled a bit of perspiration building on him, and it enhanced his alluring scent. His eyes slightly dilated, but she noted that he recovered well. The fact that he was a bit nervous made her feel more comfortable, and she smiled back.

"Beautiful. I hardly ever see you smile. Tonight, I hope to see it more often. Let's go in the room with the gang. Uh, you go ahead... and, Shamira, I better take that ring," he said and grabbed her hand. She looked at him and held his gaze while he slowly slid Thor's ring off her finger.

She didn't say a word when she slid her hand from his firm, soft grip. Ending eye contact, she turned and walked out of the lab as calmly as she could fake it. *At this rate, he'll have me crying in a puddle of tears when I've served my purpose and he leaves me for someone beautiful and alluring like Hedi. He won't want to stay with a freak with an anger problem—someone like me.*

"Hey, what the heck is this junk?" Shamira heard Hedi say.

She walked in on them opening the box that Valens told Hedi to bring in the room.

Anthony towered over Hedi while looking in the box. "I don't know. I thought we were going to play a videogame or something. What the hell is this archaic crap?"

Valens came from behind Shamira, and stood beside her. "It's playing cards. I know it's an old game, but my father loved it. He made sure we had lots of decks, and he collected them over the years from Earth antique auctions. I think they discontinued this game over 100 years ago in the year 2060. My father was fascinated with this game and chess, but tonight we're going to play a game of cards."

Mitch cleared his throat. "You're kidding, right? 'Cause, dude, I don't like to play old games." He crossed his arms over his chest.

"You'll like it if you give it a chance. Besides, the winner gets a prize," Valens said. He walked around Shamira, pulled out a chair for her, and sat down next to it. She didn't budge.

He grabbed her hand and tugged her forward. Pulling her hand away, she walked around to another chair and sat down. She saw Valens smile from the side of the gaze she landed on Anthony, who had pulled up to sit across from her. Hedi walked around the table and with an indecisive frown, turned toward Shamira and sat down next to her. *Now what is this about?* Shamira wondered. *Why would Hedi, who has been chasing Valens all this time, want to sit next to me?* Mitch decided to sit next to Hedi after he quirked an eyebrow up as the scene played out before him.

The game started slowly with a grunting Mitch, who didn't like to lose. Anthony joked most of the time, Shamira figured as a way to get everyone's mind off of the dire situation. Hedi squealed like a child whenever she won a hand.

Shamira studied her hand and picked out a card. "We need to find out who this Renu really is. He's the head of Monev, from what Thor says. Also, something is up with Thor. He shouldn't have been considered for rehabilitation here on Mars. He was too violent an offender with a history of brutal crimes. But, he mysteriously cleaned up his act five years before they started evaluating candidates for the Mars New World project." She threw down her card with a slap.

Anthony smiled and picked up the hand. "Oh, yeah, baby, this is my game. Kiss my butt! That prize is as good as mine," Anthony said with a wink to Shamira.

Hedi smacked her teeth. "Stop teasing. We girls are still up by two games, meathead, so don't count your winnings before you get them, sugar," Hedi added with an exaggerated wink to Anthony.

"Seriously, though, this Renu dude is so far underground we won't get him unless we bring down some of his head cronies. I know where they all hang out, and I know who can help us get them too," Anthony added and slammed down his card.

Mitch stood and slapped down his card. "The first one I want to bring down is Fisher. If he gave my sister to Slasher, he should die. I want to be the one to do it to him," Mitch said when he scooped up the hand he'd won.

"Slasher may be one of the untouchables. He's usually well guarded, at least that's what I heard from the underground," Valens said and then threw out the next card.

Hedi bit her lip while searching for her card. "If we get Kimble and Fisher, we can get the information we need. I bet Fisher knows about the head guy because he was part of the original gang. He just ticked someone off and got demoted. He was supposed to be running their hunt and capture division... you know, the one that Strong took from him when he cut off Fisher's ear. Lucky for Fisher, that could easily be repaired, but everyone that sees him without his hair long can tell he has a totally different ear than the other. It was a chop job I heard, done before Mars got licensed surgeons here to do reconstructive surgery." She snickered and threw out her card.

"Well, girls, it looks like your lead has come to a bitter end. Bam!" Anthony chided when he threw out the last card that made him the winner.

Hedi leaned close to Shamira's ear. "Shamira, I'm going to snatch the prize, and you run with it. We can't let these guys have the last laugh, can we?" Hedi whispered.

Shamira jerked her gaze to Hedi. She didn't trust the girl. Hedi had been putting moves on Valens since she met her, but Shamira figured she would play along just to see what Hedi was really up to. "Fine, I'll play along for now," Shamira replied cautiously.

Valens got up and left the room to go get the prize. They all looked around, and their eyes landed on Anthony, who was grinning from ear to ear.

Anthony leaned back in his chair. "Don't hate me, ladies. I can't lose a challenge. Let's face it; I haven't gotten a present in over eight years since I was captured by Monev." Then his face clouded over with a grim look. He looked intently at Shamira and said, "Shamira, by the way, there's something I need to tell you. Thank you for saving Mitch. By saving him, you saved us all."

He sniffed and turned away from them, then stood up and walked to the wall, which he hit with his fist. "Damn, to finally be able to taste revenge. I'm afraid to wish it, but now I can start to believe in justice again. It seemed so unattainably impossible before," Anthony said, then dropped his head and turned around.

Mitch stood and walked over to Anthony. "Shamira, you don't know this, but the night you came, they were going to kill me. I threatened to leave and tell the Security Force what I knew. Stupid, stupid, I know. I let my anger make me slip. When you and Valens came, you were like angels." He looked Shamira directly in her eyes.

Shamira looked at Hedit who said nothing. She lifted an eyebrow in disbelief to see tears streaming down Hedi's face.

Hedi leaned forward and hugged Shamira and whispered to her, "Don't forget, grab the prize and run." Shamira smiled, thinking, *Hedi may be a watering pot of tears, but the girl definitely has grit.* She could appreciate that.

Valens walked back into the room. "Hey, what happened? I go get a prize, and everyone cries because they're mad they didn't win? Well, get over it. One winner per game, and that's Anthony this time. Here… the keys to my dad's car. This car is fully equipped with enough firepower to bring down Olympus Mons, and I haven't even started to go down the list of other gadgets," Valens said then slapped Anthony on the shoulder while handing him the keys.

Shamira didn't hesitate. She snatched the key and ran to the training room. There were many places to hide in there, and she felt the thrill of a fun chase in her first ever game of hide-and-seek with people she had begrudgingly started to think of as friends. Hedi, her accessory to the crime, was right behind her, laughing along the way.

"Get her!" she heard Anthony yell with a sliver of laughter in his command.

Hedi came up beside her. "Shamira, take this. It's a water gun. Valens' dad had a ton of these in the play closet in Valens' sister's room," Hedi said and threw two small water guns at her.

Shamira pumped the guns, which pulled moisture from the air, filling the small barrels up with water. She entered the training room, with Hedi right behind her.

Hedi ran and slid under a small table near the entrance to the room. Shamira ran to the room just past the entrance that looked like a utility closet. She tucked the water guns in her pockets and looked around for something soft she could throw at them when they got there.

189

"Hey, I bet they came this way," Mitch said. The guys stood in front of the doorway.

Anthony's deep voice cleared. "Wait... we need a plan. These girls were up to something before the game started, I bet."

"Oh, I got it. This is what we'll do," Valens said. Then, they didn't say a word.

What are they up to? Shamira wondered. Valens must've been aware of her above average hearing, because they definitely weren't talking or whispering. Shamira tucked the key in her bra. *Hey, girl's have great hiding places!* She frowned. *He better not even think about going to get it. If he does, I'll break his fingers.*

She heard them tiptoe deeper into the room, and then Hedi attacked. Shamira pushed her sight past the walls of the closet to see Mitch fall forward flat on the floor, breaking his fall with his hands.

"That's it! Hedi's mine!" Mitch said, and then pushed up quickly to catch a running Hedi. Mitch and Anthony caught her and mercilessly tickled her feet and under her arms. She was laughing so hard she barely got out a cry for help.

"Sha-Sha-mira! Get... get them before I pee my pants. Stop! Not my toes! Stop it! Mitch! Ha ha!!" Hedi laughed.

Shamira smiled and turned around to grab a few of the soft one-pound foam training balls. *This will do.* She took a quick look through the wall and saw that Valens was looking around for her while Mitch was sitting backwards on Hedi's legs and tickling her feet. Anthony had one of her arms up, still tickling her unmercifully.

190

"Give up the information, Hedi! Where are Shamira and the key to my damn superhero car?" Anthony laughed.

"I'll, never... nev-er sell out my be-best friend. Ever! Ha hee... oh my God, stop with that foot. Oh, Shamira, hurry! I ca-can't hold out much longer," Hedi laughed.

Shamira figured she needed to take out Valens first, since he would be the first one to try to get her. She giggled to herself because she had never had this much fun with anyone besides David. At this rate, the ice around her heart would melt, and she would be hurt again, but in this very moment, she felt so good that it didn't matter. It seemed worth it even if it would not last.

She slid out of her hiding place and threw the first red weighted ball at Valens' left foot, causing him to lose balance and slide to his knees. Valens recovered and ran toward her. Shamira giggled as she faked him out and ran to the side. She slid forward and threw the blue ball at Mitch's head.

"Ouch! That's it! Get Shamira!" Mitch yelled, and then he, Anthony, and Valens were in hot pursuit. She scrambled up, then did a fake-out to the left. Sliding toward Hedi, she came to a stop and grabbed Hedi's hand, yanking her to stand. They ran out of the room and down the hall. Shamira looked through the walls to find another good hiding place for them and found a small hidden closet in a little girl's room. She jerked Hedi around the doorway and pulled her into the tiny door in the closet of the bedroom.

They were both breathing heavily and laughing at their

escape. Hedi held up her finger to her mouth and said, "Shh." They looked at each other and grinned, feeling completely safe and hidden.

Shamira heard the boys running up and down the hall. They paused to rummage through all the rooms. They even split up, but they still couldn't find them. The girls started to feel safe since the boys took off toward the other end of the hall to search for them.

Hedi turned to Shamira and smiled hesitantly. "Look, Shamira, I'm so sorry. I'm sorry I didn't thank you for saving us. I'm also sorry for throwing myself at Valens. I know he likes you, and I can see you like him too."

Her eyes lowered in shame. She took a deep breath and returned Shamira's gaze. "I... well, it's just that I thought he was the one to save us. I had a bit of hero worship for him, I guess. I'll stay out of it. He really does like you, and he put me in my place about how he feels about you that first day. I just, just didn't want to listen."

She reached out and lightly touched Shamira's arm. "Will you be my friend? I never had one with Monev. I was too scared to get close. So many kids were killed since I was captured that I didn't want to cry when I lost another friend. Mitch and Anthony promised me they would find a way out and would come back to save me. I had to believe them. It was the only way I could get through the days in that hell. But, the hell I was in is nothing compared to the hell those kids are in now—the kids we plan to set free. You have no idea how grateful we all are to you. Say you forgive me, Shamira. Please?" Hedi begged, more tears streaming down her beautiful face.

Shamira's heart wasn't that cold, and the ice around it broke when she felt Hedi's trembling hands on her shoulders. "Forgiven. Now, please, please stop crying, or you will make me cry, and I stopped crying a long time ago," Shamira said hoarsely.

"I didn't cry before I escaped. I thought I had no more tears, but now it seems I can't stop. That's why I wanted to have some fun. I haven't played since before Monev took me. It feels like heaven," Hedi said, then grabbed Shamira's hand and raised a finger up to her lip.

Shamira heard it too. Someone passed by the room and doubled back. Her heartbeat sped up, and the thrill of the chase was back on. She heard one of them enter the room. He hesitated, and Shamira peeked through the wall to see that it was Anthony. He took a moment to motion for Mitch and Valens to enter.

The lights were on in the room, and they moved quietly throughout, lifting blankets and moving chairs to look for them. She noticed slight smiles on their faces and smiled as she realized that for the first time, Mitch wasn't frowning. *Hedi doesn't realize how much we all needed this.* Hedi's body was shivering with excitement, and she turned to Shamira with a grin on her face. Then, she leaned over and whispered to Shamira, "They'll never find us in here."

Shamira doubted that, because as soon as those words left Hedi's lips, Valens pointed to the closet that held the door they'd slipped in. Not wanting to give her secret sight away, she held her tongue while she watched Mitch tiptoe forward to the open closet door. She could've kicked herself for not closing it, but she thought if she left it open, they wouldn't think it was their hiding place. *Oh well. The gig is up.* Mitch threw open the door and grabbed a squirming, yelling Hedi by the foot to drag her out.

Shamira grabbed Hedi's hand and pulled. She and Mitch were now in a tug of war, and Shamira braced her feet on either side of the door for leverage. Valens joined in and pulled, jerking Hedi's hand free from Shamira. Mitch swung a squealing Hedi over his shoulder and put her on the floor for another tickle interrogation with Anthony.

Shamira slammed the door to the hiding place shut and then turned the lock she'd just discovered. Spotting Valens heading in toward her, she struggled to keep her excitement at bay.

"It's no use, Shamira. I have the key to the door. You know what? It's opening right... now!" he said. With frustration and a rush of pleasure, the door opened, and Valens held it casually while smiling his usual cocky self-assured grin.

"Well, I'm not ticklish, you know, so don't even try making me confess," Shamira said, then crossed her arms protectively over her chest where the key was hidden.

"You know, I know your weakness. I could threaten to kiss you," Valens said and winked.

"And I could threaten to punch you in the face." Shamira winked back. He laughed out loud, and then threw his head back as he held his stomach in laughter.

194

"I don't doubt you'd punch me, but a kiss from you would be worth the pain," he said and winked at her. He grabbed her foot and pulled her out. She spread her arms out to grab the frame of the door and struggled not to laugh when he started to tickle her bare feet. Then, she felt someone tickle her other foot, and she couldn't hold it in. She giggled.

"Where is my key, Shamira? Your friend over there is doubled over in laughter. Now give up the key!" Anthony choked out a laugh.

"Fine, fine! But you have to let Hedi go first," Shamira said between giggles.

Valens tugged at her foot. "Let's pull her out and put her next to her partner in crime."

She let them pull her out and escort her over to Hedi, who was still trembling with residual laughter. "I won't talk," she giggled.

Hedi fought her foot away from Mitch, but it was jerked back. "Okay, okay! She'll only give up the key if you promise to let us girls drive it after we kick Monev's butt!" Hedi wiped a tear from her eye with the back of her hand as she struggled to hold in her laughter.

"Deal. Now give me the key," Anthony said and reached out his hand.

Shamira struggled to hold a straight face. "I can't. I put it... well, it's somewhere that I have to take it out in private." They all stared at her with a shocked look. Hedi's look of recognition turned into a grin.

"Oh, no you didn't!" Valens said as the sides of his lips turned up to a smile.

Mitch sized up Shamira, and then jerked Hedi's foot back for another tickle. "I don't trust them. They'll just take off again. She has to get it while we are in here." His face wrinkled while he tried to hold back a laugh. He won and put a frown on his face.

Valens nodded. "Fine. Anthony, you cover the door, and Mitch, you stand in front of the closet. I'll turn around. Shamira, you have until the count of ten to pull out that key," he said, and the boys took their positions.

Shamira looked at Hedi, and Hedi winked at her. Shamira followed Hedi's line of sight to the door and between Anthony's spread legs. Hedi stood up, ready to run. Shamira smiled at her and ran around Valens, who'd already counted to five, then slid between Anthony's legs through the door. Anthony let out a howl at the pinch Hedi delivered to his calf as she tripped him up behind them. They got up and ran toward the front room before Anthony regained his composure. She reached in her shirt and snatched the key free and placed in it her pocket as she grabbed each water gun in her hand. She slid to a stop, knelt on the couch, and fired the water pistols at the boys when they ran toward her. Hedi backed her up by throwing pillows at the boys from behind a nearby chair.

"Get her and tickle her until she begs for mercy!" Anthony commanded.

Valens flew over the front of the couch and tackled Shamira. He placed his hand behind her head to brace her fall, and she smiled, remembering how he had attempted to save her that first day. He scrambled over her and pulled her arms up over her head and said, "Tickle the sweet spot under her arms, guys!" *Traitor,* she thought and laughed until tears streamed down her face.

"Okay, okay! It's in my pocket. I surrender," she laughed out. Anthony reached in her front pocket and held up the key.

"Yes, yes!" Anthony said and stood up. He pulled her up, and Valens and Mitch followed. She looked passed them to see a genuine smile on Hedi's face.

"Alright, guys, let's turn on a movie and talk about recruitment," Valens said and snapped his fingers. The movie started, and they all ignored it as they started to come up with a list of trustworthy kids to recruit.

Shamira started to doze off during the second movie, and her head fell to the side, then down as the music video of the latest Earth hit start playing. She felt Valens' firm, muscled arms come around her shoulders, and she was too tired to fight him this morning. They had a long night in front of them, and she needed the comfort he offered her. Her head rested on his shoulder, and she inhaled his unique scent and dreamed of all of them after the fighting was over— friends laughing together and riding in the new Mars, a free Mars, a safe Mars.

Chapter 18

Shamira woke up with a jerk. *Where am I?* Her memory was still blurry from a deep sleep. She hadn't slept this deeply in weeks. *What's wrong with me?* Taking a quick look around the room, she jumped up and realized everyone was gone. *Figures.* It was just like she expected. She'd been set up for a joke, and the others left her behind to go after Monev. "Just great!" she yelled. Listening for any sounds of life, she heard nothing. They'd definitely deserted her.

She walked over to the door and remembered that Valens had

this place locked, and it was virtually impossible to break out of. Deciding he may have left the labs open, she headed toward them only to discover the door was locked. "Looks like you have secrets also, Valens," she said to the door. Running her hand along the wall, she hoped to get the door to open. She gave up with a punch and turned her back to the door.

"Hello, Shamira. So, you're finally awake? We went to go recruit the others to fight Monev. We'll be back before nightfall. Grab something to eat in the kitchen. By the way, don't break anything," the hologram of a grinning Valens said. She looked around to make sure no one was really there. Then, she bent forward and kissed the hologram on the lips and laughed out loud.

Turning around, she walked to the kitchen, hoping Valens didn't catch that on camera. *Dang*, she said, and hit her hand on her head. He could've seen that if he'd been watching her or had the surveillance on. What was she thinking? Now she really felt stupid. She sucked up that feeling and pushed it aside like she had so many times before. *No regrets – they're a waste of time.* Survival and saving her brother would be her only motivation from now on.

The kitchen was full service with all the fixings for any large family. She wondered if Valens invited these kids here because he was lonely from the loss of his family. This place was huge and a bit much for just one person. The kitchen island had a plate of croissants and other pastries on top. Miniature milk and juice containers were scattered around, she guessed from the others picking over it before they left. She quickly stuffed two croissants in her mouth and washed them down with milk.

Feeling edgy, she washed her hands and went in the direction of the bedrooms to take a quick shower. She walked down the hall to a corridor off to the left and looked through the wall to a boy's bedroom. Guessing it was Valens' bedroom; she headed in that direction, anxious to get a peek at where he slept. His scent tickled her nose when she got to the doorway. Smiling at her secret pleasure, she walked forward, and the lights came on for her. His room had vivid colors that reminded her of him and drawings of Earth on the wall. All kinds of vehicles, from motorcycles to spaceships to fly packs were scattered on his walls and his bed. His full sized bed was rumpled with a black blanket, and pillows were thrown all over the floor.

She went over to the side entrance of the bathroom, figuring she better hurry up and wash before they got back. Hurriedly, she tossed off her clothes and washed. Hearing sounds in the distance, she knew she needed to finish. She jumped out of the shower and got dressed. Stumbling through getting dressed, she ran out of Valens' room so she wouldn't be caught there. Taking a deep breath, she walked toward the main room. She feigned calmness, hoping her blush didn't crawl up her cheeks to give away her secret.

"Shamira." Valens smiled upon seeing her.

She looked up and then beyond him to see about fifty kids in his game room. Taken aback by the looks of admiration, she swallowed then frowned. They ranged in age from ten on up, she guessed. "Who... where did all these kids come from?" Shamira asked while she tried to hold her voice steady.

"Everywhere. Some of these kids are forced to sell dream, and others have been living—or rather, hiding—on the streets hoping not to get recruited by Monev," Valens said and stepped forward.

She pointed at the kids behind him. "How are these kids going to be able to fight Monev? We're fighting grown men with guns. Did you forget that? I'm not going to have these kids' deaths on my head!" She yelled, angry with him for putting her in this position.

He looked at her calmly and unyielding. "Trust me, they'll be ready. I can make them ready. I know this." He reached out and touched her arm.

"Look, I don't know about this. I'll rip every door apart until I find my brother, but I'm not stupid. I know I can't get him and save everyone by myself. Who is going to stay back and train these kids to at least survive?" Shamira asked, then jerked away from Valens and ran her hand threw her damp hair in frustration.

He dropped his hand. "These kids and us. We're all going to do more than survive, Shamira. They've been fighting for years to survive, and most of them are already trained to fight for their lives. I have suits for all of them that'll enhance each kid's power by ten, as well as a chip that'll give them the reflexes of born fighters that will make them more than survivors. It will make us all defeaters."

She jerked away, pacing the room in thought. She couldn't

help it. She wanted it all—to save David and to bring down Monev.

"Alright, here is the plan. Tonight I need to get close to Cutter! He will give us some answers about Renu before we break into Olympus Mons," Shamira said.

Anthony stepped forward. "Okay, but you know that is impossible, right? Cutter cannot be touched. He's a cruel bastard, and we'll get killed trying to get to him. Hmm?" He put his fist under his ching. "Hey, we can go after Cutter's best man, Fisher, and if we're lucky, he will be with Tiger, who runs Olympus Mons. Fisher used to be top dog, but being demoted, he may have a lot more information than the others. They hang together occasionally when Tiger gets a break from running hell."

Mitch shook his head, and leaned against the door. "There's no way we can get close to Strong, who is a trained assassin for Monev. He's the tracker that brings Tiger his prey. He has a well-trained bastard named Keeper under him. They're good - really good. I believe the only one that can take them is Shamira. They have some nasty weapons, but nothing like what I've seen in Valens' closet. We can take them." Mitch hit his fist in his hand.

Shamira nodded. "Okay. Then Valens and I'll go after Keeper. Anthony and Mitch, you better bring me Fisher. We need to get some information from them, and we need it before we get into Olympus Mons."

"Where are we going to put Fisher when we get him?" Anthony asked while grinning and shaking the key to his new car.

"I have a cylinder about two miles from where you put Thor. Drop him there. We need to suit up with our gear," Valens said.

Shamira looked around the room at the sea of new recruits. "Do any of your newfound friends know where we can find these guys?" She waved her hands toward the many kids that crowded the front room.

"Uh, my name is Kaylin, and I know where Keeper will be tonight. He's meeting with some of Monev's upper-class customers to talk about the organ smuggling to Earth. He was pissed off about this rich guy trying to get him to come down on his prices since Earth shut down all unauthorized space travel from Earth to Mars. He'll be there, and I wouldn't be surprised if Monev wasn't on the prowl for the Elite Security Force members they are bringing down. If you want, I can draw you a map to where the meeting is. I just can't show my face, or he'll kill me," Kaylin said, then pulled nervously at her long brown pigtails.

"How do you know this?" Shamira asked suspiciously, studying the girl and smelling her fear. She just wanted to make sure the girl wasn't a mole, leading them to a setup.

"I... I was his pet. He was training me," she stammered.

Hedi walked over to Kaylin and placed an arm around her shoulder. "Monev's gang members select what is called a 'pet' or a trainee from the new kids when they are kidnapped, blackmailed, or recruited in order to break them or destroy their hope of escape. Some kids don't make it through the training. Look at her arms and neck, all those fresh bruises and cuts. Kaylin is a new recruit, and if they put her on with Keeper, that means she was a real fighter and very valuable," Hedi said, her voice dropping in sadness.

Shamira looked at Kaylin closer and saw the girl's look of relief and a bit of anger on her face. She figured the girl was genuine, so she let it rest. "So, is this all we got?" Shamira asked Valens.

"No. We still have a lot of kids on the inside. They're willing to give us access where they can in order to get their freedom after we bring down Monev. They will be loyal, because squealing in Monev means death to the messenger," Valens said.

"Does anyone here know of Renu or his relationship to his head goons?" Shamira asked the group.

A voice behind Hedi called out. "No one's ever seen him. He runs things from underground, so to speak. It's rumored he changes faces like a chameleon and can switch sides easily. Truth is, only the top three men of Monev know him or what he looks like. They all left Earth together to come to Mars and rehabilitate. Oh, my name is Kurt." He walked forward and bowed to Shamira.

Shamira took in his dark, handsome face and almond shaped eyes, which looked sharp and assessing. "What about the kids they took? What are they doing to them?"

"You don't want to know. I'm afraid if I tell you, you'll be afraid to fight them, and I need you to lead us in fighting them. I want my life, I want my freedom, and so far you have proven yourself to be the one able to give that back to us," Kurt said.

"Let's suit up and get going. We don't want the trails to run cold," Shamira said.

"If you don't mind, I'd like to go with you. I know where the meeting is, and I'm one of their assassins in training, so I can hold my own. I'd love the chance to use what they did to me against them. Vengeance will be ever so sweet," Kurt said with a solemn look on his face. Then, he pulled up his sleeve revealing an arm riddled with large scars over zigzagging cuts that matched the faint scar on his dark brown cheek.

"Fine. You'll ride with us. Valens, can you enhance those who are coming with us? I think it might get a little dicey tonight if we're going where some high rollers are. I don't want anyone to get hurt. I'm taking no chances," Shamira said before she went to the training room to get her gear.

"Shamira, I have something for you too. Can you follow us to the lab?" Valens asked and then looked directly at her with a serious expression on his face.

"You go with them. I'll be right there," Shamira said.

Hedi stood up on her toes and held her finger up high in the air. "I'm taking everyone else to the fitting lab. I have to set their fighting gear to their physiological makeup. Everyone follow me and form a line. Then, we will start training." Hedi walked down the hall.

Shamira looked at her and smiled, realizing Hedi was a leader in her own right. All the kids followed her silently. Shamira waited for everyone to leave and fell to her knees in the corner that held her gear.

  Taking several deep, calming breaths, she started to shiver. "What have I done? What am I doing?" she asked herself in a whisper. Saving David had been her only plan, and now she was saving hundreds of kids she didn't really know. Not only that, but she had to depend on them and trust them to save her and maybe even David in the end. Being blind was not hard, but being their savior was something she hadn't intended to do. She shook off the feeling of dread, the same feeling she shook off every day of her life when she had been told that being blind was a handicap that wouldn't enable her to have a "normal life," whatever that was. Her life after this would never be normal, and she would definitely never again be the same.

  She leapt up to a stand, warming up her muscles for the fight ahead of her. *So many things to fight, fighting this ball of power that I'm afraid will consume me, and for David—always for David, who is so worth this risk.* She had to focus, drown her fear, and build strength while squashing her doubt in her success. She would win even if she had to lose herself to what raged inside her. *Saving David means this much to me.*

  Taking a deep breath, she walked to the labs where the others were getting in gear for the night's capture mission. Bringing back some of Monev's heads would definitely alert them that something was going on. It would also put all of them in danger. They would have to act quickly on their infiltration of Olympus Mons.

"Ouch! That hurt! What is this going to do?" Anthony growled at Valens.

"Remember the tags that I had to stick in your scalp? Well, I perfected it. Now this needle inserts them under your skin, giving you enhanced strength and virtually teaching your muscles all the martial arts moves you've been trained to do. It enhances them by taking memories from your training and making them reflexes throughout your body. I can easily extract them by programming them to come out through your bowels," Valens said proudly.

Anthony's eyebrow went up with disgust. "Man, that's nasty." He slowly stepped away from Valens with a frown on his face.

"Hey, all of you are done here. Go to the training rooms and get the weapons and suits I made for you from Hedi. We'll meet you at the door to the garage. I need to talk to Shamira," Valens said. Shamira watched them leave, and without a smile, she turned to Valens.

"I see you have on your fighting face," Valens said lightly.

"I'm not in the mood to chat. You've endangered all of these kids, you know. And worse, you've put their lives in my hands!" Her voice rose in her frustration with him.

"Yes, yes I did. I did it because I know they'll be safe in your hands. Besides, Shamira, you're not doing this alone. I'm here, and I'll help you. Hey, I got a device to enhance your strength also," Valens said as he came toward her with a needle.

"I have enough, thank you. I have more strength than you

could possibly fathom," she responded and knocked the needle from his hand.

Valens shrugged. "I know. I've seen you. I also know you're afraid of it. You pull back. Why?" He bent down to pick up the needle, which he placed on the table next to him.

"My business, not yours. I'm not your business, Valens. You've bugged me since the first day I've met you. Why were you even there that day?" Shamira asked with her legs spread defensively and her arms folded over her chest.

Valens chuckled softly before adding, "I was following the creep you were luring. He was one of Monev's men that worked the dream trade. You just happened to be there, helpless, I thought. I took you for a victim, but I know now I was wrong. Little did I know you were like a black widow, luring him into your web for a strike."

"Well, now you know my secret. What's your story? Why do you create all of this stuff? How do you even know how?" Shamira sized Valens up to make sure he was being honest.

"My father. This is... er, was his hobby. He and I would spend hours here working on some new technology or toy. It relaxed him. My sister would sometimes come along, but we mainly played videogames and watched movies with her. After their disappearance and my mother's death, I had nothing else to do to fill this void that seemed to fill my soul—that is, until I met you." He walked to stand in front of her as his voice lowered and his eyes held hers.

Shamira stepped back. "Well, let's go. The others are waiting."

Valens reached out to hold one of her hands. He leaned in toward her ear, and she stood stoically still while his soft breath blew lightly when he began to speak. "By the way, thanks for the kiss," he said, his voice deepening. He hesitated as her hand started to pull away and then added, "And grab the bullet-proof jacket by the door."

Jerking her hand away, she headed to the door. She felt his gaze on her back. Breathing deeply, she grabbed the jacket and put it on before heading down the hall to meet the others. Her cheeks burned in a blush of humiliation at the not-so-secret kiss she had given to his hologram that morning.

When she got to the door, she pulled on the jacket and saw the guys waiting there in solemn silence. Figuring they were preparing for their attack, she said nothing. Valens came up behind her. She could feel his presence, and she straightened, placing her hand in the jacket pocket. Feeling around, her hand landed on the gloves he'd given her that added electric shock to her punches. She smiled.

Valens walked over to Anthony without sparing Shamira a glance. "Anthony, you can take one of the motorcycles. The car is more difficult to get out of tight spots. Mitch, you grab the gold one. Kurt, there is a black one next to mine for you,"

Shamira went to the garage and called Pearl. She climbed on and let Kurt take the lead as they took flight to Sector Five.

Chapter 19

They came up to a large building, which stood taller than the rest on the city block in the business district. Looking around, Shamira realized the building wasn't far from the Security Force Headquarters. *You have got to be kidding me. They're conniving right under the nose of the Security Force, mocking the Force by doing this within a few miles of the Force's home base.* Pulling up behind Valens' motorcycle, she came to a stop and climbed off her bike. She took off her helmet and walked over to the others.

Valens stopped his bike next to Mitch's. "Mitch and Anthony, your target's not far from here. We'll meet you at the location of the cylinders. Stay alive," he said.

"No one's going to kill me now. Thanks to Valens' implants, I'm one bad mutha. I survived before, but now, I'm going to crush a fool," Anthony said, pimping his walk as he sauntered over to Valens to get ammunition for his gun.

Mitch smirked while he put his gun in his belt. "Please. You always thought you were a 'bad mutha'. Remember, you were the one to promise me and Hedi that you'd get us out of there."

Anthony slapped Mitch on the back. "Well, looks like you were the lethal one, Mitch. Valens told me you took one of them out to save Shamira. That's bad mutha in my book, man." Then he headed to his motorcycle.

Stonefaced Kurt warned, "We better get going. I contacted Ryan, who is going to let us in the office next to the conference room so we can eavesdrop on that meeting," Kurt said.

Shamira looked at Kurt and saw a face of cold calmness. She nodded at him, and he nodded back.

"We'll follow you, Kurt. How do you feel, since this is the first time you have used the enhancements?" Valens asked while he watched Anthony and Mitch ride off.

"I feel powerful, and I'm going to use it to bring these bastards down. I hate them for what they did to my family and me. I'll die trying to wipe them off the face of Mars," Kurt said and then spat on the ground before taking off.

They parked their rides in a hidden alcove behind the building and went to one of the doors in the back. Kurt knocked lightly on the door. It opened almost immediately, and a boy with black hair streaked with purple stared back at them.

"You came! You really came, man. Kurt, I'm starting to think we can actually do this. Everybody follow me," the kid named Ryan directed. He led them down the well-lit hall to an office next door to a conference room. He quickly shoved them inside the double doors while looking around to make sure the coast was clear.

Ryan grinned, adoration shining in his face. "Hey, you must be Shamira and Valens. Kurt told me a lot about you. I'm honored to help. There are other kids here tonight that work for Monev, but you have our loyalty. You'll make a safe exit. You have my word on it." He slowly nodded his head in assurance of their safe departure.

Shamira acknowledging his claim with a nod and smiled. "Who will be at this meeting, Ryan?"

Ryan rubbed his hands together with glee. "Oh, you guys hit pay dirt today. Renu is actually going to be here. He's meeting with Slasher and his gang before the rich heads get here. But here is the kicker... one of the invitees is a Security Force guard. He works for one of the Security Force Elite."

Shamira frowned. "What? Do you know the guy's name?" Shamira demanded. *This is getting uglier by the minute.* Her temper simmered. The adrenaline pumped through her, but she pushed it down. She didn't want to lose control too early. Needing to think clearly without rage at this moment, she forced herself to breath calmly.

"No, but he comes around now and then to pass on information to the upper crust of Monev," Ryan said.

Valens asked, "What do the rings mean? The ones they all wear?"

Kurt crossed his legs and leaned back on the desk. "The rings signify their brotherhood and the blood they had to shed to build Monev, or at least that's what they tell us. Only thing is, it wasn't *their* blood that was shed. These bastards knew each other before they even came to Mars. They had this planned out. It was to be a breeding ground for them to gain power and become kings. The Security Force and everyone else just got in the damn way, so Monev knew very early they would have to bring them down. The kicker is - no one really knew how."

Shamira smirked. "Someone in Monev found out how. Otherwise, they would not have been able to bring any member of the Force down"

"If anyone knows that answer, it's Renu," Kurt responded.

"Well, if that's the case, then he's the one I want," she said, then placed her hands on her hips as her lips thinned in anger.

Kurt leaned on the wall and put his hand in his pocked. "Yeah, well I'm impressed if you think you can get to him. He's the one who teaches the assassins everything they know. I heard he is as twisted as he's beautiful."

"It's not surprising. They're all twisted, these men who hurt the innocent. But our day is coming, and we will bring them to their knees—to their knees begging for mercy!" Valens said with a voice heavy with anger and distaste as he punched down on his open palm.

"The meeting is beginning. I'll check on you later. I have to send Ty to attend to the meeting members," said Ryan as he left them alone.

Valens reached in his pocket. "Here, take these so we can see through the wall," Valens said and handed out shades for them to wear. Shamira pushed his hand aside.

Turning to the wall, she pushed her sight through to see the first members of Monev walk through the door. Upon laying her eyes on the first to enter, she felt a punch in her chest at her discovery. It was Broc! He was the Security Force member whom Ryan mentioned, and when she saw him there with those thugs, a piercing pain filled her heart. Broc had been a close friend of her family's, and she couldn't understand his purpose here. *Why is he betraying us and the Force?* She growled through the pain as if she were some seething, wounded animal.

She had to turn away from Broc's smiling face as she did a double-take at the last person to enter the conference room. "What the freak? It can't be. No way. That's Cal, the head of the friggin' Security Force!" Shamira said in menacing anger as her eyes studied Cal's familiar face. He looked rather different from the day he had walked into her father's office and almost caught her fiddling around with the supercomputer. He looked harsher somehow, with stubble sprinkled on his chin and jaw.

Kurt pointed at the wall where Renu stood. "No. If that was the Security Force leader, you'd know by the brand on his neck. All Monev's head guys get brands on their necks. See there? He has it just under his cheek. You'd have picked that out easily."

Shamira tried to concentrate. She couldn't seem to get past Broc's betrayal, and now she remembered how strange Cal had looked and acted that day. She didn't remember seeing a brand, something she was sure would have stood out. *Besides, Cal looks way more professional and cleaner than this Renu guy*, she grimaced. *Maybe they just looked similar.* "Valens, call Hedi and have her do a search on the Earth computer records on criminals released to be rehabilitated in Mars. Have her check birth records of Cal Long and Renu," Shamira said to Valens while looking intently into the conference room.

"Done. I think you're onto something here," Valens added.

"Okay, they're starting," Shamira said, and the room went into total silence.

Valens placed a flat circular device on the wall, and he and Kurt adjusted their earpieces so they could hear into the next room. Valens held out an earpiece for her, but she shook her head. He looked at her and nodded while placing the piece back into his pocket. She closed her eyes to block out images around her so she could hear clearly into the next room.

Renu lashed out and grabbed the guy named Slasher by the shirt. "Before our illustrious paying guests show up, I want to ask you one question, Slasher. What the hell is going on? Where the hell is Thor? Why can't we find him with the tracking device in the ring he never takes off?" He dragged Slasher across the table to stare at him face to face.

"We're... we're on it. He was after some girl. Said she stole his ring off his finger. We can't find him or the damn device," said Slasher. The words sputtered out. Renu's other hand, which was now wrapped around his throat.

Renu narrowed his eyes in anger. "You have two days, Slasher, and then you'll see just how much I can slash you and how long I can draw out your pain," Renu spat bitterly. Then he bit down hard on Slasher's ear. A spray of blood shot out from the side of Slasher's head as Renu spit out a piece of his earlobe on the table. Everyone in the meeting room watched stone-faced as the grotesque scene played out. They seemed completely unaffected. Slasher growled through the pain and calmly picked up the discarded piece of his ear with a shaking hand. Renu casually took a napkin to wipe his mouth clean, offered to him by a teenage Asian kid who Shamira figured was Ty.

"Sir, would you like a briefing on our clients?" another guy who sat beside Slasher said.

"Why not? You may start the briefing," Renu said while he

216

leaned back in his chair at the head of the table.

"Telwell Industries, which built and maintains the Mars air management systems and hardware, will be joining us. They want to add a little side business to their empire. Trafficking of human parts and fetuses for Earth's wealthy is a high priced business. We know that because it's been profitable to Monev in the past. Now that our airspace and travel to Earth has been stunted, Telwell is willing to cut a deal with us. They still have permission to travel to Earth and back. The want a 50 percent cut of all the proceeds from these sales in exchange for assisting us in smuggling the cargo to Earth," the young man next to Slasher said.

"Richard, would you like to tell me who the hell they think they are dealing with? We're still shipping our cargo even now without their help. Who's showing up from their company today?" Renu asked calmly.

"George, Steven, and John Cruz—a family operation. We know this John has a mild scream addiction and comes to the gaming hells frequently enough to give us a small interest in Telwell. He's signed over about ten of his twenty-five shares already. I must say I was happy to help him find money to play with. George is the father and a very seasoned negotiator. He has a lot of connections on Earth that would allow us entry into the Earth markets. We could start selling dream, the addictive drug we sell to those who aren't gamers or gamblers, unnoticed while using his connections. It seems as if scream production will have to stay in the Mars domain since Earth doesn't allow the gaming or gambling dens. Also, the Earth Security Force is difficult to penetrate. They're the most loyal bastards around. Therefore, we can definitely focus on the sale of dream on Earth and our flesh sales," Richard said smugly.

He's definitely confident, Shamira thought.

"Now I must admit, control of the air management system will bring Mars to its knees. We may be willing to negotiate something," Renu said, as the door opened and owners of Telwell walked in.

After their brief hellos, they found their seats at the opposite ends of the table. George faced Renu from his end of the table and had the stern, unforgiving look of a true negotiator. He began by giving the history of his company and the benefits of Monev's alliance with them.

"Well, I'm sure Richard clued you in on our expectations. I'd like to add that doing business with us is your only way to mainstream your services. Hell, I can even get some of them legalized," George said confidently.

Renu exuded calm detachment. "What exactly makes you think I'm going to give you 50 percent of our profits?" Renu smiled wickedly, never taking his cold gaze from George.

Shamira smelled an inkling of fear in the air, and she noticed a faint bead of perspiration on George's forehead.

George gulped then recovered. "We're the only company currently allowed to travel and land in Earth's airspace. I believe that is an uncompromising benefit of our union, one I know you won't refuse or regret," George added with fake bravado.

"Well, let me clue you in. My production, sales, and delivery to my Earth market for flesh replacement have not been hindered in any way. Not only do I own my own ships to transport our goods, but I also use a most trusted source to send and deliver anything I desire to or from Earth. You, sir, don't really know who you are dealing with here, do you?" Renu said, slowly rising from his chair. He casually walked down to George and grabbed him by his hair. George's sons tried to stand but were immediately held down by Renu's guards.

Renu grabbed a fistful of Georg's hair. Then hissed, "Now, let me make this plain. Your company WILL give me 51 percent controlling interest in Telwell in exchange for your life, your sons' lives, and the lives of every living relative you have. If I'm not given this, I'll personally hunt down and kill everyone with the last name Cruz who is related to you, knows you, has spoken to you, or is connected to you in any way. Do I make myself clear, Mr. Cruz?"

"I can't. I won't do it. This is my family legacy," George forced out in anger.

"Really? Then why is your son John squandering it away in my gaming hells? Ask him how much we already own of Telwell," Renu said, then glanced over at John and winked.

John hit his hand on the table as his eyes watered from the pressure of the guard's hand on his neck.

Shamira's head turned when she heard Ryan enter quietly. Keeping an ear on the conversation, she looked at him questioningly.

"You better get outta here. Ty tipped me off that the meeting is ending soon. I can split them up so it's easier to ambush them. I'll take Slasher to one exit and then send Renu and his guards to another," Ryan said quietly.

"Valens, you can get Slasher, and Kurt and I will get Renu," Shamira said, knowing she could trust Valens to get the job done. She was still figuring out Kurt's loyalties, so she wanted to keep a close eye on him, and taking him with her to ambush Renu would show where he really stood.

Ryan said, "The exits are near one another, and I have some kids willing to play lookout and keep the perimeter guards busy while you take the scum out. Valens, you can follow Ty, and you two can follow me. Let's roll." Then he turned around and led them out the door.

Before Shamira left the room, she heard Renu's raised voice, "... and don't think the Security Force can save you! I have them completely under my control. You contact them, you sign your death certificate!"

Shamira wondered on that. He did have them crippled, but she knew he didn't have a complete hold on them. Tonight she would get answers, and she would bring Renu down now. She followed Ryan down the hall they came through earlier, and he took them out the door.

"Kurt, give me a lift. I'm going to completely disable this camera. I got a guy scrambling the cameras and surveillance. We started when Valens tipped us off you were coming," Ryan said. Kurt easily lifted Ryan up, and he disabled the camera above the exit door. Kurt turned to stare at Shamira while Ryan was at work. She returned his hard stare with her own. He nodded to her and smirked before he put Ryan down.

"What's the setup for the ambush? I still can't believe we hit pay dirt getting that bastard here," Kurt said.

Shamira figured he had started to relax now that he appeared to trust her.

Ryan chimed in, "You can catch them when they come out the door. The guard comes out first, and Renu follows with three guards behind him. Watch Renu, though. He carries some nasty weapons on him. We'll keep the rest of security at bay. We set up some traps for them, so don't mess this up. If you can't get Renu, run. Run fast as hell away from here, because he will track you down like dogs and kill you if he knows what you look like. He has an uncanny memory and ability to do things you can't even begin to imagine. Damn, I gotta go. They're on their way out." Turning, Ryan took off another direction.

She looked over at Kurt, who moved to the opposite side of the door and took out his gun. Shamira smiled at him and put on one claw glove with retractable knives and one of the gloves Valens made on her opposite hand.

Smiling back, Kurt whispered softly, "I'll take out the guards, and you get Renu."

The first bulky guard walked out as the door slid open. Kurt moved with lightning speed and fluency as he attacked. Shamira was impressed at the gracefulness of it. She listened to see if Renu was closely behind. She didn't hear a sound, and she found that odd. Slowly, she moved closer to the door and pushed her eyesight forward in barely enough time to slide out of the way of Renu's lightning attack. A punch landed on the side of her face, and she fought piercing pain unlike any she had experienced before. Her head snapped back as a reflex of her years of training. He stared at her with a slight look of recognition. *How does he know me?* Shamira wondered.

Renu whipped out at her fluidly and grabbed her by the neck before she could sidestep. *Crap! He must be enhanced*, she thought as she rose above him by the neck. A cough stuck in her throat as she let him choke her. Pushing her sight further, through his skin and into his blood, she saw them. *He has nanonytes of the Elite or something! This is too close. Enough playing around!* She punched him in the face with enough power to bust his lip.

His head swung back just slightly, and she heard Kurt fighting with the other two guards. Staring at him, she smiled, and he smiled back, lifting her a bit higher before punching at her face. Shamira's hand came up to grab his fist, but he was too powerful, and his punch landed on the side of her face, knocking her head backwards. Shaking off his punch with a daze of pain, she realized he was much stronger than she had expected. Lifting her knees up as she watched him cock

222

back to land another punch, she wedged her feet between them for leverage and forced herself back. She landed with a back flip onto the floor, and the two sized each other up.

With the grace of an experienced and merciless fighter, Renu struck forward and landed punch after punch before Shamira could recover. The raging power built inside her and strengthened her, and she lunged back, slicing Renu on the jaw with her clawed glove. He ignored the pain and blood spurting from his wounds. Shamira heard Valens come with their bikes in the distance. She had to get him down. She reached into her belt for a disc and threw it at him to cut him down. It bounced off his shoulder as he slid out of its path. Raising his gun from his hip, his cold brown eyes looked directly at her, and Renu pointed his gun and shot at her heart.

Kurt acted swiftly and jumped in front of her, and she caught him in her arms as Renu fired his gun. The bullet hit him in his chest. She went for her gun, only to hear a shot from behind her. The bullet hit Renu in the head, causing him to drop.

Valens tapped her on the shoulder. "We gotta go! Now! The guards are coming. Slasher's on my bike secured and in a death sleep. You help Kurt to your cycle, and we ride. I'll put his bike on auto control to follow us," Valens demanded, and for once, Shamira didn't want to argue.

With her anger strong and unleashed, helping Kurt to her bike caused her little discomfort. He walked as best he could, and she dragged him as she ran. Securing him quickly, she heard gunfire in the distance and wondered how many kids she had caused to die today.

Valens took off, and she followed. She glanced at Kurt's empty bike and held him tightly as she let Pearl drive automatically. A tear escaped as the regret of her recklessness stifled her. *What the heck went wrong? He shouldn't be enhanced. How could that be? He's even stronger than my father.* She knew she had to act quickly, or all of them could die. *He'll track me down until he gets me. We've got no more time. Acting now is our only option.*

"No one else will die because of me," she affirmed and leaned over a slouched Kurt. "This has to end."

Valens dropped Slasher in the cylinder after he administered an antibiotic to an unconscious Kurt. Mitch and Anthony met up with them on the way to the hideout. They all rode quickly in silence. Deep in thought, they sped across the sand, and the dismay for Kurt's condition hung in the air. They rushed through the door. Valens easily carried Kurt, who was still unmoving. Running, they went to the lab, and a scattering of kids followed. Her heart raced as she chanted to herself, "Live, live, live, Kurt. Please live."

Chapter 20

"Hurry! Pull back the covers on the bed. Hedi, bring over the stabilizer and activate the antibiotic into his system. Now!" Valens yelled as he carried Kurt over to the bed, waiting impatiently for Anthony and Mitch pulled back the covers. Anthony lifted Kurt from Valens' slightly shaky hands.

Shamira felt the slippage of her control. Her bottom lip started to shake ever so slightly, and she bit it to snap herself back to reality. She needed her edge if she was going to bring them all out of his alive. "How can I help?" she asked steadily.

"Grab that syringe in the wall cooler. It's on the top shelf encased in a clear tube marked SILVEN," he forced out while furiously keying in a sequence of words on his virtual keyboard. "Hedi, up the dosage of healing agent emitted from the nanos in his system," Valens directed while he grunted in frustration.

Hedi replied, "Valens, I don't think he can take it. There are side effects, you know. That scum would put poison into his shots."

"I know, damn it, I know," Valens said.

Shamira returned with the syringe. "Do it. Save him. He fought this long for his life. He can fight the possibility of the addiction. Do it, but slowly." She looked at Kurt's sleeping face. Closing her eyes, she walked up to him and touched his chest, then held his hand.

"Okay, give me the SILVEN. The nanos should minimize the possibility of addiction to the latent drug that accelerates the power of the antibiotic. It's a risk, but we have no choice," Valens said gravely. He took several calming breaths before he started the process of gradually increasing the antibiotic that would fight the poison emitted when Kurt took the shot from Renu's gun.

Shamira bent down to Kurt's ear and said, "Thank you, my friend. Thank you for saving my life. Now we will try to save yours. You have so much to live for. We need you. We can do this together." A tear fell from her eye and landed on Kurt's ear.

"Let's begin. Mitch, hold his legs. Anthony, hold his shoulders. He may begin to jerk and convulse. If we give him too much, he will bleed out, so if you see one drop of blood, tell me to stop," Valens said as he watched Hedi give Kurt the needle connected to the computerized IV which controlled the dosage of the medicine that could save Kurt or take his life.

Shamira looked up at Valens, then reached her hand over and touched his. He returned her gaze, his eyes slightly glassy with unshed tears, and he nodded. Then he began the series of dosages that caused Kurt's body to shake, jerk and foam at the mouth.

After several doses, Kurt started to groan, and his eyes rolled back in his head before closing. His shakes ended, and he quieted for a short while. *Oh no, we're going to lose him.* There was a slight fluttering of his eyelashes. Shamira grabbed his face and forced her sight into his body. She saw his body winning the fight against the poison.

"Stop! Stop! He's recovering. It's working!" she yelled as she held up a hand to get Valens' attention.

"Oh, thank God. Another dose would have landed him into addiction – if he'd lived. Besides, I wouldn't have been able to give it to him. That kind of life is not a life," Valens said, standing up. He walked toward Kurt, who was still being held down by Mitch and Anthony, and then smiled as Kurt's eyes slowly opened halfway.

"Thanks, dude. Thanks," Kurt said hoarsely as he slowly closed his eyes to sleep peacefully.

Shamira noted his strong breathing pattern, then took one more look deep within him to verify that his wound was closed from the inside out. Comfortable that the wound would be completely healed within several hours, she gently put his hand on his stomach and stepped away.

"Anthony and Mitch, take turns staying with him. Hedi, watch his vitals. Shamira and I need to talk," Valens said, and they all looked at him with understanding.

Shamira looked up and started to follow him out the door. "Hey, guys, get one of the kids you feel will be responsible to watch him after about an hour. We need to question the captives and call in for some backup. We'll meet in an hour to set the plan in motion to bring Monev down. There's no more time to wait. We've opened a can of worms, and we've got to act now." Then she left the room and closed the door behind her.

She slowed down slightly and noticed he was leading her toward his bedroom. "Hey, wait, uh, I don't think... where are you?" Shamira said as she came to a stop.

"Shamira, you trust me, don't you?" Valens asked while smiling through the pain she saw on his face. He turned back toward her.

Still afraid to expose her feelings, she walked past him and led the way to his room. She heard him as he walked closely behind her, and the door to his room opened upon her arrival. She glanced around when the lights flickered on and gave in to her guilty pleasure of slightly closing her eyes to inhale the overwhelming scent that was distinctly Valens'. She jumped slightly when his hands lightly touched her shoulders, and swallowed as he slowly turned her around. Looking into his eyes, she saw it. There was longing and desire mingled with something else she was afraid to name— something she was so afraid to hope for that she immediately shut her eyes to regain her composure. She opened her eyes and slowly stepped back out of his reach.

"Valens, I don't know how to say this, so I'm just going to spit it out. Thank you. I can't believe you'd have killed Renu to save me. I can't fathom Kurt giving his life for me. I won't be that careless again. Not ever," she affirmed to him.

"Shamira, you were never careless. We just didn't anticipate him being stronger than you. No one else we've encountered was able to completely overtake you. You, though, must realize that you're so worth saving, and I would've done what Kurt did for you in a minute—any minute, every minute." He returned her gaze with an intensity that made butterflies flutter through her stomach. Then he reached up to tentatively caress her cheek, and she stared at him when his gaze dropped longingly to her lips. He slowly moved his eyes upward from her lips to return her gaze. Moving his hand back to his side, he stepped back slightly.

They stared at each other during that awkward moment. She wanted to give in, but she just wasn't ready to let go of her protection over her heart, knowing that giving it could end in worst pain than dying.

"Valens, I'm so sorry that you lost your family. I can't imagine being as alone as you are here on Mars with no one to call family until you can reunite with your father and sister," she said, sadly reflecting how she would feel.

"I do miss them more than anyone could know, but all these other kids have become my family also. You've become much closer to me than anyone, and with you in my life, I have hope to truly rescue my family and to bring down the organization that has done this to us," he said as a dimpled smile touched his face. "There's one more thing. I know from back there with Renu that you have gifts that could've helped you bring him down. You seemed to have been holding back. Why?" he asked as he studied her.

"To be honest, it's because I'm afraid of what I'll become if I unleash this rage I hold within me. It's been with me since before I can remember. I suspect it's a side effect of the enhancements they injected in me to bring me back to life upon my death during a freak accident when I was a baby. In fighting for my life, I gained a power that can't be explained, unlike any other side effect of the Security Elite Force members that were enhanced in the same manner. I have never pushed myself past the limits of my control," she said softly, as though she were afraid to acknowledge her fears out loud.

"I know if you had, you'd have brought Renu to his knees. Next time, don't hold back. Just let it go and control it the way I know you can. You're a lot stronger than you know. I've seen a lot since I lost my father and sister, but when I first saw you, I knew you were a fighter. I believed in you and connected with you even though you

230

fought me. Next time, let go and be the hero I know you are, Shamira," he said with a direct and appreciative stare.

She felt awkward from his praise and refocused her thoughts on the task ahead. "I believe now is the time to clue my parents in on the situation with Renu. We need to question these guys and get answers fast so we can attack them and get in there to save the kids being held. I'm afraid he may recover and seek me out, which would endanger all of us. My parents will be able to vet out the trusted Security Force members to regain control of the Force and assist us in assuring Monev doesn't have the capability to rise again. I only hope we are not too late. He knows me. I know it sounds weird, but Renu recognized me when we were fighting. Also, he's enhanced in the same way the Security Elite are, and that's nearly impossible. That technology is not available on this planet or outside of Security Force control. Not only that, but I believe you must have certain genetic markers for the enhancements to bond." She placed her hands on her hips while she thought out loud.

He smiled briefly, conceding to her change of subject, and then frowned in thought. "You said you recognized Renu as Cal, the leader of the Security Force Elite? That cannot be. My father only spoke highly of Cal, and he would never turn rogue against an organization he helped to build. We have to talk to Hedi, who's been researching a possible connection while we were gone. If he does know you, there could be some serious repercussions to him discovering you are partly to blame for Thor's capture, not to mention Slasher and

Fisher."

Shamira responded, "We need to sabotage all of Renu's holdings, but I don't want innocent people to get hurt. Anthony knows the best places to attack, and we can send the younger kids to place time bombs in different locations. The only problem is - how will they get the firepower and initiate the bomb sequences?"

"I have some miniature computerized beetles we used to burrow underground for some of our experiments. I could program them to go to certain locations and blow up. They're extremely combustible. We can put the younger kids in strategic positions to help warn the endangered people in those locations to get out. These kids are survivors and have been practicing escaping out of difficult situations for years. Niles, one of the older runners, can organize them. Also, we still have a lot of kids on the inside that are willing to destroy the holdings in which they have been captives," Valens said while crossing his arms in front of his chest.

"Our time is up, Valens. Let's go meet with the others," she said and attempted to walk past him to get to the door. He moved in front of her quickly to block her departure.

"No, Shamira. Our time together is just beginning. I'm never going to leave your side... never," he said and looked steadily down into her eyes. He slowly stepped out of her path while she hurriedly walked to the front room to meet with the others.

Chapter 21

Her eyes landed on Anthony when she entered the front room where a large gathering of kids was anxiously waiting for her to arrive. Anthony looked at her with his deep chocolate brown eyes and nodded his head in respect. Mitch came up beside him and repeated the gesture of acceptance of anything asked.

She took a swallow and nodded her head in return, then looked around the room at the solemn but eager faces of the kids surrounding her. Without seeing him, she knew Valens came up behind her. His quiet presence reassured her friendship and bond with these kids that had joined the fight against the men that had changed Mars into a prison instead of a home.

Shamira looked into the assembly of kids. "We're running out of time and have to act quickly to bring Monev down. I'm going to need everyone here to stay alive and join us in bringing down the entire operation. Monev is built on the oppression and abuse of kids like you and me, and it ends now. We're not weak. We can all fight back, especially when we do so together. I'm honored to have your trust and will do whatever I can to see this through." Shamira smiled at the kids staring at her in agreement.

"I'm ready, Shamira. Let's do this!" Anthony responded with a punch of his fist in his hand.

"We're going to have to attack every holding they have where we have eyes and ears. Valens, what places don't have any kids on the inside?" she asked, turning her eyes to Valens as he stepped around her.

Mitch stepped up. "We don't have anyone in Olympus Mons or the Outlands, where we broke in and got surveillance. That facility is strictly for their adult captives. They don't seem to hold kids there or even to want them there." He folded his arms in thought.

"They don't hold kids there, but they do have a runner there at this moment that would run sabotage for us," Hedi added as she came into the room with her long red hair swinging behind her.

"Good, Hedi. Recruit him. Valens will send his beetles in for attack to all of their holdings, and I plan on sending some trusted Security Force members to save the prisoners held in the Outlands," Shamira said, then turned to Valens.

"Hedi, did you get any information on a possible connection between Cal Long and Renu?" Valens asked as he glanced at Shamira, who moved closer to him and Hedi.

Hedi smirked and smacked her teeth. "Boy, have I hit a gold mine for you. There was nothing in the databases here on Mars. Heck, I couldn't find anything in the Earth's system either. Then, on a lucky gamble, I tapped into Earth's archives and destroyed records databases. Seems like the word 'destroyed' just means well hidden to the Earth officials. Turns out that Cal Long and Renu have a longstanding history with each other," Hedi said with a lift of her eyebrow.

Anthony grunted. "Girl, will you stop with the teasing! We're all on the edge of hell here," Anthony said with an angry frown on his face. However, Shamira noted the frown didn't continue in his eyes as he squinted at Hedi.

"Hold your horses, bullhead. I was going to tell you, but it's just too golden to spit out. Here is the scoop. Cal and Renu are twin brothers!" Hedi said, then paused for effect as she put her hands on her hips and nodded. She was proud of herself, rightfully so.

Shamira shook her head in disbelief. "Brothers? What the freak? Were they both groomed for the Security Force Elite?" Shamira took a deep breath to calm her shock.

Hedi rubbed her hands together, eager to share her secret knowledge. "The records prove they were both destined to be in the Security Force initially. Their parents were part of the original founders on the Earth rebirth team that came up with the concept of the Mars project. An assassin killed the parents when the twins were around three years old, and the boys were placed in the program that groomed the Mars Security Force Elite. All seemed to be going well for the double duo, but soon, trouble appeared when they got older. Renu proved to be the evil twin when he killed two fellow trainees that were their main competition for the leader of the Security Force Elite team on Mars."

Hedi put her hand on her hip and walked close to Shamira. "Renu was just fourteen when he murdered those kids in their beds. He escaped and lived underground for about two years until he got caught robbing a bank. Cal Long, the good son, went on to become the successful prodigy he was groomed to be. His brother served his time for his crimes and appeared to be completely rehabilitated, which got his sentence greatly reduced. Since he was a juvenile when the crime was committed, he received mind reorganization and was released by his eighteenth birthday. Renu's juvenile record was wiped clean, and both his and Cal's records were sealed," Hedi said with a smirk.

"I'm impressed, Hedi. I've been trying to figure out how to get that information for weeks," Shamira said with a look of deep respect when she smiled at Hedi.

"What can I say? A girl's got to have some mad hacking talents to stay alive these days. Bringing big men to their knees might be your forte, my BFF, but hacking into systems to obtain unsuspecting victim's money is what Monev trained me to do," she said and smiled back at Shamira.

Shamira's heart melted with the thought of Hedi calling her "BFF," her "best friend forever." Shamira pondered on it, remembering when she thought she would never have friends. Now she had so much more than friends. She had loyalty and friendship that would last a lifetime. It was a dream she had never let herself wish for, and now that it was here, she was too scared to trust it.

"That still does not solve the mystery of how Renu got enhanced. The Security Force Elite didn't receive enhancements until they went through their acceptance ceremonies. Also, none of them knew they were going to be enhanced. They were trained in all arts of war but with their enhanced strength only during the two years after their acceptance into the Security Force Elite. Now the mystery is - does Cal know his brother is the leader of Monev? Is he protecting his brother, working with him, or opposing him?" Shamira pondered while she bit her bottom lip in confusion.

Valens added, "None of those options sound promising for Mars. I hope Cal is not privy to the fact that the leader of Monev is his brother. We have to get the facts before we attack a leader of the Security Force Elite. That would be considered treason, and we would be the ones placed in the executioner's Waters on Earth for all of our hard work at bringing Monev down."

Mitch hit his fist to his opened palm. "Screw! Looks like either way, something fishy is going on. I don't like it, but we can't wait around to figure it out either. Ryan called and tipped us off that Renu is fully recovered and angry as hell. He knows who Shamira is and wants her dead. He has sent Strong's crew to get her at any cost. Ryan said his and the others' alliance with us has still gone undetected, but he doesn't know for how long. Renu has increased surveillance. He said he got a tip from Vinny, a runner for Monev in the Outlands, that they are preparing to question the kids that were recently recruited. The vibe is that our days are numbered. Renu is evil enough to round up the remaining kids and terminate them simply for thinking about retaliating against Monev. We don't have much time, and Ryan wants to know what he can do to help," Mitch said solemnly.

Shamira's shoulders fell. "Okay. Let's go question the scum. Everyone else get the beetles ready to attack. We attack tonight. Hedi, find someone capable of directing the younger kids where to release them and send them out to prepare to do damage. Then come and join us in the lab," Shamira said before she turned and followed Valens to the lab.

Chapter 22

Upon arriving in the lab, Shamira watched while Valens activated the large wall screen that displayed their three captives in a vertical line down the left of the screen. The right side of the screen showed vitals for each captive.

"I had Matt here take one of your truth ticks and manufacture a gas that I can release in the cylinders," Valens said while he typed in the command. The gas released into the cylinder holding the angry and restrained prisoners. She glanced over at the curly haired teenager sticking his chest out beside Valens with a grin on his face and figured that must be Matt. Glancing around, she realized several other teenagers were standing around.

"Thanks, Matt," she said and smiled at him. His cheeks instantly turned pink with a flattered blush.

"Okay, we're on. They're awake, angry, and drugged—just the way we want them," Valens said while giving Shamira the direction to start questioning.

Shamira turned back to the screen. "Fisher, what do you know about Renu?" she asked clearly while she studied him for signs the truth tick gas was working.

"Go to hell. I ain't telling ya nothing. You don't know who you're dealing with, little girl," he snarled.

"Okay. He's not ready." Shamire looked away from Fisher. "Slasher, what do you know about Renu?" She noticed his eyes were dazed from the affects of the drug.

Slasher looked dazed with saliva dripping from his slack mouth. "We met on the run. Been friends since the beginning. He followed the plan to a tee, and we became kings… kings of our own world," Slasher forced out while fighting to keep his words within.

"How did he bring down the Security Force Elite members?" she asked.

Slasher's head fought side to side like he was trying to regain control over his words. "Virus… it infects their suits, makes them weaken, but only for under a minute before their nanonytes regenerate and counteract the virus. We put pain modulators on their skulls to immobilize them. They're drugged into constant pain to confuse the nanos into thinking the body is being attacked by multiple strains of the virus. Perfect... it was a perfect plan from the beginning."

"Are they still alive?" she asked, hoping for the best.

Slasher grunted. "Not for long. We tried to get all the information from the ones we captured, but they all hold different parts of the passwords and codes that control the Security Force computer systems on Mars and Earth. We need information from just a few more Elite to have it all. They're supposed to die, but we couldn't cut through the suit. We have to cut them at the neck. It's planned and has to happen soon. Got to get them all before Renu finds out the deed is not done. It was to happen tonight, after all the Sector leads were captured." Then, he slumped forward as his mumblings slurred and he fell victim to the side effects of the gas.

"Fisher, how did Renu plan Monev's domination of Mars? How long? Why?" she demanded.

"Don't know. He never tells all. He gathered us and told us to be good if we wanted to be rich. I listened. He's convincing, especially when he kills. He enjoys it so," Fisher said groggily.

"Where are they holding the kids they captured?" she asked, realizing her time for this little interrogation session was running out.

"Olympus Mons," he said while his eyes started to glaze and

241

tear from the effects of the drug.

"What about the Security Force members? Where are they? Where!" she said forcefully.

"Outlands... deep in the underground chambers. Ugh," he forced out as spittle came from his swollen lips.

She knew she was running out of time before he succumbed to the effects of the drug. "Are all the kids alive that were captured from the Security Force Elite families?" she forced out, trying not to give in to the emotion of fear she felt contemplating his answer.

"Maybe, or maybe not. All kids work the mines, and if they are strong, they survive. If they ain't worth the fight, we kill them. We don't care whose kids they are. Mining dream is our gold mine. They all work to stay alive," he spat out, as his eyes closed and the drug took effect.

"Thor! Where are the kids held in Olympus Mons? How can I get in undetected?" she yelled at the screen and watched as Thor's head jerked up at her request.

"Kids held underground tombs... they take the tunnels up into the mountain and around the top of the volcano. If they survive the day of work, they go back to the tombs where they're locked into their cells. Maybe they get fed if they meet their quota. If not, they get beaten, maybe killed. Most get beaten. I like the beating part and the killing too. Sometimes I get to help with that," he said with a sadistic grin on his face.

"How can I get in undetected?" she demanded again, trying

desperately to get him to answer before the drug knocked him out. She wanted to hurt him for the way he taunted her even while under the influence of the drug.

"You figure it out," he said before spittle trickled from his lips and the drug took him.

Hedi stomped her feet. "Bastard! I hate that scum," she yelled out from behind Shamira.

"I agree, but we don't need him. I know how to get in," they heard clearly from the back of the room.

Shamira turned around to see a smiling Kurt walking toward her. His posture was a little hunched, but without a look of grimace, he straightened and walked toward her like he felt no pain at all.

"Kurt! Look at you! You recovered. Welcome back, and thank you for saving my life," Shamira said. She looked over a healthy-looking Kurt who sauntered in the room as if he hadn't been near death just over an hour ago.

"Saving you was my pleasure, and thanks to Valens, I'm alive and well. I want in. I may have family in those mines, and I want to be a part of bringing it down," Kurt said and came up to Shamira. He placed a hand on her shoulder. She welcomed it, knowing how much it meant to Kurt that she accepted him.

"Welcome back, man. Glad to have you back," Valens said while he looked Kurt over with the practiced eye of a scientist.

Anthony slapped hands with Kurt. "I knew a trained Monev assassin wouldn't miss the chance to recover and beat up some more

Monev scum. Welcome back, my man."

"Well, I can't say I'm 100 percent, but I'm damn close. Definitely could be better, but I'm still in," Kurt laughed.

"We're attacking shortly. Everyone of age, gear up. We need someone to be our eyes and ears here at the command center," Shamira suggested.

Hedi grinned at her in return. "Of course! I'm good at multi-tasking and delegating. Oh, by the way, the younger kids are gone, releasing the beetles. I also took the liberty of contacting Ryan and the other kids at all the Monev holdings. A lot of places already have some explosives attainable by staff members, so the kids at those locations are starting to set up for sabotage. Say the word, Shamira, and it will be done."

"Well, I've one more call to make. Valens, transmit to my parents on your screen. According to my earlink, they're at the Security Elite Headquarters in my father's office," she said while looking at the screen waiting for her parents' faces to appear.

Her father was seated at his desk with her mom on the edge facing the video wall. They looked like they'd somehow been expecting her call. "Hello, Shamira. We were starting to get worried. No signal is coming in from your earlink, and things are only getting worse here," her father said, a look of relief passed over his face upon seeing Shamira.

Shamira took a deep breath and prepared to share her news with her parents. "Dad, Mom, I don't have much time to talk. I want to send you a video feed of a meeting from Monev, the crime organization bringing Mars to its knees. We need to attack tonight. I'm depending on you to lead the Security Force attack on their holdings in the Outlands. That's the holding that will have the captured or murdered Security Force captives. I'm sending the feed over now." Shamira gave Valens a nod to send the video feed of the meeting they observed.

Her parents watched intently, and their faces turned from observation to anger as they watched Broc and then Renu come on the screen. Her father stood and walked closer to inspect Renu's face, and Shamira watched while his look turned from anger to dead calm. The feed finished, and Shamira's parents stood, quietly waiting for her to come forward with more information.

"I've been tracking them with friends that were recruited from the inside. They have information and long-term relationships within Monev. Renu, the head of the organization, is the twin brother of Cal, and we believe he has infiltrated the Security Force and recruited support team members and Security Force members. Not just here on Mars, but possibly on Earth as well. I've three of his men in captivity and have questioned them about Monev and Renu's recruiting tactics," Shamira said, hoping her parents wouldn't interrupt with anger and reprimands for her actions.

Her mom stood and smiled. "Well, I'm impressed. We have trained you well. I was worried initially when your father said we should allow you to continue your independent investigation. He said you will be a future leader in the Security Force, and I wasn't ready to let my little girl go, but now I see you're no longer a little girl. You're a force to be reckoned with. We never knew the extent of your abilities. You, Shamira, are an anomaly."

Eyes tearing up with guilt, her mother continued, "When you died, the Security Force scientists were forced to inject you with the nanos only intended for Security Force Elite members when they were inducted during their final ceremony at eighteen, a time at which the body has matured in order to counteract the toxins used in the enhancements. The side effects of your death and the unexpected large amount of the enhancements needed in order to jolt you back to life caused you to become blind. Security Force Elite members' children are the only people who have the genetic markers to bind to the enhancements. All of you who are children of Security Force Elite members were genetically selected to be the continuing Force to govern Mars."

Her mom's eyes glanced at all of them, and she cleared her throat, and then added, "The preliminary enhancements you received when you were nine years old were only the beginning of your journey. The Security Force Elite, in desperation to win this war against Monev, were forced to allow you into action much earlier than we ever would have anticipated. Monev also realized your worth to us and sought to kill, manipulate, and enslave you until the dormant nanos in your systems made you too physically strong for a normal adult to control. It would allow them control of the future.

Prior to that turning point in your development, they would terminate the selected few of you that were enhanced specifically for the purpose of becoming members of the Security Force Elite."

She looked directly at Sharmira then said, "But you, Shamira, were hand selected by the Earth board of officials as the Security Force Elite Head. You were being groomed for Cal's position, which was why your trip to Earth was so important and security was heightened. After you were secured with eyesight, Earth was free to close off its airspace to Mars and allow the Mars Force to handle the Monev problem before it further infected Earth. We always knew that the Security Force had been infiltrated, but I have to tell you we never expected to find that Renu was behind it. Neither would we've thought Broc would be disloyal. After viewing this, we believe Renu has been posing as Cal for quite some time now." A look of appreciation reflected in her mother's face. Shamira found it addictive.

With her mother's words, Shamira reflected on her brief encounter with Cal and how different it seemed from her past interactions with him. She had expected him to recognize her initially, and she had thought his actions odd.

"Are you saying they purposely chose which kids to enslave and which kids to kidnap? They killed many kids before the age of seventeen simply because they didn't know who was to be a Security Force Elite and who wasn't? I don't know what to say. You trusted *me* to do this? I'm honored, and I won't let you down," Shamira said as her eyes watered softly.

Valens cleared his throat. "You mean all of us are special? Born to be Security Force Elite?" Valens questioned.

Shamira's father looked fondly on Valens. "Yes, Valens. We went to school with your father, one of the creators of the enhancements we received. He was a brilliant inventor since he was a kid. He was just an understudy who helped out with the experiments during training when he discovered a way to keep the powerful enhancements from being misused by others not genetically groomed to be Elite."

"Hedi, Kurt, and Anthony, I knew your parents also. I'm so glad you have come back to us," her mother said.

Her father's expression turned serious. "Now, back to the problem at hand." He spoke as if they were his Security Force Elite colleagues.

"What about the tattoo on Renu's neck that would have been a noticeable difference between him and Cal?" Shamira asked, remembering how Ryan had pointed that defect out to her when she first had the idea that Renu was Cal.

"That's something that can be easily covered, and since he has the same genetic markings as Cal, he could have easily come inside the Security Force undetected," her father stated.

"Is Cal or Renu at the Force Headquarters today?" Shamira asked.

Her dad lifted an eyebrow. "No. He's been on an extended

mission to seek out and terminate the leader of Monev. Funny how we fell for that one, and Broc being a part of his infiltration team just sickens me. Send us the coordinates to the Outlands, and we'll go there with our team to bring it down."

"Valens is sending them over. It's important we attack tonight. Renu is on to me, and I believe he recognized me. I'm hoping he doesn't put two and two together and figure out that David is already in his possession," she said, nervously raking her hand through her hair at the thought of the consequences.

"Don't worry about it. We've got the Outlands covered. I trust you have the destruction of the other areas of Monev under control. Did you find out where David is?" her father asked with a hidden look of concern in his eyes.

"Yes. He's in Olympus Mons, where I plan to lead the attack. He'll be my first priority. He's the reason I must go there. It was my responsibility to train him, and I failed. I will not fail in getting him back. I can tell by the look in your eyes that you really want to go after him, but I need to do this, Dad. I really need to do this, so please don't interfere," Shamira pleaded as a lone tear slipped from her eyes.

Her mom put a staying hand on her father. "I can't say this is easy, Shamira. I trust you can do it, but we really want to be there to get David," her mom said with a softening voice.

"We trust you, Shamira. Bring him back. Bring him home. Send us a signal—two beeps through the earlink when it's time. We'll be ready to move to action tonight. I already know who'll help us, and I've a pretty accurate summation of whose loyalties are in question. After we storm the Outlands and recover the prisoners, your mother and I are going to reorganize and restabilize the Security Force and Mars. As much as it hurts to admit, I knew Broc was playing two sides. I was just in denial. We went through training together, and I thought he was still the boy I remembered. That is a mistake I won't make in the future. We love you," he said before Shamira's mother placed a hand to her lips and blew her a kiss as their image faded.

Chapter 23

"Alright, we have no time to waste. Valens, we need everyone outfitted with bullet- and laser-proof enhancements. We also need a lot of firepower if we are going to clean out Olympus Mons. Kurt and Anthony, tell us what you know," Shamira directed.

Anthony answered, "Kurt was a frequent visitor to the Mons. He would be the greatest source of information. Whenever I ran supplies for the dream factory, I was only allowed on the first level, but let me tell you, it's heavily guarded with surveillance of the surrounding outer perimeter. It's definitely a place we have to prepare to attack. Just give me the word, and I'm ready to use my big freakin' car to blow the joint down."

Kurt sat on the table near Sharmira. "The place is a fortress but also a living hell for the kids held there. They never see daylight, and they pray the volcano never erupts because they would be the first to go. It's heavily guarded on the entrance level. The lower level where the kids are held in carved out cells is extremely hot. Since Mars is typically a cold place, the kids can bear it, but not without discomfort. They wake them up early in the morning and work them for fourteen hours straight before slop time, and then they are sent to their cells."

"How can we move through the place?" Shamira asked.

"There's an elevator used only for moving the dream, which is in the form of molten rocks, down to the dream collection level. The pre-teen kids sift through the dream at the collection site until their fingers grow raw and bloody. There's a tunnel that winds around the elevator that has tiny steps leading up to the dream collection area near the mouth of the volcano. The youngest kids are well prized because only the smaller ones can get through the tunnels and gather the dream. Now, the grownups (or 'dream freaks,' as we kids call them) work in the lab under the collection floor. They manufacture the dream and get it ready and packaged for sale. There are two possible entrances we can sneak into. There is a sunken hole used for the core heating system just short of a quarter mile from the Mons.

Maybe we can find a way to tunnel in that way," Kurt said, then scratched his hand on his head in thought.

Valens snapped his finger. "I got that covered. Those core heating systems have small tunnels that run completely underground. I can pull up a map of the service tunnels, and I have a device we can use to tunnel in. It would bring us up into the underground cells. We can set the kids free there," Valens said while pulling up the map of the service tunnels. He mapped out the closest tunnel to the volcano and highlighted the portion of rock they would have to cut through to penetrate the underground prison.

Shamira pointed to the map of the tunnels. "When we send the signal that we've recovered the prisoners, we need another group to attack through the front entrance while we plant the incinerators to burn through the openings in the volcano. Devices for stabilizing the guards until the Security Force arrive are needed. After the Security Force arrives to take the guards into custody, we'll incinerate the place to close it down forever," Shamira said, crossing her arms while studying the map of the service tunnels.

"Question. How do you plan on moving all these people out of there? Anthony's big bad car can't do it. All his car can do is blow crap up," Mitch asked with his usual pessimistic face showing the beginning of hope.

Hedi smiled and wiped her hands together. "I have that covered. I tapped into the computer system that controls the Mars World Construction distribution vehicles. We can fit over 100 kids in each of the vehicles and take them directly to the Security Force Headquarters. Then we all can hop into Anthony's car and ride off while watching the Mons close down permanently."

Anthony raised an eyebrow, and they all laughed at his obvious displeasure at the idea of all of them being in his car.

"That is so not happening. The only person riding shotgun with me is Mitch, my road dog. Yeah, boy," he said as he slapped hands with Mitch.

"That's fine. I'm riding on the back of Shamira's ride so I can cover her. Seems she likes getting shot at," Valens laughed.

Hedi joined in, "Then I guess I'll ride behind Kurt since he is a recovering invalid."

"No I ain't. I'm already recovered, and I don't need a mousey redhead covering for me," he said, looking at Hedi with irritation.

"I'm so far from mousey I'd make your head spin. Lucky for you, I take pity on the weak," she smiled back mischievously.

"Weak? Girl, I oughtta... well, you're lucky I don't hit girls," Kurt said with the frown softening on his face.

Mitch looked at Anthony with a smirk, then winked. "Hitting doesn't work on her."

"Aw, c'mon, guys. It's not time to play around," Shamira said, eying Mitch and Anthony sternly.

"Who's playing?" Anthony said and put his hand behind his back.

"I know I'm not," Mitch said and also put his hand behind his

254

back.

"Uh, uh. I mean it. Don't you dare…" Shamira said just as she watched both Anthony and Mitch pull out water guns and point them at both Hedi and her.

"Don't what?" Valens asked as he caught the water gun Mitch threw at him. She watched as Anthony threw another water gun to Kurt, who caught it perfectly. Unlucky for them, Hedi and Shamira were caught in between the boys.

Hedi just looked at them and laughed. "Take your best shot," she said through giggles.

Several other kids in the room came and gathered around, enjoying the water gun faceoff and hedging bets. Movement started in the back of the group of kids, and as Shamira suspected, they were passing out more water guns.

"Okay, I'm not playing. You better not shoot me with that! We have business to take care of here," Shamira said sternly and then burst out in laughter when Mitch squirted her in the face with water.

"If you want me to stop, then lift up your arms," Mitch said, breaking out in a genuine smile while shooting Shamira with the water gun.

She turned to Hedi and laughed when she saw Anthony shooting her in the face. Hedi looked smug and unaffected while a smirk rose across her face. Valens and Kurt were smiling with their water guns ready to fire. She spied the kids surrounding them and heard their laughter, realizing they all deserved to play a bit considering many of them rarely had the chance before.

Hedi reached out and grabbed her hand, and Shamira went quickly to a squatted kick, causing Mitch to stumble. Hedi gracefully copied Shamira's move, and Anthony didn't budge. He laughed, and Hedi quickly recovered to snatch his water gun out of his hand. Shamira didn't waste time as she tickled Mitch under his arm and grabbed his gun.

"How about you put your hands up, Mitch?" Shamira laughed and squirted him in the face. Hearing the commotion around the room, she looked around to see that all the kids had water guns and pointed them at Valens, Kurt, and Anthony.

"Oh, you boys are in trouble now. We have backup," Hedi laughed.

"What makes you think I don't have something up my sleeve for just these types of situations?" Valens asked with fake bravado.

"Um, they look like they're pointing the guns at you guys, not at us. I'd say no trick you have will top this treat," Hedi replied.

"A faceoff, huh? I love it. Well, if I'm going out anyway, I may as well take my best shot. Ha!" Kurt said, firing his water gun at Hedi. The room came alive with water spraying everywhere. Kids were running and spraying water at each other. The room turned into a playground, and Shamira smiled while she took it all in. Mitch took the opportunity to attack by tickling her. She doubled over and held her stomach in laughter as a wet Valens easily lifted her and carried her out of the room through water fights and laughter.

She let him carry her over his broad muscular shoulder, and she held on to his back, feeling guilty from the tingling in her fingers when she felt his firm muscles under his shirt. "Put me down!" she laughed, but his arm just secured her at the back of her knees more snugly.

"Not until I show you something," he said, his voice turning serious. She stopped fighting. He walked down the hallway and took her to the little girl's room she and Hedi had hidden in days earlier. He carefully walked with her through the door. The lights flickered on, and she saw that the room was decorated in girly pastel colors. He gently and slowly slid her off his shoulder and down his chest. She closed her eyes as her feet landed on the floor and he held her briefly in a tight, warm hug. His head was tilted, and his lips were so close to her that she could feel the warmth of his breath.

"I want to show you something—something really special to me," he said deeply. Her eyes remained closed, and the knowledge that she wanted Valens to give her that first wonderful kiss seeped into her thoughts. She pushed those thoughts from her mind, knowing she had to put them behind her.

He slowly turned her around and then placed one hand on her shoulder. Her eyes followed his pointing finger. Her gaze fell on the picture of him tickling his sister, who looked up at him with dark brown hair and sparkling eyes of adoration.

"When I look at Mina's picture, I want to punch someone for taking her. If I don't find her, I will have failed. My father tried to train me for the Security Force, and I refused. I wanted to be an inventor. I wanted to leave Mars and live on Earth. And now, I can't take my selfishness back. If Dad is dead, I'll never have the chance to tell him he was right. Mars is my home, and building a home safe for everyone is my destiny. I'm not going to fight it anymore. Looking at those kids out there, I realized any one of them could have been me. My sister could be dead from trying to mine dream," he said, his voice breaking in emotion.

"Oh, Valens, I'm so sorry. We'll save her," Shamira said. She softly and hesitantly took his hand and wrapped his free arm gently around her waist. She felt him breathe out slowly.

"Shamira, before we do this tonight, I want to tell you something. I need to say it so you know how I feel about you... what you mean to me," he rushed out, and for once, Shamira realized Valens wasn't as controlled as he tried to be all the time.

"Shh. Don't you say it, Valens. Not now. You give us something to fight for. Save it for when we have saved them," she said, feeling unfulfilled at putting off his words she selfishly wanted to hear, words that would break the wall she had built around herself. She wasn't quite ready to totally let it go.

"You're right. You're not ready yet, and I'm sorry," he said and removed himself from her slowly. His presence was immediately missed. She stood and stared at Mina's picture. Valens' sister and thoughts of her brother came into her mind's eye. She heard him quietly leave the room and her while she stared. A silent tear dropped from her eye. It was a tear for David and all the other kids taken like animals by Monev. She would fight and release this raging power inside her if it meant she could save them all.

Chapter 24

Breathing in the scent that was Mina's, Shamira was ready.
She left the room and walked toward the lab. A few kids were still
cleaning up water, but she noticed most of them were gone. She
looked in the lab to see Valens alone at the computer with his back
turned toward her. *Just great. I'm not quite ready to face him alone
again.*

"Hey, where's everyone?" she asked. She'd expected mayhem
and play to still be going on. However, she saw the serious and
purpose filled faces of the kids she had passed along the way to the

lab.

Valens didn't bother to turn around. "Hedi, of course, managed to get everyone calmed down and to the training room. I'm upgrading our suits to include protection from firepower and the poison from the laser shots. No one will get shot at or hurt on our team," Valens said while staring at the screen before him. She inhaled the heightened scent of him and realized he was indeed affected by their earlier conversation.

"Valens, I—" Shamira started, wanting to explain and apologize for her earlier actions.

He lifted a hand to stop her, never turning around, and said lightly, "Go see how training's going. We can meet in the front room with final directions for our attack. I have to get these finished and tested quickly, before we fit everyone with them. I'll see you then." He continued to work as though she wasn't there. She bowed her head and left with her heart feeling as though it were breaking.

She headed straight to the training room and realized it was rather quiet. Upon walking in, she noticed kids of all ages silently and seriously following through with the ancient martial arts moves, mimicking Kurt, who stood in front of the group. None of the kids missed a step. They acted as though their lives depended on memorizing every move. Hedi quietly made her way through the class and took a moment to wink at Shamira. Shamira smiled back. She couldn't believe how Hedi had become her best friend, and that was something she definitely needed—a saucy, fun friend to tease out the part of her she only ever shared with David and her father. It felt good to be free. She pondered how she hurt Valens, someone that had come to be a friend and so much more. Hopefully, he would forgive her for pushing him away. One day, she would make it up to him.

She started to walk slowly around the room and was impressed with the kids large and small. A young kid around seven years old was biting his lip and growling slightly when he punched. Shamira reached out and straightened out his arm, then ruffled his hair. The boy smiled up at her with adoration in his toothless grin.

Nothing missed Hedi's practiced eye, and Hedi nodded to Shamira. She crocked her finger for Shamira to follow. They walked toward the back of the room, and Shamira followed Hedi into the walk-in supply closet. Hedi waited for Shamira to enter, then reached over and closed the door.

"Okay, spill. I know you and Valens are having some problems. I can see it in your face," Hedi said, looking at Shamira with true concern.

"There is no real problem. I'm just not ready for..." Shamira trailed off.

"Oh? You're not ready to trust him? Are you crazy! He saved your life! He loves you, and everyone can see it. He looks at you as if you are the last piece of candy on this planet, and you're afraid? Look, I have seen so much pain in my life, but I have had hope. You've got more than just that. You have someone that loved you even when you were blind," Hedi said. She waited for the shocked look on Shamira's face to fade.

"How did you know about that?" Shamira asked as she waited to see how much about her had been revealed.

"Oh, Valens told us how he met you and that when he first encountered you, you were being attacked by one of the Monev lowlifes who worked the dream ring, and you were one of his chosen victims. The guy had been tracking you for weeks, and Valens had been tracking him. Valens thought you were helpless because you were blind and seemed to stick to the shadows most of the time. Boy, was he in for a surprise when he realized that in your own way, you *could* see, and you were strong and well trained in protecting yourself. At first, he thought he would be your champion, but you turned out to be his," Hedi said and reached over to touch Shamira's shoulder in support.

"This is all new to me. I've always been alone, partly by choice and partly by circumstances. I wonder if this is changed because I can see? It's a struggle for me, but I'm getting better," Shamira replied evenly.

"None of us care if you're blind, deformed, or flawed. We're all flawed. I have scars so deep they may never heal, but you have friends here—more than friends, really, because we have become family. We love you any way you are, and we will follow you anywhere. You've proven your worth as a friend and a champion, and I don't doubt Valens will forgive himself for pushing you just a little too hard too fast. His scare with you being shot at shook him more than he could handle. He'll pull it together, and so will you. Now come here and give me a hug," Hedi said with her mischievous smile lighting up her face. Shamira hesitated for just a moment and let Hedi give her a quick, friendly hug.

"See! That wasn't so hard. Now, let's get out there and whip these kids into shape so we can kick Monev's butt," Hedi said and briskly walked past Shamira out the closet door.

She took a moment to ponder Hedi's advice and nodded her head in agreement before she stood and followed her out the door. Anthony nodded at her when she came out of the room, and she stood in front of the straight line of kids eager to do her bidding.

Shamira closed her eyes, placing herself back to a time when she moved purely on instinct and with her second sight. She started the sequence of moves she wanted them to remember, moves that would save their lives. She showed them the tactics that would bring their opponents to their knees, no matter how large they were, and they followed her every move as quietly as she delivered them.

Chapter 25

She knew he entered the room because his scent tickled her nose. The kids in front of her slipped as they briefly glanced at Valens. Shamira figured it was time to get ready for the attack. Valens walked toward her with the look of a person coming to conduct business. She ended her lesson and stood waiting for him to approach.

"Shamira, I've finished the new designs. We have to get everyone fitted. Mitch is preparing the vehicles some of the others confiscated in the name of freedom from various Security Force impound lots with the help of your parents' loyal networks," he said steadily.

Shamira lifted an eyebrow at the mention of her parents helping with the confiscation of vehicles. She wondered what Valens had said to her parents when she wasn't present. *No point in pondering on that further,* she scolded herself. She knew Valens' purpose was to move forward in the attack.

"Good. I want everyone to meet in the front room after we have all prepared the vehicles and have on full gear," Shamira added and glanced at Hedi, who was already organizing the kids in lines leading to the lab.

"I have something special I made for you. I don't want you to get hurt if we get separated. I left it in Mina's room. I'll see you in an hour in the front room," Valens said flatly. He dropped his eyes and turned then walked away. *Great. Now I may have scared him off for good.* She figured she'd think about how to fix that later. Now was definitely the time to focus on preparing for their attack, and anything else would have to be dealt with later.

She followed the others out of the training room and headed straight to Mina's room. When she entered the room, she noticed it smelled like roses, sweet and seductive. Valens must have set the scent settings for the room. She surmised from this that he must not be too angry with her. Her eyes traveled around and landed on the white box on the bed with a handwritten note on top.

She walked over to the box, smiled to herself, and picked up the note.

> *I designed this while thinking of you. I've been working on it since the day I came to your house when you returned from Earth. I knew we would do this together.*
>
> *PS. I wasn't angry with you... just at myself.*
>
> *Valens*

Her eyes watered at his words and the knowledge that he'd believed in her when most people would have taken a look at her and counted her out. She thought back to their first meeting and realized that even without seeing him, she knew they were connected somehow. Now, the thought of him not being part of her life was unimaginable. She trusted him more than she did anyone other than her family, and after this was all over, she promised herself she would let him know it.

She reached for the box slowly and opened it. Another note was inside that pointed to the bathroom she could use to change. A smile slipped to her face, and she removed the tissue that covered the suit he had created for her. She gasped upon seeing it. It appeared to be black, but when she shifted it, the color changed, as though tiny crystallized glass was within the fabric. Her thumb rubbed against it, and it felt like the softest leather.

"Wow! This is beautiful. Oh, Valens," she said in a whisper with a tear dropping from her eye. This was so special. No one had ever given her something this beautiful. She pulled the fabric, and it stretched just a bit then retracted. *Leave it to Valens to put something extra into the design*, she thought with a smile. She couldn't wait a moment longer to put it on.

After a quick shower, she rushed out and put on the suit. She walked over to the full-length mirror and was impressed. It even had a belt that held all of her weapons, which Valens had carefully arranged on the floor by the bed. The matching gloves were also an upgrade from the previous gloves he'd given her. She pulled her hair back in a firm bun and sucked her lips as she placed on her gloves. Taking one last glance at her image, she headed out the door and to the front room to leave for the attack.

Chapter 26

Kids were piled everywhere. There was very little room for Shamira to get by. As she walked through the masses, the kids chanted while they reached out and touched her. A pat, a finger, and an arm squeeze all came when she walked through the crowd of kids leading up to the front room and the main entrance to Valens' hideout. She forced a shiver of discomfort down deep. These kids loved her and didn't shun her like so many others did. She had something within her grasp they wanted—freedom and justice with just a taste of revenge, something she desired to give them all. She relaxed and enjoyed it all. Allowing herself for once to relish in the comfort of friends, she smiled as she stood before them with Valens and Anthony on either side of her.

"Everyone, are we ready?" she asked, her voice rising above the chants.

"Hell, yeah!" Anthony said, and all the kids repeated and applauded.

She looked around and cleared her voice in awe at the mass of kids before her that wanted this as much as she did. Her eyes landed on a tall, broad boy just in front of her who looked eager to speak. "Hey, you, what's your name?" She looked over the kid with chestnut brown hair and brown eyes who stood about Valens' height at six feet.

"Dion, and I want to offer my experience in any way. Kurt and I were trained together. He can vouch for me. I'll do anything you need," he said steadily.

"Dion, I have the perfect job for you. I need someone to lead up the rescue and attack crew that will make sure all of the kids we free from the Mons get out safely. You'll also have to take on any guards that try to kill or retrieve the captives. Can I count on you?" she asked, and after sizing him up, she knew he was her guy for the job.

"Consider it done," Dion replied. Shamira detected his elation at her trust.

"He's good for it," Kurt concurred to affirm to Shamira that he trusted Dion also.

"Uh, I offer my services also. I have a skill you will need," a petite kid that looked like he had missed more than a few meals stated as he stepped in front of Dion.

"What's your name, and what can you do?" Shamira asked, not able to stop the smile that formed on her face.

He grinned widely. "You'll need someone small and wily like me to climb up the tunnels in the Mons to recover any of the kids in the dream mines." His eyes got wide as though he dared her to tell him no.

"What's your name? How old are you?" she asked, thinking of David and the other kids in the Mons. She didn't want to risk this kid's life.

"Manny, and I'm ten, but I'm a bit small for my age. A side effect of a few missed meals and small parents, I guess," he said and puffed out his chest to look intimidating.

"I don't know. We're going into dangerous territory, and we may not come back alive. I can't risk your life, Manny," she said.

"What? I risked my life every day I hid out and ran from Monev. I've been on my own since I can remember. I'm tough. I can do it. Give me a chance. It's all I have to live for—the chance to get back at them. I know the mines. I've escaped them – and Monev," he said loudly. Gasps and whispers went around the room.

Anthony squinted his eyes in disbelief. "You what? You've

escaped? When? How the hell was that possible?"

"To be honest, it was an accident. I didn't get inside, um, actually, but they were taking me there. While we kids were being transported and moved from the vehicles to the door, a few of the guards started to argue while the door to the back of the truck was open. Since we were being transported, they took off the handcuffs they used to keep us immobile. I slipped out of the truck unnoticed, then took off before they knew it. Lucky for me, they had another truck taking off that was transporting waste to the Outlands. That's where I got off and moved through the night back to Sector Five," he said and pushed his chest out in pride.

Mitch crossed his arms and looked over Manny with scrutiny. "I'll be damned! I think the little runt is telling the truth, or should I say, he'd better be."

"You lucky bastard! I think we should bring him with us. He will be small enough to get through the tunnels, and he's mature enough to help the other young kids get out alive," Anthony said with his hands on his hips while examining Manny with a look of respect.

Valens moved hand off his earlink. "We have the team set to release the beetles. They're on the street and ready to go when we give the word. We have Rob on the inside of the Mons, a runner who was sent there an hour ago. He said he'd make sure he shuts down the surveillance, lights, and security system. We have limited time for him to help, though, because runners are only allowed in the Mons for several hours before they are forced to leave. In most cases, they can't wait to get out."

Shamira zipped her outfit up to her neck. "Okay. We need to get moving to the strike location near the Mons. Valens, Anthony, Kurt, Hedi, and Manny, we are going into the Mons first. We'll send the signal to Dion and the others to start the complete attack. Let's go."

Valens opened the door, and Shamira walked to her bike, then watched as the others got comfortable on their vehicles. She gave a nod and followed Kurt to the location within a safe distance of the Mons that would shelter them from discovery.

Chapter 27

The Mons stood like a giant before them. They were about a mile outside the security perimeter, and night had begun to fall. They came to a silent stop, and Shamira nodded at Dion while he voiced the command to the mini-computer on his wrist to send the vehicles from the Mars World Construction distribution warehouse to the site. The vehicles were computer operated and would drive on autopilot to the specified location.

She took a moment to scan the area, and on a need to be

cautious, pushed her sight beyond the hard packed ground surrounding their pathway to the manmade entrance to the Mars core heating piping.

"Crud. I knew they wouldn't make this easy. We have a problem," she said loud enough for her team to hear.

"What is it?" Valens asked.

"There are heat sensor laser landmines that separate us from the entrance to the core heating piping tunnels. If we attempt to walk, drive, or run in that direction, we'll be burned to a crisp," she said and frowned.

Hedi smiled at the challenge. She worked on her mini-computer on her wrist. "No problem. I can fix it. Just give me about five minutes." They all looked at her in shock and with a bit of doubt.

"Uh, what the hell you going to do? Lastly, who is going to test it? It won't be me," Anthony said and shook his head from side to side.

Shamira bit her lip in thought. "We don't need someone to test it. I can tell when they're deactivated. You just follow me." She looked out to the vast landmine farm ahead of them.

"Uh, how in snot is she gonna do that?" Manny asked in a whisper to Kurt.

"She has gifts, so leave it at that, little man," Kurt said and smacked the back of Manny's head.

"I hope so, 'cause she said she was the one going first," Manny replied and ducked out of the way of Kurt's hand as Kurt prepared to

275

smack his head again.

"Hey, while she's working on the landmine issue, let's put these vehicles in stealth mode and scramble this area from any surveillance," Valens added.

Mitch looked up and said, "I got that covered."

"I'm going to try to get Rob on to see if he's in the security center yet and can deactivate this," Valens said, then tapped on his ear to connect to Rob.

Shamira's frustration started to rise at this unanticipated delay to their attack. Everything hedged on them getting inside.

"Okay! Rob gave us some good and bad news. Good news is - he's deactivated the landmines. Bad news is, it's rumored that if there is a breach, the whole place is rigged to blow up. That could be a major problem," Valens said.

Shamira replied, "Oh, it won't be a problem because we'll get them all out alive. David is in there, and I'm getting him no matter what. Returning without him is not an option."

Hedi sighed. "Okay, then I'm in. I can only deactivate a few so that it goes undetected by the main security system. That means we have to stay really close to one another until we get to the tunnels. I can deactivate them in a stair step mode when we clear a few, then they'll reactivate. The system does a random pass, so the security system expects a few to deactivate throughout the area. I'm tricking it into deactivating them in our path. It's slick, but not tricky enough to stop me from using it to our advantage. We only have five minutes before our path starts, five minutes and counting."

Shamira watched the illuminated underground laser mine deactivation pattern move in the direction of the path ahead of them. "First team, come close. I'll lead the way. Get your weapons ready. We may need them." The deactivation pattern was just large enough for them to follow with less than a foot between them. "Manny, you get behind me. Anthony, pull up the rear. Let's move," she said and started the mile trek ahead.

She crouched down and moved slowly across the terrain while she watched a few of the mines ahead of her dim as they deactivated. Manny moved anxiously from side to side behind her, and she had to whisper the command for him to be still time and time again. She wondered why she risked bringing such a young kid with them. He would either get them caught or endanger himself. She felt his movement yet again, and this time she reached back to squeeze his arm in a silent reminder to be still. He calmed down again, but she wondered for how long. The trek was slow, and sweat built on her forehead from the realization that with one slip, someone could get burned alive. The activated mines lit up the ground like blue radiant discs under a brown mass.

"This sucks. I can't take it. I don't want to fry," Manny whined.

"Shush up!" Shamira said.

Mitch forced out in an angry whisper, "If you don't, I'm going to throw you on the mines, so walk and keep your whining to yourself."

Hedi warned, "We've got to move faster, people. I think the system is on to us. The mines behind us are reactivating faster than I can deactivate the ones in front."

Manny cried out, "You have got to be friggin' kidding! This cannot be happening."

"Get a grip or you'll get us all killed. Take it slow and stay steady, you hear?" Shamira commanded. Her patience was slipping, and she reached back to grab Manny's arm to steady him.

Manny forged forward and didn't realize she had stopped. His surge frontward pushed Shamira into the active mines ahead of her.

"What the hell!" Mitch yelled.

Shamira breathed in deeply as she fell forward. She quickly placed her hands strategically between the active mines directly in front of her. Her patience with Manny disintegrated, and she glanced back to see that Valens held Manny by his shirt so he wouldn't fall forward on her. She took a deep breath and mumbled, "I knew I should have left him behind."

"Hey, I heard that. I can hold my own. Hmph," Manny argued.

Valens swore, and Manny's shirt ripped, leaving him to tumble onto Shamira's back and slide off to the side to pass over an active mine. In an instant, Shamira heard the beep underground that set off the mine and sent a wide laser light from under the red packed ground and up into the air. She acted speedily and grabbed his shirt, then threw him behind her at a waiting Valens, who caught him. Still, she slipped, which caused her shoulder to set off the mine on the opposite side of their path.

"Shamira. Watch it!" Valens yelled out when he tried to stop her slip. With a flash, she felt the fire and heat emitted from the mine she had activated. She moved quickly out of the way, but not before the shoulder of her suit and the bottom of her glove was burned through. Pain hit, and the direct and heated pain of the burn started to anger her. She quickly jumped up and back out of the laser path, pushing the pain deep within. It settled into a throbbing ache as she refocused on her determination to save her brother.

Frustrated, Sharmira grunted. "Hedi, we need to speed this up. Give us one minute to cover the quarter-mile path ahead. Can everyone keep up with that?" She glared at Manny.

"Yep, I can do it, but that's all. It'll set off the entire system if it's more than that. At the count of three, take off, Shamira, and we'll be close beside you. Oh, and one more thing, no wider than three people. We need to travel close," Hedi replied.

"Just great. Who is watching the shrimp? Don't even ask me to do it," Mitch said angrily.

"I'll carry him. He definitely doesn't weigh much," Anthony said.

"Hello, guys, I can hold my own. I don't need to be carried," Manny whined.

"Shut up and let Anthony carry you! We don't have any more room for mistakes," Shamira forced out, annoyed.

She heard a muffled complaint from Manny's lips followed by

some sort of rebellious grunt as he realized he was outnumbered and conceded.

Anthony cleared his throat. "The shrimp is quiet and secured. Ready when you are."

She smiled, because, knowing Anthony, he had found a funny way to subdue Manny. Lucky for Manny, Mitch didn't decide to help. Mitch had much less humor.

"Let's move. We're running out of time," Shamira said as she signaled Hedi to start the countdown.

"On three... two... one... go!" Hedi said, and Shamira took off.

She looked ahead and saw the path before her of deactivated mines moving in sync. They came together to lead in the direction of the manhole that held the underground heating grids and pipes for Mars. The path cleared, and she listened to the sound behind her to make sure her team remained safe. She heard a complaining Manny and then the sound of a slap.

"I'm being abused here!" Manny yelled.

Then she heard a directed slap and another muffled compliant from him. She figured Anthony probably covered his mouth. She smiled and shook her head. She really had to get used to working with others. It was hard not to lose patience and control with Manny's distractions. She supposed the others were similar to her in survival training, but this Manny hadn't been trained, and it showed.

The manhole was close ahead, and her excitement at the impending confrontation sent tingles up her back. Mouthfuls of air came fast. She heard the others feet hit the ground in determined pursuit of the next barrier. Quickly, she slid to a stop, and Valens came forth to dislodge the top of the manhole for them to go inside.

Immediately, she felt blazing heat as it came from the hole when Valens and Mitch removed the top.

Manny started to squirm. "Oh, heck no! I'm not going in that hole. Dude, how are we going to walk in there?" Manny yelled out.

"Can I remind you that you volunteered for this, you little weasel? If you can't remember, I can gladly take you out of your misery and save us a lot of trouble by throwing you to Monev when we are done with you," Mitch spat out.

Valens dug in his jacket. "Look, we don't have time for threats. I came prepared thinking we would have this problem. I have a cooling device, but I don't know how long it will last, so we are going to have to move on this quick."

Hedi yelled from the back, "Hate to be a party pooper, but we've got to get in there fast. Our pathway is disappearing, and we'll all be fried toast or discovered if we don't get in there now!"

"I'll go first. Let's get going. I see Manny's about to get burned if we don't move forward, like now." Shamira said hurriedly with a slight grin at the sight of Anthony holding Manny over a soon activated mine while the boy squirmed uselessly.

"I've got two coolant devices. Shamira, you take this one, and I'll pull up the rear with the second. Let's go. I started the coolant. You have about six feet of leeway. I don't know how long it will last,"

Valens said.

Manny peered over the edge of the opening. "Uh, I ain't going in there. That place is dark and probably stinks, especially from the smell of burning flesh."

"Sorry, Manny, I don't have any glasses for you. But we all can see and will guide you. Trust us. We know what we're doing," Valens said as Shamira shook her head at his offer for eye specs to see in the dark hole.

Chapter 28

Shamira dropped down several feet into the dark manhole that held the piping. She sprayed the pipe below her before she landed, swiping the coolant so it cooled enough for her to move forward. Darkness surrounded her, and she quickly moved ahead, not taking the time to look around. She moved swiftly to make room for the others. Her enhanced eyesight easily adjusted to the darkness and gave the area around her a bright green hue. The piping under her was cool, but she noticed that ahead of her, heated steam rose from the untreated piping. *This is not going to be any fun either.*

"Oh, this ain't so bad. You want me to go in the front? I'm a real good lookout," Manny interjected from above.

They all ignored him. Anthony slapped him on the back of the head before he dropped him into the hole. Shamira realized Manny was behind her. Valens dropped down behind Manny and nodded to her, then winked as he gave her the thumbs up to move forward. She ignored the tingle within her belly at his flirt and turned to move forward. She glanced down and realized there were several layers of black steamy piping.

She took a deep breath and secured her legs around the pipe that was several feet wide. Shamira looked up at the ground above her and realized that several feet above her were solid rock and dirt. The piping went on for miles below, and she saw smooth barrier walls of separation that looked like silver. She leaned forward in order to better grasp the pipe and prepare to cool the path ahead of them. Sweat built on her forehead. She moved forward.

"Ugh! Help!" Manny yelped out.

She quickly squeezed her knees tightly on the pipe and reached behind her to steady him as he started to slip. "Look, put your arms around my waist and hold on tight. Don't squirm or scream out, understand?" she whispered sternly at him.

Mitch called out angrily, "One more slip, and I'll throw him off. I swear it, Shamira! I'm sick of him. I didn't come all this way to save my sister for some jackass to mess it up." Mitch reached around

Valens to hit Manny on the arm.

When Manny jerked his arm away, he started to slip again but held tightly to Shamira's suit without complaint. She knew Manny had grit since he was the only one of them that couldn't see what was around him. He didn't cower from the hit and shook it off quickly.

Manny exclaimed, "Hey, the pipe is getting warmer. Can somebody do something, like now?"

Shamira cooled the path in front of her and pulled him along. Looking up, she pushed her sight ahead. Finally her sight revealed the location of the underground holding cells. She didn't have time for a scan to see how many kids moved about, but she was relieved they didn't have much further to go. She smiled, knowing that finally, they would get in, and she would get David. Determined to get there quickly, she rushed forward while cooling the pipe ahead of her. Everyone moved quickly and silently. She was glad Manny now held firmly to her without a fight.

At last. They'd made it to the floor just beneath the underground prison where the child prisoners slept.

"Valens, I need a device to cut through this. Looks like it's about three feet of rock separating us. I hope what you have is quiet," Shamira said while she looked above her. She noticed quite a few little bodies roaming the cell above. After she counted, she realized most of the kids must be in the mines.

Valens called out, "Here, Manny, give this to Shamira. Be careful! It's the only one I have. Shamira, you have to start a small hole and then slowly move in a circular motion so the rock melts and has time to cool to smoothness. Otherwise, you'll have some melted rock drop down on the pipes, and that's not a good thing." He gave the handheld device to Manny.

She glanced behind and noticed that Manny held the device as if his life depended on it. In that moment, Manny reminded her of David, and she regained her patience for him and smiled at him with thanks. His eyes widened in appreciation. She handed him the coolant, and he took it gladly.

"Keep it cool, but use it sparingly. We have to make it last," Shamira whispered to him.

"Valens, give the others permission to prepare for attack. It should only take me a short while to cut through," she called back. She started to cut through the rock above her.

Time passed fast. The device worked well at melting and pushing excess rock to a smooth surface on the sides of the hole. She continued to work quickly while she slowly widened the hole above her, and then she saw it. Several of the children became aware of the faint noise of the cuts through the rock. Some leaned their heads to the floor to listen to the faintly muted ring of the beam.

"Valens, the kids can hear this. Do you have a silencer? I don't want them to alert the guards. They're starting to gather around where I'm cutting. I can't cut anymore without hurting someone. Right now it's only large enough for Manny to fit through," she said, frustrated by the small hole she made.

"Sorry, no silencer. We have another problem too. We're running out of coolant. There's only enough for about twenty minutes," Valens said calmly.

"Friggin' great," she replied.

"You can hoist me up there, and I can widen the hole for you. I'm sure the kids up there will help me. From what I remember when I was captured, they all wanted freedom and were a close group," Manny said.

"Looks like that's a plan. C'mon, climb up on my shoulders," Shamira said. Manny quickly obliged her. She stretched a little to adjust to Manny's slight weight while he adeptly crawled onto her shoulders. Then she balanced him on her shoulders and held onto his ankles.

"This is good. The small tunnel you made has dents where I can put my feet. It won't take me long," Manny said.

"Good. Take the cutting device and cut the few inches through, and then the rest of us will come up, okay?" She patted his leg when he hoisted himself up through the tunnel.

"You better tell him to work fast. Our time is running out here. My second coolant is so low I have to shake it to get the coolant out," Valens said. He tried to speak calmly, but she could sense the slight tremble in his voice.

"Manny, please be quick. Our time is running out," Shamira yelled up at him.

"That's fine. I'm breaking through now," he replied.

287

She looked past him to see that the kids in the cell above him had spread out from the area where he cut. Some of them appeared to walk around the area like they didn't notice the slight *hum* of the device Manny used.

"Damn! Move up. It's heating up back here," Anthony said, irritated.

Shamira felt Valens move in closely behind her. He put his head within a breath of her shoulder in order get a close look at Manny up above.

"Good. It look like he's in," Valens said, and she shivered a little at his close proximity.

"Let's hope the clumsy shrimp will come through," said Anthony.

"If he doesn't, we'll all fry," added Kurt.

"I'll go up first to get them ready. You tell everyone to start the attacks. Seems to me we're going to have to fight our way out of their holding cells," she replied.

"All is clear. Come on up," Manny yelled down. Valens gave her a push as he firmly gripped her thighs just below her behind.

"Watch where you put your hands, Valens," she warned.

"Oh, I'm watching alright," he added with a naughty smile.

"Cut that crap out! We're in danger here," Mitch added and pushed on Valens' back.

Shamira shook off the slight jerk in movement and jumped up and secured her feet within the makeshift tunnel. She quickly moved, and Valens and the others were right behind her with Anthony in the rear.

"My tail is burned. Damn, this hurts," Anthony complained.

"You weren't the only one that got burned, you big baby! Shut up and stop complaining. We're about to try out these new suits Valens made for us," Hedi added.

Chapter 29

Shamira climbed up and out of the makeshift tunnel to get into the underground cell. She moved quickly and climbed out on her knees so she wouldn't alert the guards. Kids gathered around her and spoke softly, immediately understanding the danger if they spoke too loudly to alert the guards. The others quickly came up behind her, and Shamira took a moment to look around the holding cell.

The smell in the cell reminded her of burning metal and was so overpowering that she coughed. The cell was carved out of the rock within the volcano and had silver crystals within the rock. She assessed the room to see if there were any other possible ways out besides the cell door. Then she pushed her sight beyond the barriers of the room to see the structure beyond the cell.

One of the kids put their hand up to their mouth to motion for her to be silent. She nodded and smiled in thanks. The others stayed low also so their height wouldn't give them away while they, too, searched the room. In the dim light of the cell, she frantically looked for David but couldn't find him. Then she looked around for Mina, Valens' sister and didn't see her either. She motioned for the kids to come to her and gave a signal to her team to investigate the area further.

Shamira looked into the cluster of unkempt kids. "Do you know where they took a boy named David? He has brown hair. Or a girl named Mina? Anyone?"

All of the kids were dirty, and various kids had bruises, scratches, and cuts over the exposed areas on their frail bodies. She simmered with anger at the thought of what David and these kids had endured.

"Are you here to save us?" a girl that looked to be about seven years old asked meekly.

"Yes, we are. Do you trust us?" she asked the girl.

"I trust you. We have hoped for so long. The guard took the boy David this morning, and the girl named Mina is a small one. She's still in the mines. My name is Taren, and I'm happy you are here," the little girl said, and tears fell from her eyes.

Shamira motioned for her team to come closer. They all complied—even Manny, who now had a goofy grin on his face in hopes of a show of appreciation.

"Manny, you did great. Now, it seems like the only way out of here is through that cell door. I looked past the door, and the place is swarming with guards. There are only two other cell areas, but there is no one in them. We're going to have to fight our way out. The exit on the next level is going to be even harder to secure, but we can do it. Hedi, I need you to find an opening during our assault on the guards and take the kids out to Dion. Valens, your sister is in the mines, and the guards took my brother," she said and looked at them for their response.

Mitch whispered, "I found my sister here and Anthony's brother! We trust Hedi enough to know they're safe with her. We're in on the assault and saving your brother and Valens' sister."

Anthony nodded in agreement. Shamira noticed the sheer happiness on Mitch's face when he hugged the blond haired girl close to his side. The looked up at him with adoration and love.

"I appreciate your sacrifice for us, guys," she said.

Valens squatted in the middle of the kids. "Okay, do any of you know how to get the guards' attention so we can get them to open the door?"

"Um, they will come in if we fight. They don't like us to hurt each other. They say we are more useful alive while we're small enough to do the mining," Taren added.

Shamira asked, "Well, if that is so, how did you get those bruises and cuts?"

Taren whispered, "It's what happens when we do the mining. We pick the dream until our hands bleed. They wrap them so we can mine again. If we don't meet our quotas, we get hit, but only on the face, because we need the rest of our bodies for mining. If we do well, we get to eat." Taren confirmed how cruel Monev was to its captives.

"Can you all start a pretend fight for us when I give you the signal? We need to get them to open the door," Shamira asked and gently rubbed the girl's arm as she put her thumb up on her other hand.

Taren hugged Shamira. "Anything. I'll do anything you ask."

Shamira returned Taren's hug and motioned for the others to take attack positions. She went over to the door and crouched down on the opposite side of the door jam. Valens was beside her, and the others flanked the wall and corners of the room. She gave the signal to Taren, and the kids started to argue and roll around the floor. They yelled and cheered on the fighters.

Shamira peered through the wall and saw that the noise attracted the interest of several of the guards, just as Taren had said it would. One largely built guard punched a shorter one on the arm and gave him the signal as if it were the shorter guard's turn to check on the captives. Shamira gave the signal to the others to let them know a guard was on the way. A rush of anticipation came. She felt every hair on her neck stand up to signal her state of awareness.

The guard unlocked the cell door and hesitated before he peered in. The kids that fought on the floor increased their efforts to imitate a true brawl. The cheers from the kids got louder in order to get the guard's attention. Shamira prepared herself for her assault and smiled at finally being able to make someone pay for how Monev hurt these kids.

Short and well built, the guard walked into the room, unsuspecting of the danger. Shamira took the opportunity to land a front-kick to the guard's cheek. It landed with such power that his head hit the metal door, which dazed him in preparation for her next assault. She immediately bent her knee to knock him forward with the kick of her heel. The force of the kick knocked him out cold as his head slammed against the stone floor of the cell. She took a quick look behind her and confirmed that Hedi held the kids at bay while she led her team into the hallway to finish the attack on the remaining guards that stood between them and the exit out of the complex.

Guards flanked them on both sides, too many to count. Her team started to fire, and the guards fell, but not without a fight. They returned the firepower, and Shamira worked hard to stay clear of it. Then, seeing an opportunity to clear out the barrier of guards, she unleashed her power, and her body charged with electricity at her release of adrenaline.

Her vision held a red hue as she felt a hot river of power flood her system. She ran forward and attacked the largest guard in front of her, not giving him time to fire his weapon. Her fist connected to his nose, and it broke instantly as he was thrown back into several guards that stood behind him, causing them to fall. Her suit deflected the firepower and without thought, she kicked, hit, and broke the bones of numerous guards that were focusing their fights solely on her.

The onslaught of the Mons defenses thundered toward her as she grabbed the closet victim that challenged her and rammed his head into her knee, causing him to fall in a convulsing heap on the floor beside her. With each punch, kick, and challenger, her strength grew, and her body heated to the point where she felt on fire.

The barrier ahead of them was blocked by the guards that remained, and she smiled at them knowing this was their end. The beast within her was callous and cold, and its only directive was its mission to defend and protect. Burning with heat and ready for attack, she ran into a sea of adversaries. The firepower initiated by the guards bounced off her suit during her assault.

During her angered haze, she heard Valens yell out. Anthony confirmed to Mitch that a stray bullet had hit him. Without thought or question, Shamira increased her onslaught and grabbed the large guard in front of her that had fired the shot that hit Valens. Fire pulsed in her veins, and she punched him over and over again, and threw him to the floor as she charged on the remaining guards. With each punch and kick, the victims fell and convulsed like their bodies were on fire with electricity.

She looked around and saw a scattering of felled and twitching bodies and realized there was no one left to attack. Looking behind her, she saw her team and the others staring at her in shock. Her eyes landed on Valens as she realized he'd taken off his form-fitting protective hood and blood trickled through his fingers at the wound caused by the attack.

"I'm okay, Shamira. It's just a scratch," Valens yelled out to her.

At Valens' nod, she kicked in the door riddled with holes from the battle.

"Is it me, or did she just let go of a can of whip-shod on them?" Manny asked and then laughed. He instantly crouched when Anthony slapped the back of his head.

"Shut up before I do that to you, squirt. Hey, Valens, do I have that power filled shock juice in my suit like she does in hers?" Anthony added as Mitch snickered. Then they followed Kurt and Valens out of the cell.

"What she just did was all her. The suit I gave her can't carry that much power or send electrical shocks through its victims. Besides, she damaged the suit when she burned a hole in it at the landmines. Whatever power it had in it's long gone," Valens said while he watched the felled guard at his feet twitch with convulsions from her blow.

"I guess she is a bad ass," Mitch said before he spat on the rocky floor. His gaze fell upon her with respect.

Chapter 30

Valens turned his head when his earlink beeped. "We've got confirmation from Rob that the mines and surveillance systems are shut down," Valens confirmed.

"New set of guards are coming fast. Prepare to fire. Now!" Shamira yelled while she crouched down and prepared for another faceoff.

Shots fired past, and she went for her closest target. Now able to control the burning power, she kicked the guard in the face, and he hit the floor, knocked out cold.

"We'll clear the path! Hedi, get them kids outta here! Dion is ready and waiting," yelled Valens.

"Got ya! Still waiting for Warrior Girl badass to clear the way. Manny, you stay there until I give the signal, then make them run like hellhounds are behind them until they get out," Hedi yelled back while she fired. Manny and the kids hid behind the doorway and waited for Hedi to give the signal.

In her haze of movement, Shamira smiled when she heard her friend's praise until a huge guard demanded her attention as he charged at her. His momentum slid her back several feet and slammed her into a nearby wall. Her head hit the jagged and rocky surface and caused her to daze out for a moment. He seized his opportunity and tried to stab her in the gut as his fellow guards shot fire around them. Her suit protected her from the assault as she shook her head to clear the haze. Her team countered the ambush of guards quickly, and Mitch threw a mini-bomb at the guards that charged forward.

Shamira's large opponent's fist pounded her face from left to right as he held her up by the neck. Fighting to regain her focus, the burning fire of power built from the adrenaline rush incited by his attack. She licked the blood off her lips and steadied her face from his attack. She grabbed the hand he punched at her and broke it at the wrist with a painful sounding *snap*. With her free hand, she punched him out cold. He fell loudly, and she landed effortlessly on the floor.

Pausing, she smiled at the remaining guards and ran forward into attack, focusing on making a clear pathway for the kids she had promised to free.

Hedi, seeing the way clear, directed the kids around the fallen guards and out of the entrance to the Mons. Dion's crew was waiting with the large trucks that acted as a safe haven and getaway. Children of all sizes, dirty from the debris of battle and slavery, ran, stumbled, and fell on their way to freedom.

"Don't look back! Just run and don't look back! Go straight in the trucks! Now!" Hedi yelled, and the kids eagerly obeyed.

"Is that all of them? Where are Shamira and the others?" Dion demanded as he confirmed his team got the kids into the trucks and drove off safely.

"They're still in there. There are still some kids working in the mines. They won't leave until they save them all," Hedi said.

"I hope their time doesn't run out. There are booby traps that will still set off the incineration mechanism – and with it reactivate the landmines," he said gravely.

"Oh, they'll get out. Shamira and Valens will see to it," Hedi affirmed while she shot at guards who tried to escape the compound.

Chapter 31

"Let's head to the mines," Shamira commanded.

"One of the kids told me your brother was taken to the tombs. We need to go there before he burns or worse," Manny called out.

"The tombs? Why there?" Shamira asked while she looked at the fallen guards around her. She made her way to the elevator that led to the next level where the dream labs were.

"They were ordered to send him there. The kid said that's where they take kids who are unable to work or are problems. He said the guard was told to take him there by Renu himself. The boy mentioned he heard the guard bragging about it to another guard," Manny said solemnly.

"Where are the Tombs? Tell me! Did he tell you where they are?" she demanded. Her heart broke at the thought that she may be too late to save her brother.

"He said they're in the back of the dream lab. The workers in the lab are made to hear the victims scream while they burn to remind them of their fate if they make any mistakes," Manny replied.

"Damn, that's messed up. That insane bastard would think up something cruel like that," Anthony added as he pounded on the elevator button in frustration.

"Hey, Rob's warning us there are guards waiting for us when the doors open," Mitch said.

"Good! It's our turn for some hand-to-hand. Shamira, we'll take care of the guards. When you see the chance, you can go straight to the labs to save your brother," Valens said.

"Yummy! I can't wait to kick ass. Like now," Anthony said.

The elevator jerked to a stop, and Shamira hung back, now with the knowledge that her power didn't control her, but she controlled it. She also knew that even with her earlier loss of control, she had not yet reached the full potential of her strength.

She watched as her team fired with no hesitation. Manny squeezed behind her to dodge any stray shots. Turning to look at him, she smiled and then winked. He smiled back and gave her the thumbs up when he secured the protective bulletproof hood and mask combination over his face. She secured hers and then turned around to see her team had moved forward to follow through on their promise to make a way for her.

Proudly, she observed that Anthony's power and anger showed in his combat with several of the guards. He grabbed the wrist of his attacker and then landed a powerful kick at his charging opponent, yelling after his victory.

"Yeah, baby, I've been waiting to do this all damn day! Come on, scum! Feel the pain!" Anthony roared, as he elbowed another charging guard while he dodged an incoming bullet with the sleeve of his suit.

Her glance landed on Mitch, who was cold, merciless, and deadly. He had a knife as well as a gun, both of which he used to slice and shoot the guards when they swarmed toward him. Shamira figured they misjudged his size and thought him to be the weakest. She knew they were indeed wrong as she watched Mitch slice the face of the guard who attempted to pull the trigger of his gun at point-blank range into Mitch's cold, unsmiling face.

Kurt, her graceful savior, was beautifully deadly as he attacked. His years of training as an assassin kept his kills clean as he downed the opposing guards. He seemed to work at shedding as little blood as possible and made his assaults neat. It was almost like a dance, and the power suit Valens created for them appeared to make Kurt's deadly strikes effortless. *I wonder what caused the electrical charge of power that emitted from me. Who am I kidding? It was me. I felt the electricity leave my body. God, what have I become now?*

A grunt came from in front of her, and she saw Valens as he shot the guard that stood between her and the labs. His resolute and sharp-eyed expression never wavered while he meticulously downed the guards that were a barrier to her mission to save her brother. He kicked the guard that was bold enough to replace the first, causing his opponent to fly several feet into the air.

"It's clear! Go now! We'll stabilize the hall leading to the mines," Valens shouted to Shamira.

Manny pushed her on the back, and she took off in the direction of the dream labs. Tables upon tables of shimmering silver dust sparkled as she ran into the dream lab. The workers ran in pandemonium in all directions while they avoided attack and attempted escape. She slid to a stop and pushed her sight past the walls of the lab. Her eyes landed on a rock-enclosed room in a small hallway at the end of the lab where a boy pounded furiously at the door and scratched to fight his way out—the boy from the picture in her brother's room. She pushed forward and saw he was starting to sweat from the intensity of the heat within while he struggled to get out. *It's David,* she knew. *Free him!* Her power burst forth, and she ran to the door to kick it in.

"David! David! Get away from the door!" She slid to a stop in front of the tomb. The pounding had stopped, and she heard him struggle to talk.

"Shamira! Shamira!" he called, as his raspy voice fought for volume.

Deeply, she pulled air into her lungs and kicked repeatedly at the thick metal door. It dented, then squeaked, then finally burst open to hang jaggedly on its track.

David stood before her, bravely and frozen. Noticing the harshness in his features, her heart broke for him. She ran toward him and knelt down before him. He watched her quietly, and then his face broke out into a smile.

"It's about time you came to save me," he said with a voice much gruffer and harsher than she remembered. A tear dropped from her eye, and she pulled him close.

"Sorry, David. When you save me next time, will you make sure I don't have to wait for as long as you had to wait for me to save you?" she choked out. Greedily, she inhaled the sweet scent of him she so remembered.

"You can see me now?" He slowly relaxed and gradually inched his arms around her.

Her soul cried at how he had changed from the abuse he received at the hands of Renu. "Yes," she answered with a choke.

"I'll save you next time, Shamira, because I'm going to keep training until I'm strong enough to fight anyone that tries to hurt you. I don't ever want you to be hurt," he stated bravely.

She pondered his words and realized he was as brave as she

always believed. Touched, she knew he would be different after this, that he would be a force to be reckoned with. He had changed, but she just hoped he would still be the one to make her laugh. At that moment, he snuggled his nose into her neck. She removed the tight protective hood from her head so she could feel him close to her, and she held him as though they were the only ones left on Mars.

Then, just under all the noise of mayhem beyond the tomb doorway, she heard the *click* of a gun and the heavy breathing of someone nearby, confirming they were still in danger.

"Touching," a deep, angry voice behind her boomed in sheer disgust. The butt of the gun jabbed her behind the ear. David's head shot up and looked at their attacker with a flash of fearful recognition before anger filled his eyes.

"Leave her alone, Tiger!" he shouted.

"Shut up, boy. Don't even think about moving, little huntress. I have another gun pointed at your brave little brother here, and I really want to use it so he remembers his place," he said.

Shamira remembered the name and knew Tiger was Renu's henchman, the one who ran this evil place. "Do you know who I am?" she said evenly.

"Of course, Shamira, and you have been up to no good. The word is out that whoever sees you is to kill you. Since this is my operation, I figured this little bait would bring you back here. I just didn't realize you are such a little fighter. For a blind girl, you sure are good at seeing things," he said, then pushed the gun further into her skin.

"Renu doesn't like to do his own dirty work? He's so much of a punk that he has to send you to clean up his messes? What, he can't even handle a blind girl that kicked his butt and liked it? He's a friggin joke," she said smugly to tick him off all the more.

"Oh, it's my pleasure to do this for him. This place was my dream. He just gave me funding to run it. Don't worry, though. He's long gone anyway, and I'm the nice one between the two of us. Consider this mercy, because if I gave you to him, you'd be screaming for eternity. But, you look like the type that likes that kinda stuff." He jerked his other gun at David. "Boy, if you move another inch, your little body is going to hit this floor a lot quicker than I had planned to put you there," he warned, glaring at David.

"Long gone?" she forced out, her anger building with her strength. She held it back in order to get more information from her captor.

"Oh, you don't know, do you? Hmm, like hell you do. All of our holdings are under attack. There is nothing left but the Mons, my domain. At least for now, or should I say at least for the next twenty minutes or less. Thing is, I can't decide if I want the pleasure of killing you myself or letting you incinerate with the rest of the meat in here. Decisions, decisions... hell, I just have to tell you, killing you will be a lot sweeter," he said in a deadly, determined voice. She heard the *click* of Tiger's gun. But as the shot rang out, it was Tiger who fell dead beside her on the floor. She jumped and looked back to see Valens holding his gun.

"Bastard! I enjoyed taking that scum down. Let's go, I gotta get Mina before this place blows. Shamira, get David, and let's go!" Valens called out.

She didn't falter as she got up to run out of the tomb door. Looked back, she saw David kicking a fallen Tiger. The burley man's dead face was just as evil and menacing as he'd been while alive. She felt no guilt in Valens bringing down such a vile, cruel man, as she pondered on just how many more kids he would have tortured and killed to meet his sadistic gains. She surmised no rehabilitation Earth had tried on him had worked. His very being refused to change.

"David, let's go!" she yelled and watched him land one final kick before he took off behind her.

Chapter 32

"I knew you'd come and get me, Meera! I told them. I told all the kids not to worry 'cause my sister would save us," David said, as though he was totally unaffected by all the mayhem around him. She watched him as he casually walked over the strewn bodies left by her team and hoped he would indeed recover from his ordeal at the hands of Monev.

She grabbed his arm to speed him up and said, "Soon, David you will be the one kicking butt. Let's hurry, though. We're running out of time."

"This way! Rob said we don't have much time. He hacked in and added another ten minutes, but that's all he could do for us. Even the guards that were left have cleared out – or tried too. They got the word about this place sanitizing, and without a cooling system, anyone left in here will be incinerated," Valens called back. The others followed Valens and ran toward the tunnels that led to the mines. Shamira dropped David's hand and he kept up.

They ran through the dimmed hallways toward the mines. David ran quickly in front of Valens and pointed him in the direction where they could get up into the mines. They slid to a stop at a platform at the end of the dark hallway. It was opposite the exit to the Mons. They climbed the stairwell leading to the mine entrance, a tunnel with stairs that wound its way up toward the top of the volcano.

Valens started to climb up in the tunnel when David pulled at his leg and said, "You won't fit! I'll go get them. I know the way, and I climb real fast."

"I'll follow him and help send the other kids down to you. Yes, finally this is my show," Manny said. He rubbed his hands together and climbed up behind David, who'd already started his journey upward through the tunnels.

Within minutes, kids started jumping through the hole of the tunnels. There were about twenty or so, and Shamira's heart broke as she watched Valens look desperately for his sister, to no avail.

Watered eyes of frustration looked up, and she watched him help the kids break their falls. She gave Mitch the signal to get them out of there. The stream of kids ended, and only David, Manny, and hopefully Mina remained.

Anthony tried to pull Valens and Shamira away from the mine entrance. "Damn it, Valens, time is ticking. Rob can't hold it back any longer. If we don't get past the exit, we'll get fried. He said the mines outside would start to reactivate!"

Shamira pushed Anthony away from them, and he slid several feet. "No!" she yelled. "We're not leaving without them. You go!" She was determined to get to David and the others in the tunnel, and she moved in front of Valens to climb her way in.

"Fine! Then we won't leave either!" Anthony yelled. Anthony motioned for Mitch to take the kids out while Kurt stood back, refusing to leave. Mitch hesitated, angry he was the first one to go, and then he shrugged his shoulders as he led the kids to freedom.

"Shamira, don't come up! You won't make it!" David yelled down as he hurriedly climbed from the hole.

"Where is Manny? Mina?" Valens forced out on the edge of losing control.

"Right here! I'm dropping her down. Be careful. She's got a sprained ankle!" Manny said. Tears filled Shamira's eyes when she saw the look of relief on Valens' face when he held out his arms for his sister. Her small, malnourished body fell into his arms.

"Valens!" she yelled in a raspy whisper.

"I told you, Mina, that I would always save you!" he said and kissed the top of her forehead.

Manny jumped down, and they didn't waste time before they took off running toward the entrance. Other than the strewn bodies of felled guards, there was no one around. They burst through the entrance with the *beep* of the alarm behind them as they finally cleared the door.

"Hurry! We've got to get clear of the landmines!" Valens yelled.

Anthony grabbed Manny, lifted him up, and tucked him under his arm as they ran. Kurt grabbed David and tossed him up on top his back, and they took off in the direction of their waiting team and past the ground with buried mines. Behind them, they heard the sound of the Mons burning from the inside out. A loud roar emitted from its mouth, and the landmines closest to the entrance started to spontaneously activate.

"Move! Now. Faster. It's gaining on us!" Shamira yelled at them when she heard the faint beeping before the mines reactivated. The ground blew up as the burning lasers burst through the ground to point toward the sky. Her arms pumped as the air in her lungs released painfully from the sheer physical exertion of it all.

Shamira looked ahead and saw Hedi and Dion leading the surrounding kids in a chant, "Faster! Faster! Faster!" They all reached the others just as the last row of landmines activated. A large burst of fire and explosion erupted from the opening of the Mons and caused the landmines to explode into flames and die out.

312

They flew forward with the final blast. Stumbling, they all stood as they watched it finally burn down to a calm fire as lava slowly oozed from the top of the volcano. The kids burst into cheers and tears as they watched their nightmarish prison burn down to nothingness.

David and the other kids started to chant, "Meera! Meera! Meera!"

Valens lifted her up high in the air, then spun her around as he cheered and stood her in front of him. He looked deeply into her eyes, placed his hands softly on each cheek, and then waited for her to hesitate. Surprise registered on his face when he realized that she didn't resist, and he slowly leaned in to kiss her. Butterflies filled her stomach as his firm lips softly touched hers. *Heaven... he feels like heaven.* Filled with love and trust, she wrapped her arms around him as he deepened their first kiss. He pulled away softly and whispered in her ear, "Be mine, Shamira. I love you." He pulled back to look at her as he waited for her response. She took in the hope on his face, the urgency, and the hunger that was only for her. Her heart melted, and her barriers fell.

"Yes, I will. I love you too," she smiled back at him. He quickly embraced her in another kiss as he held her tightly in a strong clutch.

"Um, you better stop before her parents show up, dude," Manny said.

All the kids burst out in laughter as she and Valens broke apart, embarrassed. She couldn't believe everyone witnessed her first kiss, but the whole time, she felt like they were completely alone.

"It's about time. I got sick of him looking like a starving animal every time you walked by," Mitch said, then came up and hugged a surprised Shamira. Before she could recover from that shock, the rest of her friends came up and embraced her and Valens in a huge group hug.

"We did it. Everyone, we did it. We bought Monev down!" She led them in a chant. Her eyes landed on her parents, who ran from their car as the skies around them filled with helicopters and the ground thundered with the Security Force Elite vehicles.

Her father ran up to her, picked her up, and threw her up in the air as her mother leaned down to hug David.

"I knew you'd do it. All of you. Our new trainees for the Security Force of the future!" her father yelled loud enough for all the kids around to hear.

"Dad, did you get him? Did you get Renu and save the real Cal?" Shamira asked, anxious to hear his answer.

"I'm sorry, but regretfully, Renu and what remained of his crew escaped. Our work is not done. As of next week, you will be training under Cal. You, Valens, will be training under your father, Jason Andrews. You, Hedi, will be training under your mother, Rachelle Goodwin. You, Anthony, will be training under your father, Peter Williams. And lastly, you, Mitch, will be training under your father, Carl Poole. The rest of you all will be training under Shamira, who will be the next Security Force Elite Leader!" her father yelled and threw his fist up in the air.

Shamira saw her friends cry as their parents came out of the cars surrounding them when her father named them one by one. With her heart filled with joy at their reunion, tears fell from her eyes.

Shamira's mother came up to her and gave her a hug and a kiss. "That's my girl. I love you."

Shamira looked around her and realized that for the first time in her life, she felt like she belonged. She had a purpose, and it included every one of these new friends she had grown to love. She held her family close, and thought to herself, *Now this is home!*

About the Author

LM. Preston was born and raised in Washington, DC. An avid reader, she loved to create poetry and short-stories as a young girl. With a thirst for knowledge, she attended college at Bowie State University and worked in the IT field as a Techie and Educator for over sixteen years. She started writing science fiction under the encouragement of her husband who was a sci-fi buff and her four kids. Her first published novel, *Explorer X - Alpha* was the beginning of her obsessive desire to write and create stories of young people who overcome unbelievable odds. She loves to write while on the porch watching her kids play or when she is traveling, another passion that encourages her writing.

www.lmpreston.com

You may write to LM. Preston at Phenomenal One Press, Attn: LM. Preston, P.O. Box 8231, Elkridge MD 21075

lmpreston@yahoo.com